# Permission

## Jo Bloom

Legend Press Ltd, 51 Gower Street, London, WC1E 6HJ
info@legendpress.co.uk | www.legendpress.co.uk

Print ISBN 978-1-91505-4-562
Ebook ISBN 978-1-91505-457-9
Set in Times. Printing managed by Jellyfish Solutions Ltd
Cover design by Rose Cooper | www.rosecooper.com

Printed and bound by CPI Group (UK) Ltd, Croydon CR0 4YY

**Jo Bloom**'s debut novel, *Ridley Road*, was published in 2014 and recently adapted into a major four-part series for BBC One. Jo has worked as a freelancer in the communications field for over twenty years, with a focus on arts publicity and e-learning. She also contributed to the book review section of *Time Out, London* for a few years. Prior to this, she lived and worked in Prague and New York. She now lives in Brighton with her family. *Permission* is her first contemporary novel.

Visit Jo
www.jobloom.com
or follow on Instagram
@jobloomauthor

"*The grand illusion of committed love is that we think our partners are ours. In truth, their separateness is unassailable, and their mystery is forever ungraspable.*"

**Esther Perel**

# 1

Fay and Steve are each struggling with a drunk person in their living room, only she is pulling Katie up and he is holding Matt back.

When Matt's voice grows even angrier, Fay pushes Katie into the kitchen and quickly locks the door. Katie clutches a countertop, then slides to the floor with her back to a cupboard.

'Hey, none of that,' Fay hears Steve shout. 'Come on, mate. Behave.'

Katie moans and tucks her lowered head into her arms as Fay steps over her to get to the sink. 'I'll only be a sec,' she says, her hands trembling as she pours a glass of water.

The speed at which Katie and Matt's relationship has disintegrated makes Fay feel vulnerable and scared for herself, like she might be passing by a terrible accident on the motorway. Part of her would like to ask them to go straight away, so they can sort themselves out in their own home, but something in her is also compelled to look. Irritatingly, she hadn't even felt like having people over this evening, but Katie kept dropping hints about having a free weekend and offered to make her mum's jerk chicken if Fay did the rice. And actually, it had been a fun evening until ten minutes ago. The chat had been lively, and Fay had drunk almost as much as the others, which she never normally did.

Fay crouches down next to Katie and hands her the glass. 'Drink this.'

Katie bats it away. 'I want red.'

'Jesus, it's water.' Fay closes Katie's hands around the glass. 'Do you think I'm going to give you more wine?'

In between big sips, Katie whimpers and has a little cry. Fay has never seen her so fragile. It is almost like she has a stranger in her kitchen, not a close friend of ten years.

'I'm sorry,' Katie says again. 'I didn't want to tell anyone. But I should have told you.'

These past few months, Katie has been writing poetry while Matt is out playing football – sweet, soppy lines about love that she stores in a shoebox under their bed. The other night on the phone, she read Fay a poem about the man in her life, which is how Fay came to tease Matt about being married to someone writing him love poems. Matt had jumped up from the sofa and bent over Katie, jabbing a finger at her. What love poems? What does she mean? He kept rubbing his face with his palms. He might not have known for definite there was another man in her life, but Fay could tell that he'd had his suspicions. She had mistakenly told him what he hadn't wanted to believe.

'What's his name?' she asks.

'Nathan. I really like him, Fay,' says Katie. 'It's electric.'

*Electric.* This isn't a word Fay has ever heard Katie use before – maybe she picked it up from Nathan – but it's a description that doesn't lie. When she starts saying that she can't get enough of him, her voice is so lit with excitement Fay feels weirdly put out. She doesn't think she's jealous, but it's hard not to feel sidelined by Katie's breathless commentary.

'How long has it been going on?' she cuts in.

'Five months.'

'Five months! Bloody hell.' Fay gets up and opens the cupboard above the oven. Reaching up, she rummages around for the pack of cigarettes and lighter she keeps hidden behind the baking trays. She's not a regular smoker, this pack is probably six months old, and the tobacco feels a bit crispy, but it's the right time for one. 'I can't believe you kept it to yourself for that long,' she says, putting a cigarette between her lips.

At least once a fortnight, Fay and Katie go to the cinema

or swim lengths at the leisure centre pool. They WhatsApp each other several times a week. At weekends they might walk Katie's dogs across the local fields, sometimes for hours on end. It seems unbelievable that Fay didn't even have an inkling.

'Are you hurt I didn't tell you?'

'It's not about me.' Fay takes a puff. 'So, it started after Matt quit his job?'

Katie nods. Almost ten months ago, just after his fortieth birthday, Matt left his job as a mortgage broker to give his songwriting one last push. Now or never, guys, he kept saying. He didn't need to convince Fay. She turned forty the year before last. Although she threw a phenomenal party, an unexpected sorrow about getting older came over her that she hasn't yet fully shaken off.

'It's hard to support him,' says Katie through tears. 'He wants so much from me.'

Matt used to complain regularly about his job, but now this has translated into regular anxiety over his decision to quit. He speaks a lot about how he's in touch with different record labels, but it always sounds like an apology, as if deep down he knows success will never come. At dinner, Katie talked about all the baking he's been doing. Yesterday he made mini Victoria sponges, the size of muffins. She laughed as she was talking, calling him Matt Berry, but it was a contemptuous laugh and Matt stayed quiet the whole time.

'I didn't mean him to find out like this,' she moans. 'Don't judge me.'

Fay puts her arm around Katie's shoulders and pulls her close. 'Don't be daft.' Fay has been with Steve for twenty-two years. She understands what it's like to love the bones of a person, yet for your heart to feel like it might suffocate under the familiarity.

'You get it, don't you?' Katie glances sideways at her. 'I mean, you fantasise too. There was that guy from your spin class.'

'Yeah. That was just a silly crush though.'

'You said you couldn't get him out of your head.'

'Okay.' Fay gets to her feet and stubs out the cigarette on a dirty plate in the sink. It's obvious where this conversation is heading. Katie needs a co-conspirator. She wants to make herself feel better by making Fay feel bad, just because Fay confided in her that she really fancied Reuben, a man who showed up at her spin class a few times, to the extent that for several weeks she got into the habit of conjuring up his imaginary presence alongside her, watching her while she went about her day.

She opens up the door. 'Stay there. I'm going to check on the boys.'

With the hallway and porch light on, the downstairs is flooded with brightness which ramps up the drama. Fay picks up coats that have fallen from pegs in the tussle and turns off the lights. Steve is outside encouraging Matt down the path towards the taxi, but Matt keeps turning to the house. 'Let me come back in,' Fay hears him say as she stands on the step, shivering.

'No chance. Go on, go home,' says Steve as the chill of the night makes Fay turn around and head inside.

'It's all kicking off, isn't it?' She looks up to where their nineteen-year-old son, Billy, is hanging over the upstairs landing, amused at this unexpected action. Since he's been working as a commis chef's apprentice in London, his hair has grown to his chin. Now it slopes untidily over his cheeks, concealing his mouth. Watching Billy make ravioli from scratch yesterday, Fay thought he looked much older than when he moved out of home nine months ago and he certainly seems far more confident than when he left school with a handful of GCSEs and huge culinary ambitions, yet no clue how to achieve them.

'Sorry, love.' She pulls a face. 'What must Caroline think?'

Billy had only come home for the weekend to show off his girlfriend, a waitress at the restaurant he's been dating for a while. It's the first time he has introduced anyone formally to them and as Fay shook Caroline's hand while Billy kept his arm protectively around her waist, she felt slightly bereft in a way she hadn't expected. Billy's mine, she had wanted to shout. Later, lying against Steve in bed, she had quietly shared this experience with him. Steve had listened, he had stroked the small of her back, but then his chest had started shaking with laughter. Billy's mine, he repeated. Glad you kept that to yourself. Fay had gently pushed against his stomach to stop him mocking her, but she also ended up laughing at herself.

'She thinks it's funny,' says Billy, coming to the top of the stairs.

'Well, please apologise to her,' says Fay. 'It's so embarrassing.'

Billy and Caroline were so quiet in his room she had forgotten that they were even in the house. She imagines they were in bed on separate devices, possibly even texting each other rather than speaking, which she had caught them doing last night. They couldn't understand why she thought it was strange. 'Anyway, show's over.'

Billy says, 'I think Rose is awake.' Fay sighs. Once unsettled, her youngest can take ages to get back to sleep. She only just started going through the night last year, shortly after her fifth birthday.

'I'll check on her in a minute. Go on,' says Fay, waiting at the foot of the stairs until he disappears.

'Christ,' Steve whispers as he comes in and shuts the front door.

'I know,' she whispers back. 'Madness.'

He runs his hands over his shaved head. 'We need new friends.'

They are both sharing a smile when the kitchen door handle rattles and Katie appears in a burst of light, scrunched up and confused.

Fay holds out her hand. 'Come on, we'll make up the sofa for you.'

'I'll get the sleeping bag.' Steve takes the stairs two at a time; they both want to get this evening over with. In the living room, Katie droops onto their worn velvet sofa. Looking at her slowly take out her dangly earrings, Fay wonders if Katie's newish afro is for Nathan. Until recently, Fay has only ever seen her hair braided.

When Steve comes back in, Katie watches him as he unrolls the sleeping bag and pushes the pillow into a fresh pillowcase. 'How was Matt?'

'As you'd expect,' Steve says reasonably.

'It's not all my fault. There are things you don't know.'

'Uh-huh.'

'Do you hate me?' Katie asks him as she nudges off her shoes. Steve stops unzipping the sleeping bag.

'You're out of order. That's all there is to it.'

She sprawls out. 'I know.'

He reaches towards her and places a hand briefly on her head. 'Go on. Sleep it off.'

Steve's hands are things of beauty – one glimpse of them when he and Fay argue and all her love for him comes flooding back. Long, thick fingers, a slight smattering of dark hair and lined, heavy palms. Proper hands. Hands that could cup the whole side of her face. Hands that held their babies as if they were weightless.

From where Fay stands, she can't understand what Katie is saying, but moving closer, she can see her eyes are shut and she is already falling asleep.

# 2

Steve has work on his mind. He's waiting to hear if his small digital marketing business has won a campaign for a new kids' clothing range that he recently pitched for. He used to pretend to Fay that he thrived off competition because she does. Now he accepts that it scares him. Every day is hard and never really over. Often the worries just seep through one dream into the next.

He puts on his watch while Fay sits on the edge of the bed in just a T-shirt and knickers, applying moisturiser to her pale shaved legs and talking about some copy she must rewrite for the fourth time. He's always had a thing for watches; there are six in his drawer. Some are good fakes, others are the real thing. The one he straps to his wrist was his dad's and it's the only one Steve has worn since he passed away eighteen months earlier. The woman at the hospice gave it to him in a clear bag which also contained his dad's dentures, a wallet bulging with family photos and his old-fashioned radio and earpiece – Steve cried when he turned on the radio and heard the local Greek station his dad had loved.

Wearing the watch isn't necessarily a positive thing. It shores up the grief again, but it's a habit Steve can't seem to break. He still isn't sure if he needs to get to a point where it doesn't hurt him to wear it or whether he should need to wear it at all.

'This project is relentless.' Fay stands up and pulls on her jeans and a grey sweatshirt. 'Every day the marketing guy, who's about twelve, emails me and says, "I've been thinking..."'

Steve shakes his head sympathetically. Fay's been a self-employed content writer for the past six years and, while she only works part-time, she's always got a client on the go who is tricky or demanding.

'Sorry, I know I'm going on,' she says.

'No, you're not.' He scoops up his change from the dresser and pushes the coins into his jeans pocket. 'That guy sounds like a nightmare.'

He turns when Rose opens the door, still in her pyjamas. 'Why aren't you changed?' he says irritably. 'You'll be late for school.'

'I don't want to go.'

Rose, you've only got two more days before the Easter holidays,' says Fay. 'And—'

'And after that I'm going to a new school. Without Nancy and Millie in my class.' Rose finishes her sentence with a soft, almost dreamy smile as if the thought is in her head all the time, ready to be released.

'Well, you're on the waiting list, remember?' says Fay. 'We're almost at the top. We're so close.'

Rose rubs her nose and says nothing. She has heard this promise so many times before she knows it's pointless pressing them for more details. Steve watches Fay bury her face in the space between Rose's neck and shoulder. He wonders if she is silently apologising to her like he does all the time. He can be engaged in elaborate role play with Rose, where she's the daddy and he's the child, and in his head he's apologising over and over again that they have to send her into a school where they can't seem to stop two girls bullying her.

'Let's get you dressed and fed, missie.' Fay turns Rose around by the shoulders and steers her through the door. 'Or you'll be late.'

While they are eating their toast, Steve takes his coffee into the garden. He's only become keen on gardening in the past couple of years and he likes to walk around, check how everything is growing, even when he doesn't always know what he's meant to see. Although it's easy to tell that their smoke tree is struggling a little. The leaves used to be dark burgundy and lush, but the ones coming through the past month or so have been dry and shrivelled-looking. As he twists off a few, his phone in his jeans pocket vibrates.

## Matt

Fancy a pint? Could do with some company.

This is the third time he's heard from Matt since the disastrous dinner ten days ago. The first was hours after Matt left, full of expletives and rage; the second time was after Fay insisted Steve check and see if he was okay. But this is a surprising text to receive as they've never socialised separately nor been proper friends in their own right – an arrangement which has always suited Steve. Matt can insert an upbeat energy into a crowd of people, but he's not relaxing company on his own. Uncomfortable with pauses in conversation, he has a habit of darting between random topics, speaking fast and for some time without waiting for input from anyone else.

Steve doesn't answer till he gets to the office. When he does agree to a drink without any specificity, Matt responds straight away and asks him if he's free that night. I'm lonely, he writes, which is a hard excuse to dismiss and is the reason why Steve finds himself arranging to meet at a pub in town.

When he arrives, Matt's greeting is so loud and enthusiastic that Steve finds himself glancing over sheepishly at other drinkers close by. Then Matt insists on running around to find Steve a less rickety chair, before making a show about getting in the first round. He is such a whirling dervish that Steve has to stop looking at him.

It soon becomes apparent why Matt wanted to meet. He

thinks that he and Steve are now uniquely connected because Steve had witnessed the event that saw him and Katie break up. He keeps saying, 'You were there, mate, you were there with me,' as if they had both been in the trenches together, fighting for a common cause. This makes Steve feel really uncomfortable. He has absolutely no interest in being part of their story, but he understands Matt is hurting in new and unexpected ways, so he listens to him talk about Katie and their endless rows, and how much he misses the kids since moving into his sister's spare room where the single bed is surrounded by boxes of the hand moisturiser she sells online.

'Have you thought about couples' counselling?' Steve asks when Matt stops talking to take a sip of his drink.

'Yeah. I wanted to give it another go, but Katie said she was done with all that.' Matt pounds a fist on the table. 'I should find out where that bastard lives. Pay him a visit.'

This ridiculous declaration makes Steve feel even sorrier for him.

'The thought of them having sex,' says Matt. 'It does my fucking head in.'

Steve nods. 'Try not to think about it.'

'How can I?' Matt winces as if the thought physically hurts him. 'You're a better man than me. I'll give you that.'

'What do you mean?'

'Ages ago Katie suggested trying an open marriage. Said you and Fay had talked about doing it.' Matt knits his hands at the back of his head and says, 'Is that right? You were just going to let Fay sleep with whoever she wanted?'

Steve puts his pint on the table and rubs his palms on his thighs. The exchange has taken such a surprising turn he's unable to speak at first. It's inconceivable that Matt knows about this private conversation between him and Fay.

'Of course not,' he snapped. 'It wasn't like that.'

He reminds himself that this is classic Matt, opining on something he knows nothing about. It's also likely that this conversation is calculated, that somehow Matt needs to spread some of his shame.

'Sorry. Didn't mean to make you fret.' Matt put his hands in the air. 'Mea culpa.'

'I'm not fretting. It's just none of your business.'

Steve presses the sole of his trainers firmly onto the sticky floor. It occurs to him how quickly the safety of his own feelings has been removed. He feels like he did when Fay had first suggested exploring an open relationship. Actually, he feels even more affected now that the discussion has been cracked apart for others to see.

'I need to make a move.' He has no interest in sitting for a moment longer. The evening is dead. There's nowhere to go from here. 'Got a stack of work to get through.'

'No worries.' After Matt drinks the last of his beer, they both put on their jackets, then Steve slings his satchel diagonally across his body and picks up his cycle helmet. Outside the pub entrance, when Matt shakes his hand and claps him on the back, Steve finds it impossible to put himself fully into the gesture. Not that Matt notices. He is too busy talking again, complaining about the extortionate cost of renting a decent flat anywhere in town.

/

A few months back, Steve went through a lengthy period of feeling like he and Fay weren't particularly connected. Their exchanges were either snippy or a little mean, like they were giving each other paper cuts. He wasn't too worried. It happened every now and again, usually when they had too much stuff pressing down on them, squeezing them emotionally. And they did have a lot going on: Rose was being bullied at school. Steve was still coming across people who didn't know that his dad had died, so every time he told someone it broke him a bit, even though he knew that it was not a new grief simply because he had taken it out and allowed another person to see it. He and Fay were both working hard at their respective businesses to keep enough money coming in; and while Fay would resist putting her fortieth into the mix, she did admit that it had hit her hard – she felt that her life had become more humdrum and buried beneath responsibilities.

So, it was no surprise to Steve that the invisible thread that bound them together felt a lot finer and looser, as if Fay was bobbing around in her own world some distance from him. 'I need to decompress,' she would announce, and disappear. She started running longer distances and going to boxing classes. In the evening, all she wanted was to put on her pyjamas and watch a programme on her laptop alone in bed.

They were still having regular sex, which Steve insisted wasn't necessary if she wasn't in the mood, but he appreciated it, nonetheless. One night, after they'd had what he considered great, intense sex, he opened his eyes briefly and saw her smiling at him.

'What?' he said sleepily. 'Are you going to tell me what a stallion I am?'

'Of course.' She ran her hands slowly over his head. 'So, you know… I was wondering… have you ever thought what it would be like to have an open relationship? Just to try something different?'

He opened his eyes properly, waited for her to laugh, but she wasn't joking.

'Don't look at me like that.' Her voice fluttered.

Steve bent a pillow behind his head and waited for her to expand.

'There's so much evidence about it helping couples to grow even closer.' Fay sat up, legs crossed. She had clipped back her hair but was still naked. 'Their sex lives have been recharged,' she said in an animated voice. 'They're more intimate and excited by each other than ever.'

Steve tried to appear relaxed, but really he felt scared. Fay had clearly been planning this. She had done her research and was ready to articulate a case for freedom outside of their marriage. As she talked, she rested her fingers on his thigh, but he was too confused to respond. He needed time to adjust to the conversation; his thoughts always had a narrower range than hers.

'You know how much I fancy you,' she said. 'I just like the idea of a little sexual adventure. You can understand that, can't you?'

This was Fay's subtle reminder that she had only slept with one other man before him. She had gone straight from an all-girls' Catholic school to university where they had met in the second year and been together ever since. She had always been honest about how her lack of sexual encounters bothered her; she'd even expressed jealousy about Steve's more varied past. As a young man, he'd had great hair, black and wavy like his dad's. His skin tanned easily. He was an attentive conversationalist, a rarity amongst his friends. In his first year at university, a number of girls wanted to sleep with him, which he had never discouraged.

'Give it some thought,' was the last thing Fay said after they'd kissed and before she turned off the light. 'Sleep on it. Might be great for us.'

In the morning, he woke first and watched her sleeping. Her smooth face was close to his, her light brown hair mussed up and falling forward. He particularly loved her nose, small and snub and lightly freckled. When she eventually woke and grinned at him, he guessed the first thing on her mind was probably the last thing she had thought of the night before.

He got out of bed. 'I don't want to sleep with anyone else,' he said as he stepped into his boxer shorts. 'I'm sorry. I'm not built for that sort of thing.'

Fay lay back down on her side, with both hands under her cheek. Her look was blank, and her hazel eyes didn't widen, but he knew a lot more was going on beneath the surface.

'Fair enough,' she said passively. 'I know my ideas can be a bit full on.'

For a couple of days she was distant and neutral about

everything, polite but a bit arch, so he left her alone until she came back to him, breaking the ice with a brutal but funny story about one of the mums at school she couldn't stand. When he put his hands on her waist and whispered in her ear that he loved her as she sliced into a doughy brown loaf, she said it back and later, in bed, she showed him by dragging down his boxer shorts and getting him hard. After that, things went back to normal. A normal he thought they were both happy with.

/

When he gets home from the pub, Fay is in bed watching a documentary on the heroin trade between the US and Mexico. 'You're back early. Good night?'

'Uh-huh.' He unthreads the belt from his jeans and hangs it in his wardrobe.

'What's the matter?'

'Nothing.' He silently takes off his sweatshirt and tosses it onto the green cocktail chair near the wardrobe.

'Really? It doesn't seem like nothing.' She pauses her documentary and waits. Without the sound on, the silence is loud.

'Okay. Well, I hear you told Katie that we'd discussed an open relationship.'

Fay blinks. 'Oh. Shit.' She pulls an apologetic face. 'Sorry. What did Matt say?'

Steve shrugs noncommittally; to him, that's an irrelevance. 'Why did you tell her? It was just for us, private.'

'Was it? More private than our arguments?'

'Yes. Way more.'

Fay nods and pauses thoughtfully. 'Every couple argues, so you think that's normal. I guess you feel judged about the idea of opening up our marriage.' Steve nods in an exaggerated fashion to confirm that, *yes, of course I did, and is that really so strange?*

'I'm sorry if you felt exposed. I really didn't mean for that to happen.' She lifts the duvet and crawls in her T-shirt to the end of the bed where he is sitting. 'Katie should never have told him.'

'He made it sound cheap. And like I was weak and weird for considering it.'

'Oh, Matt never thinks before he speaks.' She kisses his neck, then behind each ear. Another time, he might have hoped that she'd push him onto his back and lie on top of him. Instead, he swivels to face her. 'Are you unhappy? Like Katie was?' he asks, caught by a burst of insecurity.

'Nooo! Don't be silly. We're nothing like them. I can't see them getting back together.' She sighs. 'It's sad.'

'You don't think?' Steve likes sitting so close to Fay that they could almost slot together as they gossip. 'Have you moaned about me for not being broad-minded enough?'

'Of course not. You are broad-minded.'

Steve contemplates this. He supposes he is in some ways. They tried bondage a couple of times, but it didn't excite him. He kept thinking they were at some awful fancy-dress party. Watching porn was more exciting, but morally it really didn't sit well with either of them. It made both of them feel complicit and grubby. 'Not as much as you,' he says truthfully, because these ideas are never his. Fay always comes up with them.

'Well, I don't know if that's true. I guess I wanted to find out.' She says this pointedly but without anger.

'Do you still want to try opening things up?' he asks.

She sighs. 'We've talked about it. The discussion is over.' As she turns and crawls to the other end of the bed, Steve reaches out and grabs her ankle.

'Stop,' he says.

She stays where she is, mid-bed. 'There's nothing left to talk about,' she says over her shoulder. 'You didn't want to go there. End of.'

'Maybe I do now,' he replies with a small shrug. They both know it would never be his choice, that it's not his thing. But on the way home from the pub, Cecile, the attractive French PhD student who used to live alone in a flat across the street, came into his mind. She would always venture over to speak to him if she saw him. Steve knew there was something between them, a frisson. What could have happened if he'd been able to act on it?

'I know you don't.' Fay gently shakes her foot at him.

When he drops her foot, she crawls away, then repositions herself. She smooths the duvet with her hands and plumps up the pillows behind her. When she's ready, she puts the laptop on her thighs and restarts the programme. Steve gets up and at the window he moves the curtain aside and looks out. Nothing much happens on their street at night. Sometimes he's amazed how quiet it is, as if it is permanently coated in thick snow. Their basement flat in south-east London where they lived for eight years before moving here was steeped in noise. Permanent traffic, people always arguing or partying in the flats around them, snatches of music at all hours.

He walks back and sits on the edge of the bed close to Fay, one arm over her bent legs, his knuckles pressing into the duvet.

'And it's just about sex?' He thinks back to something she said to him when they didn't feel particularly connected, how she sometimes felt like she was on cruise control.

'Yes, of course,' she says.

'I think we should explore it.' Actually, he still doesn't know what he thinks; his thoughts are firing off in different directions.

Staring at him, Fay runs her tongue over her top front teeth. 'You don't need to do this. We're not going to end up like Katie and Matt, okay?' She knows him better than anyone else, which both annoys and diminishes him right now.

'Maybe I've changed my mind,' he says boldly. 'Can't I do that sometimes?'

She considers this for a moment. She closes her laptop and puts it next to her, then says, 'Be honest,' adding in a shy voice: 'Have you?'

# 3

Fay is on her knees, scrubbing the white tiles on her dad's kitchen floor as the sun stares down through the kitchen window and into her eyes. When she moves her head, the tips of his slippers come into sight. Rex has followed her around the bungalow as she changed the bed sheets and cleaned the toilet and emptied the bins. His presence is so oppressive. It's also the reason the agency told her they would no longer send any cleaners to him and why Fay is here instead.

Stretching to dip the brush into the bucket of soapy water, the phone in her jeans pocket presses hard against her hip, reminding her that Reuben hasn't texted back yet. The thought gives her a pain in her stomach.

'Good news about Rose getting into a new school, isn't it?' she says, sitting back on her haunches, trying to make conversation.

Her dad nods. 'It is that.'

The phone call from the school came on the first day of the Easter holidays. Fay took it sitting down. Her legs were shaky. After she'd thanked the school secretary more than once, she hung up, put her head in her hands and sobbed before calling Steve.

When Rex checks his watch again, Fay glances at the time on the oven. The pubs in Canberra will close soon. Once Gerry is kicked out, he'll walk five minutes to his flat and call them. Fay's older brother left England four years ago for work – something in software – and never came back. She doesn't know much about his life in Australia except he lives in the suburbs in a new build with lots of black furniture and wall mirrors.

Rex's landline rings, like clockwork. She's never understood why he likes Gerry to call during her visits. Neither she nor Gerry have any desire to talk regularly to each other, so she can only assume her dad must have manufactured a united version of their family in his mind because it has never existed.

'Hello, son,' he shouts very loudly into the receiver and then he's laughing for the first time since Fay arrived. 'Sounds about right.'

Everything about Gerry pleases Rex. They look similar, both average height and heavyset, with thick sandy hair and a short neck. Gerry can hold his drink, isn't interested in marriage and has a young blonde girlfriend who apparently looks terrific in a swimsuit – that was a conversation Fay could have done without overhearing.

Gerry must be talking about a trip he just took. 'Your mum would have liked to have seen photos of that,' says Rex. 'She always liked a waterfall.'

Did she? Another thing about her mum Fay never knew. Later she'll go home and write the word 'waterfalls' in a tiny notebook she keeps in the back of her sweater drawer. The last entry was about how her mum had played badminton for the county when she was young. She died of cancer when Fay was seven. She had been ill for months, but it wasn't one of those slow, intimate deaths where she and Fay cosied up in bed together, sharing everything they could, knowing they couldn't share it later. No, as Fay remembers it – and admittedly, her memories are patchy and her dad does nothing to fill them in – her mum used up all her energy either going to church or resting in the bedroom alone with the curtains closed until she faded away almost naturally, as Fay described it later to a therapist.

Once Rex has given Fay the phone and she and Gerry have talked about nothing much, Rex takes it back and says, 'You too, son. You too.' Fay avoids looking at her dad after these calls end because his smile is always hard. He needs time before he can live with the idea that it is just her with him.

Fay peels off the rubber gloves as she hears the ping of her own phone in her pocket. It could be anyone, but it could also be Reuben. Heat runs through her. She'll wait until she's in the car to look. It's something to hold on to, a thrill that can carry her through these last few minutes. She empties the dirty water down the sink as she watches two boys scooting up and down the pavement. Hearing their silvery laughs, she wonders if her dad lets the kids be or if he stands on the steps, telling them to keep the noise down. He would see that as his right.

She pulls on her jacket. 'You need to reheat the cottage pie for about forty minutes. At one-eighty.' Her eyes turn to the small plastic bags of coloured powder on the countertop. 'What are those?'

Rex follows her glance. 'Spices. From the Coxons over the road. Just back from India. *Spices!*' he repeats as she picks each one up and smells them. 'I've told them I like my food plain, but they said, oh Rex, you have to try.' His voice turns mocking. 'I bet you'll love a homemade curry, Rex. Like they know me better than I know myself.'

Fay puts the spices back down. No wonder Steve can't be around her dad for long. She often wonders what Rex's colleagues at the local police station used to think about him. Not much, she imagines. As far as she knows, none of them have stayed in touch with him since he retired. 'Will you come for Sunday lunch?'

'I will, if you're asking.' He says the same thing every time she invites him.

Her phone pings again. She's so proud of her self-restraint. She doesn't even touch her jeans pocket. She gives her dad a hug. 'Take care of yourself.'

'You too.' He pats her back awkwardly.

Fay wonders what he would say if he knew she was seeing another man that night. He'd be shocked, even speechless for once. He would probably blame Steve. 'You're such a softy,' Rex had once said to him after his third can of beer, when

27

Steve was cuddling a young, tantrummy Billy on his lap. 'I bet everyone sees you coming a mile off.'

Fay walks out, barely looking behind her. In the car she pulls out her phone.

**R**
Sounds like a plan. See you at eight. Reuben x

She stares at the screen for a moment, then texts back:

**Fay**
great x

*You're allowed to text him*, she reminds herself in a panic. You have permission.

/

A week earlier, the day after their conversation in the bedroom, Steve had come into the living room holding two glasses and an opened bottle of red wine.

'Shall we talk more about it then?' His voice had snagged a little.

Fay had just tidied up and was on her way to bed. Her stomach dipped. 'Sure.' She sat down on the sofa. Neither of them spoke while Steve poured them both a glass of wine, then put the bottle on the coffee table. Fay waited, but he still said nothing as he crossed his legs, then put a cushion behind his back. She gave him a small, encouraging smile, but he kept twisting the glass in his hand and looking at the swirl of red wine.

'It's okay if you've changed your mind.' She held her breath until he shook his head.

'I'm just not sure where to start,' he said. His arm was

resting in between them, but his hand wasn't touching any part of her. He didn't rub her calf or massage her foot like he normally would.

'Are you angry with me about it?' Fay asked.

'No. Do I seem it?'

'I'm not sure what you seem.'

'Sorry,' said Steve. 'This is new to me.'

'And me.'

'I need to know something.' Steve looked at her properly for the first time. 'You weren't lying when you said you were still into sex with me, were you?'

'Of course not.' She really hadn't lied, but his question didn't entirely cover the complexity of her feelings. Of course Steve still excited her. She loved the look of him and how he held himself, and if she glanced over at him at a gathering, she felt happy knowing that she was going home with him. But they had been together for over two decades, and it was hard to be into anything with the same vigour and intensity as they had at the start.

'Good.' He put his wine glass down and rested a hand on her foot. 'So, is this about someone in particular? That guy from your spin class?'

Steve's question was surprisingly direct, even though she could tell he was trying his best to sound casual. She felt herself flush. She must have joked about a hot guy in the class before the idea of Reuben as something more took root in her mind. 'Not really. I mean, I was attracted to him,' she said, matching Steve's spirit of honesty. 'But that was ages ago. Anyway, I'm sure you've been attracted to other people.'

He nodded vaguely, reluctant to give anything away as he massaged the ball of her foot. He did this for what felt like ages, then looked up at her and said, 'Right, let's do it. Let's try consensual non-monogamy.' He pulled a face and looked pleased when she laughed.

'Only if we don't call it that.' Her heart was pounding a little faster as she knitted her free hand with his. 'Are you sure? I mean, really? You promise that you're not just doing this for me?'

They both knew she meant his need to keep things between them happy and safe, a hangover from his mum's absent parenting. He had been thirteen when Patricia went to live with Doug, leaving Steve and his brother with their dad. After Steve had watched Doug carry three matching suitcases and four hatboxes into the car, he pleaded with his mum through the open passenger window to stay. Patricia had touched his cheek, said, 'See you very soon, darling,' then rolled up the window. It would be two months before Steve saw her again. Fay tried to get him to engage with the intense emotions she knew he had around his mum leaving him, but he wouldn't go there. 'What's done is done,' was his worn-through mantra. 'Stop trying to manage my feelings.'

Steve shook his head. 'I've had a look on the internet. Listened to a few podcasts. There's lots of positive stories out there. I'm intrigued. Kind of excited, actually. Like we're doing something we might have done before being a grown-up got in the way.' He smiled endearingly and she smiled back, nodding. Then he got serious again. 'But we need to be honest and have rules. We can't mess this up.' He moved his finger back and forth between them. 'We're the priority. Us and the kids.'

'Of course,' she said. 'Without question.' They kissed, as if sealing the deal, then she sat back and said, 'So, what rules did you have in mind?'

'Well, for starters, the kids can't find out.' She nodded her head in agreement. 'Always use protection... what else? No friends. I don't want to be having a drink with one of them and realise he's fucking you. No one is allowed in the house. And maybe a limit on how often we can see the same person?' He paused, stared into his glass, then looked at her. 'Also, I don't want to know anything. I can't imagine hearing about it.'

'That all makes sense. I don't think I've got anything to add.'

'And this isn't a permanent arrangement.' Steve tapped her knee. 'We're just trying it out for a while. An experiment.'

'I don't see it as permanent either. Definitely not.'

'Because we're just talking about sex, aren't we? No emotional commitments.'

'Of course not.' Fay stroked his face. 'I'm not looking for that. I have you. This.' She waved her hand around, then leant towards him and traced his bristle with her fingertips, imagining how other women would see him. Handsome, even if you didn't care for dark eyes or olive skin. A sharp thinker. A great dad. He was also moral and good-hearted, if occasionally too casual with their money – it was always down to her to keep them on track. There would be no shortage of women lining up to have sex with him. Fay moved the thought around her head to see if it hurt. It didn't.

'And if one of us starts to get cold feet, the other will respect that and it stops.'

'Of course,' she said.

Steve fell silent for a moment. 'It might be too hard for me. I'll be jealous.'

When Fay said, 'Yeah, me too,' he shook his head.

'Not like I will. You've always wanted more than me. Ever since I've known you. I'm pretty content with my lot.'

It was not said unsympathetically, but it revealed a painful feeling in her. She recognised that she was often chasing something new. It wasn't healthy. But it was also surprising that Steve had mentioned this, because she felt like she had stopped pushing for more a long time ago. It was hard enough to keep on top of what she did have. She bent her legs close to her chest and stared at him over her knees. 'We don't have to do this. I can change.'

'No, you can't,' said Steve tenderly. 'And I don't want you to.'

*/*

Hours after she leaves her dad's house, Fay is standing in the bar, some way from the table where Reuben looks down at his phone. This place isn't new to her, but she wouldn't have chosen it herself. The narrow, too crowded room is sweaty and loud. It will be embarrassing if she has to keep asking Reuben to repeat himself.

She pauses, pulls at the waist of her jumpsuit and shakes her hair forward over her shoulders like a veil. Reuben still hasn't looked up. He must be reading something amusing; he keeps flashing his teeth. Her breathing has turned a bit funny. She presses her hand gently on her ribcage as she inhales and exhales a couple of times. Then she walks towards the table and touches the top of the empty wooden chair opposite him with her fingertips. 'Hello.'

Reuben glances up, smiles and lays his phone face down on the table.

'You made it.' He clears his throat. She doesn't think he doubted her. It sounds like something he would say to anyone. Standing up, he sidesteps to the edge of the table to kiss her cheek and his blonde hair grazes hers. Surfer's hair, thick and messy, pushed this way and that around his angular face. An unexpected waft of aftershave reminds her how unfamiliar he is; Steve refuses to wear aftershave. He can't even bear scented soap. Fay's breath tightens again.

Reuben is grinning, one eyebrow raised. 'You're not going to believe who I just bumped into.' His low, casual voice had annoyed her when she first heard it at the end of a particularly tough spin class. He had jumped off his bike, turned around and, rubbing a towel across his face, hadn't seen that Fay was woozily getting off her bike. She had fallen but not badly. Reuben had quickly helped her up, but once he realised that she wasn't hurt, he'd teased her for being in his way. She had felt flustered, thanking him. He looked so naturally strong and fit, whilst sweat was pouring off her.

'Who?' Fay can't think of anyone they have in common.

'L-o-l-a.' He draws her name out slowly.

'Oh God.' The only other time Fay had seen Reuben since he disappeared from the spin class was at a local networking event for freelancers a few months later. The events were dull, but she had made a pact with herself to attend one a year. Reuben, who had recently set up his own painting and decorating business, was standing by the window talking to a man who had a large Jiffy bag clamped under his armpit. He was wearing a tight black T-shirt and baggy shorts and Fay saw a couple of women check him out as she tried to slink by him, unnoticed. But he stepped out in front of her and asked her with a straight face if she wanted him to push her over again. The banter between them had built unexpectedly but tantalisingly from there. For a while Fay had been able to be both witty and mocking without feeling self-conscious until Lola, a pink-haired photographer's assistant roughly half Fay's age, came over and introduced herself, then squeezed the energy out of the rest of their evening. Fay and Reuben didn't know each other well enough to overcome a person with such a high level of self-interest.

'Only joking,' says Reuben and grins as if he expects her to find it funny.

It isn't, but Fay smiles, sort of.

'I'll get the drinks in, shall I?' he says awkwardly.

She asks for a Sauvignon Blanc, then sits down and waits. When Reuben reappears, he is carrying a bottle and two large glasses. There are spots of perspiration on his top lip. He looks older under these lights, closer to thirty-five than thirty. There are faint grooves around his eyes, which is pleasing. It doesn't interest Fay to sit in a bar with a much younger man.

They clink glasses and say cheers. 'You look lovely,' he says.

'Thank you.' She asks him what he's been doing even though she already knows some of it. A couple of days after agreeing the arrangement with Steve, she had contacted Reuben via LinkedIn to say – in an attempt to be a bit clever, a bit light-hearted – that he'd popped into her head after someone else had knocked her to the ground. Reuben had responded quickly with *LOL*, then they exchanged several messages before moving over to WhatsApp. He was quick to reply there too, but still wrote short, nothingy sentences. *I'm not a wordsmith* he had said at one point, levelling her expectations.

He tells her again that he has been busy, even working at weekends to finish painting a four-storey holiday home belonging to a London-based TV producer.

'And what about you?' He pushes back the sleeves of his blue top. He has so many tattoos, coloured faces and words that sit tired and faded beneath golden hairs. It is strange to be sitting opposite him, free to examine him close up. Until this evening she has treated thoughts of him like a torch she can only turn on at certain, private times. 'You ask a lot of questions. But you don't give much away.'

She shrugs. This isn't the first time she's been told this.

'I'm talking too much,' he adds. 'I'm nervous.' He takes another sip of wine. 'I was shocked to hear from you, if I'm honest.' He takes her left hand and rubs her wedding ring a little roughly. 'Tell me about this.'

Fay looks down at her hand. Before she came out, she had sat at her dressing table staring at her ring while Rose sat on the bed and watched *SpongeBob* on the iPad. But it hadn't been a difficult decision to make. She always wore her wedding ring. To take it off for this evening felt deceitful somehow. It went against the underlying principle of the arrangement.

He lets go of her hand. 'How long have you been married? And you've got kids?'

'Been together twenty-two years. Married for twenty. Two kids.' She rolls the wine glass stem between both hands. 'So, you've got no problem with married women then? It doesn't bother you?'

'You contacted me, Fay.'

She blushes at the edge in his voice. 'Sorry. You're right.'

'I could have made a move when we met again at the freelancers' event, but I didn't,' he says self-righteously.

'Anyway, I can do what I want. I'm not married. You are. I could judge you, couldn't I?'

Fay takes a large mouthful of wine. 'My husband knows I'm here.'

Reuben has a disbelieving expression on his face. 'With me?'

'Not you, per se. He knows I'm with another man.'

There is a short silence. 'I'm really confused,' says Reuben, looking annoyed. 'What is this? Why did you get in touch?'

'My husband and I... we... we've decided to try an open relationship.' Fay feels like her entire body is shaking.

Reuben pours himself more wine even though his glass is relatively full. 'Okay. Right.' He is nodding, thinking. 'So, how's that going?'

'I don't know yet. This is the first time I've been out with someone else.' She looks down at her drink and takes a deep breath. A warmth runs through her.

When she looks up, he is squinting at her, head slightly tilted. 'Let me get this straight. You're out with me... but you'll go back to your husband tonight. And he's okay with that.' After she nods, he says, 'Well, this is a first. So, are you together because of the kids?'

His tone has shifted. There's a brusqueness that wasn't there before; she can tell he's trying to make sense of her. 'No. Nothing like that. It's a good marriage. We're both happy.' Fay shrugs. 'It's just something we decided to explore. That's it in a nutshell.' She folds her arms on the table and smiles between closed lips.

It's pretty obvious that she's not going to say any more and, to his credit, Reuben doesn't push, although he looks disappointed. She wonders if that's to do with her closing up so quickly or because she's told him she's happily married. Either way it doesn't matter. She's said all she's going to say on it. Yesterday, Steve sent her an email with the subject header, *An Additional Rule*, and in the email he told her he would feel very insecure knowing she was discussing him with someone else. *Which includes what I'm like in bed*, he said. *Absolutely*, Fay replied. She doesn't want Reuben to know stuff like that. Her marriage feels completely separate from this evening. It has to, really. It's the only way she can sit here and do this.

'Are you cross?' she asks. 'Should I have told you?'

Reuben shrugs. 'I don't know. Maybe. I would have still come though. I'm flattered. But...' He shakes his head as if he is still trying to get to grips with it. 'Personally, I don't think I could do it.'

'Maybe I can't.' Fay attempts to laugh. 'I don't know yet.'

'I can't imagine my ex-wife and I ever discussing it. Not a chance!' He laughs to himself.

'You were married?'

'Yeah. Five years. Divorced two.' A burst of loud cheering strikes up behind them. 'It's good that you're in a happy marriage and yet...' Reuben's voice returns to being slightly flirtatious and cheeky. 'I'm also pleased that you're not totally, one hundred per cent happy.' He puts his hand over hers, covering her wedding ring, then makes her laugh by following up with a comical wink.

They chat and drink for another couple of hours before Fay says she should probably make a move. She only had a couple of glasses of wine and drank them slowly, but the tension between them makes her feel drunker than she is. In the street, she looks towards the beach, feeling the breeze off the sea and noticing the flicker of a lit boat in the distance. She slowly buttons up her denim jacket. She wants to, but can't, look at Reuben. Sensing her lostness, he takes her hand and pulls her along the pavement and into the thin, dank alley that separates two of the buildings and is a shortcut to a parallel street.

'Can I kiss you?' he asks, and she nods, feeling a distinct pulse between her legs as he presses her against the wall. When he curls his hands into her hair, she is immediately aware of how different they feel to Steve's hands, smaller and surprisingly soft. Then, with his hands cupping her face, he kisses her on the lips. She hears herself gasp. The tension between her legs intensifies. She puts her arms around his neck, and she returns the kiss with her body as well as her mouth, shrugging hard against him.

They kiss for several minutes. When she hears footsteps and a man and woman talking, she turns her face into Reuben's jacket to hide herself.

When they are alone again, he whispers, 'That was something.'

'It was,' she says.

/

She is home by eleven. Steve must already be in bed – the doors to the downstairs rooms are shut. In the kitchen, where she drinks a glass of water, a neat stack of clean washing sits on the table. Rose's backpack rests on one of the chairs, newspapers and magazines are bundled neatly together for recycling by the bin. It's slightly surreal that her normal life has carried on while she stood in the street with a man who was not her husband pressing his hands down on her shoulders and kissing her.

In the bathroom, she brushes her teeth and takes off her clothes, leaving them in a heap on the floor. She's just about drunk enough not to care. On her way past Rose's room, she doesn't automatically go in as she would most evenings to stand and look gratefully at the child they had after years of trying. Tonight, with another man's touch on her, it might feel painful to be anywhere near her daughter.

Fay opens the door to her bedroom. Her nakedness feels strange and daring in the darkness, like she's about to slip into bed with a lover, not her husband. Beneath the duvet, her side of the bed is cool. Steve is far over on his side, with his back to her. She listens for a moment, for the small noises he makes when asleep, a clicking in his throat or a faint, acceptable snore. But nothing. Of course he's still awake. If the roles were reversed, which they will be, she can't imagine falling asleep while he's out. She lies there for a moment, trying to work out what to do, what Steve might need from her. She doesn't really know, and she suspects neither does he. He made it clear that he didn't want to hear any details, but she wonders if this is really what he wants, and if he is suffering more or less because of this.

She turns onto her side and kisses his bare back, then rests her head against the space between his shoulder blades.

'Steve,' she whispers. Certain that he can hear her, his lack of response triggers an unexpected sadness. For twenty-two years she has taken her life home and shared it out with him. Sometimes the best part of her evening is dissecting events with him. What someone said, who was acting in a particular way, why a film was overrated. To withhold information seems almost as strange as being with Reuben in the first place.

'Night,' she whispers, then carefully turns over.

As she does, Steve puts an arm behind him and strokes her bare leg. Neither of them move. For a second Fay feels so strange and sad that tears gather. She is overcome with an unexpected guilt, hates what she has done, as if she has cheated on Steve and diminished him somehow. And yet, she kissed another man. That feeling, when she isolates it for a moment, is thrilling.

She lies there, with Steve's hand on her leg, knowing that he is also thinking about all of these things.

# 4

Steve hurries Rose along. They shouldn't be running late, not on the first day at her new school. He opens the car door for her and guides her in with his hand, wishing that she would match his sense of urgency and stop talking about penguins for a moment. She knows a lot of random stuff about penguins, too much, so the conversation is one-sided. More of a monologue really, but that can happen when Rose gets anxious. Either she'll say absolutely nothing, or all her emotions get sunk beneath an endless stream of chatter.

This started at five thirty when she woke him by prodding his arm hard, then shouting at him about how much she needed to eat cereal *now* and crying and talking until Steve got out of bed, hugged her, then held her hand all the way down the stairs, because he really did understand that being the new girl is not an easy thing. My God though, all her talking makes his head pop.

'Penguins are better than dolphins. They have such kind faces. And dolphins don't have any yellow on their heads. Daddy? Penguins have nice faces, don't they?'

'Uh-huh. Yep. They sure do.'

He straps her in her booster and checks over his shoulder that Fay is locking the front door and hurrying to the car. When she gets into the passenger seat, she swivels around and says, 'Okay, darling... oh yes, you're absolutely right, much nicer faces, I've always thought so too...' before facing the front. Steve smiles gratefully at her as they drive off. Fay is better at dealing with Rose at times like this. She doesn't get flustered or overwhelmed.

'Did your mum call Rose?' asks Fay.

He shakes his head. 'Nope.' She had overheard him calling his mother yesterday, leaving her a voicemail to remind her that Rose was starting a new school today. 'She might not have listened to the message,' he adds.

'Maybe,' says Fay vaguely. She doesn't believe that and, if he was being honest with himself, nor does he.

'She'll probably call later when Rose is back,' he says loyally. 'See how her day went.'

'Maybe,' says Fay again.

The morning roads are clogged with cars and bikes. While they wait at the traffic lights in a patch of strong sunlight, Steve glances sideways at Fay on her phone. He wonders if she is texting that guy. He doesn't imagine so. Fay is not disrespectful. If he asks her, she will tell him, but he won't. Instead, he looks at the car ahead and reminds himself that he mostly feels prepared for their arrangement, except for random, unexpected moments when it hits him that he might share a part of Fay with someone else. Then he feels as though he is physically falling through the carefully constructed layers of his life, and it takes him a few minutes to recover.

'Katie wants us to meet Nathan this week.' Fay stops texting. 'I made an excuse.'

Steve nods. 'Bit too soon for all that. We don't want to rub Matt's nose in it.'

'That's what I thought.' She touches his stubble. 'You're a good person, Steve Ariti.' She puts her hand on his thigh and runs it up and down as he glances over, feigning a shocked expression. He also needs to keep remembering that since her first night out with someone else, the sex they've had has helped him feel a lot better about things. It's been incredible, the best it's been for ages. They even did it twice in one night. When was the last time that had happened?

'Look, there's a space,' says Fay as they approach the

school. He parks, then goes to open the door for Rose. 'Here we go, sweetheart. Come on.'

'Do you think penguins—'

'Enough, Rose. Please. Let's just get out.' He helps her onto the pavement where she stands, small and slight and silent, staring at the old school building.

But when she reaches for each of their hands, he regrets getting frustrated with her. What kind of an unfeeling asshole is he? Especially since he has many of his own difficult memories as the only mixed Greek-Jewish kid in his school. He was name-called, pushed around a little in the lunchtime queue. Small stuff that meant the bullies could say that it was nothing, it meant nothing. Worse was being seen at his dad's café where he often went after school to help clear and wipe the tables. A few of the boys would wait until his dad was in the kitchen, then stand outside on the pavement in front of the window, grabbing and thrusting their crotches at Steve. Did his olive skin, his vague hint of a different ethnicity, make him an easy target? Or was it because back then he was doughy and overweight? He won't ever know.

They find Rose's classroom on the edge of the small playground and wait awkwardly close to the door. Children run around them, barrelling into one another, while parents hold lunch boxes and jackets or fleeces, picking up and putting down conversation with a casualness that he can tell Fay envies from the small, frozen smile on her face. It doesn't matter to him if no one speaks to them, but Fay doesn't like clinging to the edge; she'll need to find a way to move quickly inwards. It isn't about being a big player, she's not gossipy or interested in anyone else's business, but she likes having the choice over her involvement, what and whom to reject.

As Rose latches herself uncomfortably to his left thigh, he plays with her hair. He imagines she's thinking about her old school, wondering whether this will be any better. Who can blame her? She has no reason to trust anything yet.

Now he can feel her body heave against his leg, a potential

precursor to some serious sobs. He gestures to Fay that he'll deal with this, then he crouches down. 'Come on, sweetie. Remember, you were excited about this yesterday.' As he says this, he recognises it to be a pointless statement. Kids can't draw on yesterday's emotions.

'You, missie, are going to have a great day, you hear me?'

Rose nods.

'Sure?'

She nods again, hesitantly.

/

The first night Fay went out to meet another man, Steve drank far more beer than usual. As soon as he'd finished reading Rose a bedtime story, he kissed and cuddled her with unusual brevity, then made his way down to the fridge.

Later, before getting into bed alone, he gargled with mint mouthwash. Fay hated the heavy smell of beer; it kept her awake. He was still looking into the dark when she returned and slipped in beside him. He couldn't bear to speak to her, but they touched each other gently and he listened to her breathing. They were physically so close and yet to him it might have been the furthest he had ever felt from her – even more than he had at moments during the decade after they had Billy when they were trying for another child. They had taken their time to get going, ridiculously cocky that it would be as easy to conceive as it had been first time around, but then they had three miscarriages in three years, followed by four rounds of unsuccessful IVF. Fay started to hate her body; she didn't even want him to touch it. After the last failed IVF, she refused to talk to anyone but Billy for days. At one point Steve had found her in the bathroom pounding her stomach over and over and he hadn't recognised anything about her, yet he felt more separate from her that night in bed, knowing she had been with someone else.

Steve kept moving around, thinking sleep would come,

but it didn't. Eventually, he got up and sat at the kitchen table with a cup of tea and his phone. A few days earlier, he had joined Tinder and a couple of other dating websites, curious about online dating, having completely managed to bypass it until now. He tapped on one of the sites and browsed for a bit. But every time, within minutes, the same thing happened; no matter how hopeful he felt starting out, he couldn't keep it up. His mood dropped. By the time he'd looked at half a dozen women's profiles, instead of being intrigued, he just felt flattened.

Steve put his phone down. It definitely wasn't the right time for this; he had too much on his mind. Instead, he opened his laptop and typed. It didn't take long to commit to a document what he was thinking, and it must have released a lot of anxiety because when he went back to bed, he soon fell asleep.

The next morning in his office, he printed out what he'd written before anyone else came in and glanced over his shoulder. That night when it was just him and Fay in the kitchen, he handed her the piece of paper and a pen. She was wearing a pair of navy sweatpants and a soft blue cardigan over a black sleeveless top. Even in her oldest clothes, she still managed to look good. When she glanced up, she seemed confused.

'You... wrote up the rules?' she said in a drawn-out voice, one eyebrow raised. 'And you want me to sign this?'

Steve nodded. 'Yep, I do.'

'But I've already been out with someone.'

'I know.'

'And I've agreed to the rules.'

'You did.' He offered no other explanation. It was just something he needed to do, his small way of asserting some personal control.

Fay sat down at the table, looking at the document thoughtfully. 'This is a bit extreme.' She sighed. 'But why not? Let's really go for it.'

'Go for it?' he asked.

'I'll sign, then let's toast the arrangement with a glass of something. I might even give you a hand job to seal the deal.'

He grinned. 'Only a hand job? It's a big deal we're closing on. A blow job feels more appropriate.'

Fay threw back her head and laughed. He loved that she wasn't squeamish, that she actively encouraged him to talk dirty. As he took out the bottle of cheap Prosecco they had in the back of the fridge and uncorked it, he heard her running through the list. 'Yes, always be honest. Don't see anyone more than about fifteen times... random, but okay... no emotional involvements... no one in the house... no friends... yeah...' Eventually, her voice trailed off. She signed her name with a flourish. 'I've even dated it, so I do believe this will stand up in a court of law.'

She handed him the pen as he handed her a glass of fizz. After he had also signed the document, they clinked glasses.

'Cheers,' said Fay. She took a sip, put down her glass and started unzipping his flies. 'Nice doing business with you, Steve.'

He also put his glass down and started to unbutton her cardigan. 'You too, Fay.'

/

Fay is standing by the fireplace, ready to go out. 'It's such a relief that Rose had a great first day, isn't it?'

Steve is only half listening. He feels winded. Fay is dressed for someone else. She is fully, carefully made-up. Her hair was cut and layered the day before, so it only drops to her shoulders, and she has a choppy, sexy fringe. Her black dress is old, she's worn it countless times, but she has perfectly accessorised it with yellow trainers, big silver hoop earrings and a compact red and yellow shoulder bag. She must have pictured herself in this outfit for days, rearranging the details over and over again. Steve knows, without doubt, that she hasn't fucked this guy yet, but she will tonight.

'Steve?'

'Yeah.' He hugs his beer between crossed arms and extends his legs. 'Yeah, I'm made up for her.'

Rose had not just got through her first day, but run out and flung herself at them, shouting about some girl called Olivia who was her new best friend and how her teacher, Miss Floss, made Rose today's guest of honour. She looked happier and more relaxed than they'd seen in months and emotion had filled his throat and brought Fay close to tears.

'You look great, by the way,' he says in a voice that doesn't entirely sound like his own. Bizarrely, now he's examining her, he can even tell that her brown eye shadow is heavier than usual, with a hint of blue in the corners. He knows this because recently he's begun to look at her even more closely. This is not about suddenly appreciating her – she's a beautiful woman; he often tells her this. No, this is about documenting her carefully. Sometimes he thinks this has to do with working out how other men might see her. Other times, he feels as if he's actually recording details about her, noting any changes, in much the same way he looked hard and long at his dad in the months that the cancer took hold. When this happens, Steve has to tell himself to snap out of it and not to be morbid, that the arrangement is in place to enrich their relationship. Will it? He doesn't know.

'Steve?' Fay pauses. 'Are you sure you're still okay with this?' she says in a whisper.

'Yes.' She asks him every couple of days; he can't keep saying the same thing.

'I don't have to go tonight. I can stay.'

'Why are you saying that?'

'Because… well, it feels a bit odd to leave. We've had a big family day.'

Steve waves his beer bottle at her. 'It's fine. Go. You've moved it once already.' She was meant to go out the previous night but swapped it so she could be on hand for Rose.

Fay nods as he speaks. She looks surprisingly hesitant. Is she about to change her mind? Maybe. Probably not.

She pulls on her denim jacket. 'I won't be late. I've got an early start.'

He nods. He tries to imagine how long it will be before she and this guy start having sex, how quickly they can feasibly get to it. Given that they've already had a night out, he imagines she's going straight to his flat. Or house. Or caravan. He has no idea where this person lives. Yet Steve knows, with a life-changing certainty, that at some point in the next couple of hours, his wife will open her dress and display her small, perfect breasts for another man.

'When are you out this week?' Fay fiddles with her jacket collar.

She has also been asking this a lot recently. What she means is, when is he going to have sex with someone else? He suspects it would make her feel better about what she plans to get up to.

'No idea.' He doesn't feel like making it easy for her. 'Not this week. Maybe next.' He's already said this once. Will he keep saying it?

'Okay. I'm going to get a cab from the main road.' She puts a small tube of hand cream in her bag, then comes over, leans down and kisses him on the lips.

'Look, do you want to forget about all this?' she says. 'Tell me the truth. Please.'

He wants to cry. He thinks she does too. She looks scared, all big eyes and a soulful expression. Without moving, he keeps staring up at her. He feels under enormous pressure to understand exactly what he is feeling. Is it that he really can't handle what Fay is about to do? Or is he jealous? When they were having long discussions about how things would work, they had talked at length about not needing to belong exclusively to each other, that it was a construct that had been forced upon them and jealousy was a shallow, destructive notion that they should move beyond. It was an interesting conversation and he'd agreed with all of it, but that was when it was all pleasantly academic. Now he wonders whether he is just too ordinary and small-minded to be the free-spirited, emotionally in-touch guy that Fay has decided she needs.

Jesus, his head is reeling. Now Fay is pushing him back into the sofa and sitting on his lap, kissing each of his eyelids and his cheeks and saying in a faraway voice, 'You know you're the love of my life, don't you?'

She is saying the right thing and he's filling up on her words, but it does feel a bit bizarre to hear it as she's about to walk out of the door and have sex with someone else.

'Right back atcha,' he says as she stands up.

He could pull her back. He does pull her back. He clasps his hand around her wrist.

'Steve.' She doesn't try to shake him off. 'I won't go.'

She might be nodding, but she's not making eye contact. If he stops her going, what then? It means that he'll have to figure out how else to give her what she needs – because clearly, she is lacking something. And he's always loved that she's wanted more. Her hunger has made him strive and push himself. He knows he wouldn't be working for himself without her at his back, forcing him forward. He would have given up at the first failed IVF, insisted they were happy as they were. And he really does want them to at least try this new experience, to grow together. He tries to claw back the tremors of excitement he has felt now and again over the past fortnight.

'I'm alright. Go on. I mean it. Go.' He doesn't move for some time after she shuts the front door. When he realises an hour has passed with him just sitting there, he gets up and walks to the kitchen. He picks at some cold chicken in the fridge and makes himself a piece of toast, then he goes and sits in the living room, but this time without any of the lights on.

# 5

'Come on, Rose. Give me a break,' says Fay. 'All I'm saying is if you go up there, sweetheart, tidy up after yourself. Don't leave empty crisp packets on the rug.'

Fay hates telling her off, but Rose has begun to monopolise her desk area in the corner of the attic, the one space that should belong mostly to her. She keeps finding Rose spinning in her desk chair with her headphones on, listening to her audiobooks.

'It's not just your office,' says Rose on her way out of the kitchen. 'It's the spare room too.'

'I shouldn't have to clean up after you. That's all.'

Just back from his Saturday morning run, Steve comes in wiping the back of his neck with a hand towel. 'What's going on?'

'I'm tired of cleaning up after everyone.' Fay presses down on the cafetière. She pours herself a coffee without asking Steve if he wants one, an act that he acknowledges with a small lift of his eyebrow, then she takes her coffee into the garden and sits on a chair on the decking.

Of course, they both know this isn't about the cleaning. No, they both understand that this is tied into the other night, when she went to visit Reuben at his flat for the first time and returned home early. So early, Steve was still up, sitting in a dark living room, watching a film. Glancing back at her as she stuck her head around the door, all he had said was, 'Hey, everything okay?' and turned back to the television when she nodded. And she had been glad, really glad, that he had feigned a lack of interest. It wasn't real. It couldn't be. Steve was a curious person. On a normal night, he would have paused the film and encouraged her to slump into him on the sofa while she ran through what she'd got up to.

She is still sitting there, drinking coffee, thinking, when Steve comes out with a glass of water. He sits down next to her and, after a few seconds' silence, asks, 'What time are you out tonight?'

'Seven-ish.' She isn't in the mood for Katie's birthday drinks, but she has to go. Katie gives the impression that she's a relaxed person, but actually she's totally neurotic about social stuff. For the past few days, Fay has received several messages from her criticising women that Fay hasn't even met. In Fay's mind, it seems masochistic to organise a birthday celebration every year if small things, like how long people take to reply to your invite, are going to wind you up.

Steve nods. 'The babysitter will take over from me about eight.'

'Where are you and Matt going?' asks Fay. 'Big night?'

'The pub. I could do without it, but Matt seems bent on dragging me out. He won't take no for an answer.' Steve picks up the rucksack that he has brought out to the garden. After a quick glance at the house, he puts it on the small, rusty garden table, unzips the main pocket, then pulls out two new mobile phones still in their boxes.

'Here.' He hands one to her. 'We'll use these phones to communicate with anyone to do with our arrangement. Keep things separate.'

'You're kidding.' Staring down at it, Fay knows she's pulling a face. 'That seems a bit over the top.'

'You think?'

Fay blushes. She deserves Steve's sarcasm. On the morning of her second date with Reuben, Rose had picked up her phone to FaceTime Steve's mum and seen a message from Reuben which said, *See you then xxx R*. Since Fay has him in her phone only as R, naturally Rose asked who R was. When Fay said it was an old friend, Rose insisted on asking Fay in front of Steve who had the same initials as her and did she have a daughter and why hadn't Rose met them.

Steve takes the phone back from her and zips them both away. 'I'll set them up later today.'

'There's no hurry.' Fay's laugh is short and forced. 'I don't need it anytime soon.'

Steve nods slowly, as if she's just confirmed his suspicions. 'I knew your mood was to do with him.' He says it matter-of-factly. 'Look, we said we wouldn't talk about things, but he didn't do anything bad to you, did he? He didn't hurt you? That's something I would absolutely want to know.'

Standing up, Fay presses her hands on the table until her knuckles are leached of colour. His kindness makes her want to cry. 'No, nothing like that. Honestly.'

'Good.' As he looks towards the smoke tree, she can see he's deliberately trying to breathe slowly and calm himself down. They both know there's more, that there's a story between them that she isn't telling him. But she has pushed for this experiment, and she must contend with the highs and lows.

/

Three nights earlier, Fay had left Steve sitting in the half-light and gone to Reuben's flat for the first time. He had told her to text when she was on the way over in a taxi. The intercom was dodgy, so he would meet her by the entrance to the building. When she texted, he quickly replied.

## R

Just so you know, my flat's a bit of a dump but it's only temporary. x

Fay could tell he was feeling insecure about her seeing where he lived, but she didn't care about any of that. Her main preoccupation on the journey over was whether her body was good enough for someone new. It had been out of public scrutiny for so long, she really couldn't tell.

As she got out of the taxi, holding the bottle of wine she'd picked up from the off-licence, Reuben stepped away from the main door, punching out the pockets of his cargo shorts. He was also wearing a white T-shirt that showed off his strong, tattooed arms, and flip-flops. It surprised her how underdressed he was. She wondered whether this signified something: if he felt relaxed with her (a good thing) or if he was sure that he'd already snared her (a bad thing). Then again, the truth was that he had snared her, hadn't he? She was there for sex, regardless of how he dressed.

'Hello, Mrs-Someone-Else's-Wife,' he said with a silly grin on his face.

'Hey.' She frowned.

'Sorry, I'm just teasing you.'

'Don't. Not about that.'

'Okay. I won't. Let's start again.' He kissed her on the lips. 'You look gorgeous,' he said, pushing aside the heavy door for her.

In the foyer, as they waited for the lift to clank down to them, he answered her questions amicably. He'd been living here for the past year. His mum and sister lived five minutes away and he played football with some guys twice a week on a nearby field. The low rent was a big help, but he knew he needed to look for somewhere more permanent.

'You're very good at getting things out of me,' he said as they got into the lift. 'That's a compliment, by the way.' She smiled as he stroked the side of her face, then pressed the fourth-floor button and leaned back against the mirrored wall.

In his flat, Reuben seemed very awkward. He kept extending his arms above his head in a fake stretch as he pointed out each room. The place was tiny. It took no time to end up in the living room where he didn't invite her to sit in one of the two flowered armchairs, so old-fashioned the arms had separate fabric sleeves. Instead, he fussed with some papers on the coffee table for a minute or two, while Fay stood in the doorway, trying to look relaxed, telling herself that the flat wasn't that bad. But this was only to neutralise the claustrophobic feeling that was rising in her. The ceilings were low, every wall was painted a sullen magnolia and, from her brief look around, Reuben had hung nothing on the walls except a dartboard. The care he spoke of lavishing on his clients was clearly lacking here.

'It does the trick for now,' he said as if he was seeing the flat through her eyes.

'We could have gone to a hotel.'

'Is it that bad?'

'Not at all.' She waved him away. 'I just don't want you to feel uncomfortable in your own home.'

'I think we both need a drink,' he said, heading out of the room.

'Good plan.' In the kitchen, he took an open bottle of white wine from the fridge and poured her a near-full glass.

Sitting at the kitchen table, Fay felt a gnawing in her stomach that had nothing to do with hunger. Now she was in Reuben's flat, she felt far less sure of him. She wasn't a snob. The house she grew up in had been bland and functional, lacking in art and books, but the feeling of this place implied a slight breakdown in self-worth. She felt some empathy for Reuben, but if she was being honest, it was also a turn-off.

She wondered if he had always lived like this or whether his failed marriage had emptied him out. Turning this over in her mind as he talked, something profound dawned on her: why did she care? She didn't need to change or save him. She was not looking for a new partner. She wanted sex. Recognising this, her anxiety became manageable again. Her breath slowed, her stomach stopped hurting and she was able to properly listen to Reuben's story about the doctor whose living room he had just started decorating. The day before, she had told him to help himself to a box of books she was about to give to charity. As Reuben extended a muscular arm towards the counter to show Fay the book he was reading, her enthusiasm for him fully returned.

She laughed at the title, *I Hate You, Don't Leave Me*. 'Is there a reason you were drawn to this one?'

'I knew you'd say that.'

Fay grinned. Now she'd rationalised that she didn't need to like everything about Reuben in order to be here, she felt so much more light-hearted, childishly so. She stared at him. It had been a long time since she'd kissed a man with hair, and it held a strangely erotic appeal. He correctly took her look to mean an advance of some sort and he leant over, put his hand on her shoulder and kissed her. They both stood up, pushed aside the chair in between them and came together. It happened so smoothly it was almost dreamlike how she got to do all these astonishing things, such as put her hands through another man's thick, lavender-smelling hair and kiss him, even though she had a husband and child at home.

And the kiss, like Reuben's other kisses, was really good. Her head felt woozy. She was moved not only by the excitement of unfamiliar, physical touch but also by her own fearlessness. She had taken a big risk with her marriage, pushing to collapse structures that had held things in a certain place for years. Here she was, getting what she had felt she needed.

Eventually, Reuben drew back and smiled at her goofily, as if he was now pleased at the way things were going. 'Shall we go to my…' He coughed into his closed hand in a fake way. '…bedroom?'

Giggling to hide her awkwardness, Fay let him take her hand and lead her to yet another barren room, in the corner of which was a double bed.

'I changed the bed linen,' he said with a hint of pride.

'Lucky me.'

'Don't knock it.' He lifted his T-shirt over his head at the same time as she unbuttoned her dress and stepped out of it.

He had a lovely body. Sinewy, long. There was nothing she didn't like about it. She reached out and grazed her fingers along his upper arm.

'My turn.' He leaned over as if he was about to touch her arm, then moved his hand and stroked her left breast through her bra.

'Hey,' she said, slightly shocked, but then they both really laughed. It was different from the laughter they had shared only a few moments ago in the kitchen. It felt like they had moved on to a new level of relaxation with each other. As exciting as the tension had been, it was also unbearable and a relief for some of it to drain away. They were still laughing when he pulled her onto the fresh sheets. As he kissed her, he lowered her knickers, then glanced down.

'Woah.' He tenderly touched her pubic hair. 'Very seventies.' His voice was quiet, as if she had caught him talking to himself.

'Seventies?' By contrast, it sounded as if she was shouting. She felt small, naive. Pulling herself up onto her elbows, she glanced down at him. 'Is that what you said?' A sense of loss blew through her.

'Yeah.' He was still examining her with a genuine, studied interest. 'Everyone I've been with since my wife has had a Brazilian. Or whatever it's called.'

'Lots of women have hair down there,' snapped Fay. 'It's mostly children who don't.'

He glanced up at her face. It would be impossible not to tell that she was seriously pissed off. She couldn't hide it. She didn't want to hide it.

'Sure.' His cheeks went a bit red. 'I'm only talking about the women I've been with.'

'You make me sound prehistoric. Am I that much older than the girls you've been sleeping with?' Fay sat up, pulling her knees tight to her chest.

'No! Not at all. Fay, I'm really attracted to you,' he said. 'I really like it. I really like you.' He kept talking. Now he was saying reassuring things in a heightened, panicked way that made her feel even more uncomfortable. She wished she was wearing a robe that she could pull tight around herself. Eventually, she said, 'Alright. Let's forget about it.'

She unfolded herself and lay back down. Almost as soon as she did, Reuben angled himself over her. He looked deep in thought. She suspected that he was still trying to make sense of what had gone wrong and was working hard to overcome it and bring himself back into the moment. One of them needed to move things along, so she reached up and ran her hands up and down the strong edge of his torso. Reuben liked that. He made a small noise, leant down and kissed her clavicle.

'It's going to be okay. It's all good,' he whispered. 'We're just getting to know each other.'

His body was on hers, their legs were entwined, and the kissing was much more searching and ferocious. Fay became involved, disappearing away from herself. Her insecurities and worries were dissolving. She felt the excitement rise up between them.

But when she realised Reuben was stopping to put a condom on, she almost gasped. So soon? Where's the overture? As she was still hoping for something more, it appeared that he was already done with that; he was making his way inside her.

'Yeah. Oh. Yeah.' His exhalations were so loud. 'Don't worry. I can go for hours.'

He looked at the wall behind her as he spoke, pushing and straining, unaware that his words sounded like a threat. The idea that this could go on for an interminable amount of time frightened Fay. She felt outside of her body, looking down a telescope at her life as it grew smaller and smaller.

'Stop,' she shouted.

'What?' He kept thrusting, pushing her back against the headboard.

'I need you to stop. Now.' Reuben pulled out of her. While she felt an instant relief, she also felt a certain sympathy for him when she saw how injured he looked. Shaking, she swung her legs over the side of the bed. 'I'm really sorry,' she said with her back to him.

She heard the snap of his underpants waistband, the zip of his cargo shorts. 'You're obviously not ready for this,' he said. 'Or you've got issues.'

Given her harsh rejection of him, it wasn't an unfair thing to say. But shortly she would leave his flat and she knew they would never contact each other again. He could reason it out however he chose. Who knew what was fabricated in her mind or what was real? It didn't matter. All she knew was that things felt right and then they didn't.

Once she heard him leave the room, she turned around and got dressed. On her way to the front door, she stopped by the kitchen. Reuben was sitting at the table facing away from her, which she was glad of. Still, she felt a warmth come over her jaw and cheeks.

'I'm really sorry,' she said again. 'I don't know what happened.'

'Me neither.' Reclining in the chair, he moved his glass between both hands without looking around. 'See you around, Mrs-Someone-Else's-Wife.'

/

Fay crosses the street outside The Nine Bar, holding her clutch bag against her black silk bomber jacket. It isn't surprising that she's never been here before; Katie prides herself on choosing venues that are new and emerging.

At first the place seems empty until Fay realises it's designed to look this way. Groups of people are squirrelled away in oval booths. The walls are fashionably dark, except for a few perfectly positioned wall lamps. It's all very mysterious and atmospheric, which suddenly feels rather tiring – she would prefer to just have a drink and a chat in a shabby old pub.

She finds the booth where Katie is sitting. It's a real showpiece, a curved red bench with a high back. Fay briefly imagines it is an open mouth that will swallow her down, which is exactly how these gatherings can make her feel. As she smiles and whispers general hellos and waits for Katie to stop talking and notice her, a couple she knows well – Tim and Tim(!) – spot her and wave. She hopes she can shuffle in next to them. They're chatty and fun and won't demand too much of her conversationally.

'Yeh, Fay!' shouts Katie from the middle of the table and waves. She is wearing a gold off-the-shoulder top and a matching hairband. 'I'll climb out in a minute.'

Now that she's been acknowledged, Fay relaxes a bit and affords herself a proper look around the crowd. Apart from the Tims, there are about seven women – thankfully, Katie decided against asking Nathan – some of whom Fay has met before, if only in passing.

'Squeeze on here,' says the thin woman closest to Fay, whose name she thinks might be Val and who, like Katie, is an HR manager in the NHS.

'Thanks,' Fay says and asks her what she's drinking.

'A Negroni. It's absolutely delicious.'

'Oh, lovely. That's what I'll have.'

'Can I get anyone another cocktail?'

Fay glances up at the woman in the long black bib apron taking the orders. She is leaning away from Fay, towards the opposite side of the booth to answer one of the Tims, who is pointing at the menu and asking a question.

Watching her, Fay is momentarily shocked. *I know you*, she thinks. *You're Emma French*. It must be twenty years since they've seen each other in person, but privately, if somewhat shamefully, she has always been a bit of a mental go-to for Fay. At difficult emotional times in her life, Fay can clearly recall picturing her and thinking, *there but for the grace of God – at least this isn't as bad as the experience Emma French went through.*

'Oh, good call. That's a favourite of mine,' Emma is saying as she taps out the order on the small screen in her hand.

Fay waits, her hand wavering towards Emma's white shirt and the rattle of bracelets on her wrist, like a schoolchild trying to grab the teacher before they turn away to someone else.

'Emma?' she asks as soon as there is a natural pause. 'Emma French?' She hears the wonder in her voice.

So does Emma. She swivels around and clutches the edge of the table rather dramatically. 'Fay Munro!'

Fay stands up and moves her hands around like a showgirl. 'The one and only.' She has no idea why she does this. It makes her look and sound ridiculous and jocular. Now everyone's eyes are on her. This includes Katie, who is scrutinising this unexpected interaction between guest and server.

'My God, Fay. Amazing. I can't believe it.' Shaking her head, Emma bites down on her bottom lip. Ruby-red lipstick specks her top front teeth.

'You haven't changed a bit,' says Fay.

'Oh, I think we both know that's not true.' In fact, it isn't true for either of them. As Emma speaks, she tucks stray hairs behind her ears and pulls the band tighter around her thick, messy ponytail. She is much blonder than in college, and Fay isn't sure it works; it's too light, almost crispy. She is more solid-looking than Fay recalls, but aren't they both? Emma still looks striking. Huge, hooded grey eyes. Clear pale skin, lovely teeth. Well-kept eyebrows. Surprisingly, it doesn't all add up to her being conventionally attractive, but Fay likes that. Emma is the sort of woman you want to keep looking at to work out what you think.

'But you, Fay. You look incredible. Honest to God, *in-cre-di-ble.*'

Fay bats her away, embarrassed. She had forgotten how effusive Emma could be. Early on in the first year of their degree, she had sought out Fay at the end of a psychology seminar, one of the few they had shared, and told her that her remarks on active listening were so spot on she had got goosebumps. She even pulled up her jumper arm to show Fay, who had probably blushed, unused to such direct praise from a fellow student. Yet she had also been touched by it, especially since they really didn't know each other.

'I had no idea you lived here,' says Fay. 'Not that I would know, I suppose.'

'I've only been here about eighteen months.' As Emma twirls her ponytail in her hand, Fay notices her bitten-down nails. Worry nails, she calls them. Rose also has them. 'My son's dad moved here for work. We're not together, but we co-parent, so it made sense for us all to make the move.'

'How old is your son?'

'Almost sixteen. Impossible to believe, but he's doing his GCSEs this term.' Emma raises both eyebrows and shakes her head. 'And you? Kids? Husband? Work?'

'Well, I married Steve Ariti. Did you know him? He was at uni too, but I didn't meet him until the second year, so...'

When Fay falters, Emma smoothly finishes the sentence for her. 'Ah, after I left.'

Fay nods. 'And we've got a nineteen-year-old son and soon-to-be six-year-old girl. I write content. Mostly website stuff, brochures, that sort of thing.' She waves her hand dismissively. 'I only work part-time at the moment, but I'm hoping to step it up once Rose settles at school.'

'How interesting,' says Emma. 'Me, I'm the oldest cocktail waitress in town.'

'I miss waitressing.' Fay immediately hates herself for saying this, for her poor attempt to make Emma feel better. Who, in their right mind, misses waitressing? Sure, she misses the simplicity of taking food in and out of the kitchen and messing around with the busboys, but she's forgetting about the long hours, bad pay and being treated as a nobody by so many customers. 'Well, I guess I miss the idea of it,' she adds more honestly.

'Exactly.' Emma leans in and whispers in Fay's ear. 'Believe me, you wouldn't miss some of the assholes who come in here. I really have to hold my tongue.'

She draws back, rolling her eyes. Now Emma has stopped smiling, her face has taken on a certain sharpness. It's not unlike the closed, tough expression she had to adopt all the time at university after what happened to her made it into the local news.

'I bet,' says Fay.

'But I don't just do this. I do a lot of art. Collages.' Emma's hand now plays with her bracelets. 'I'm thinking about a couple of other business ideas. I've had some failures.' She sighs. 'I'm trying.'

'Good for you,' says Fay. 'It sounds like you're taking risks. That's brave.'

'Em.' A man in black shirt and trousers stops alongside them. 'We're getting busy, lady. One of your other tables needs you.'

*Lady*, thinks Fay. *Who says that?* The tightening around Emma's mouth suggests that it's not the first time he's belittled her. 'I hear you, boss.'

'Great stuff.' As soon as he walks away, Fay says, 'I don't want to get you into any trouble. I'll have a Negroni, please.'

'Coming up.' Emma taps the screen, then looks back at Fay. 'I'm so thrilled I've run into you. I never said thank you.'

'What for?'

'The letter you wrote me after what happened.'

'Oh no.' Fay shakes her head. 'I've always wanted to apologise for writing it on that card. It was so crass.' She finds her mouth growing dry. She had messed up a sentence on the one bit of blank paper she could find in her chaotically messy bedroom, so she rewrote her message to Emma on an index card she'd stockpiled for revision.

'No, don't you dare do that to yourself.' When Emma puts out a hand and pats Fay's arm, Fay expects it to be brief, perfunctory. Instead, Emma holds her hand there for a few seconds, rubbing her thumb gently against the silky sleeve. 'Hardly anyone wrote to me. You and a couple of others. It meant a lot.'

Fay notices Katie struggling over everyone's laps to get out of the booth and join them. 'So how do you two know each other?' she says, approaching them.

'University,' says Emma.

'Nice,' says Katie. 'I love an unexpected reunion.'

'But we hardly knew each other,' says Fay. 'And we haven't seen each other since.'

'Well, let's remedy that. Can we get coffee sometime?' says Emma shyly. Flattered by this request, Fay says she'd love to meet up and writes her number on a bar receipt Emma digs out of her apron pocket. Emma always intrigued her from afar, so it will be interesting to get to know her better.

'Cool. I'll give you a shout this week,' says Emma, smiling, as she folds the receipt between her fingers, then says she'll be back shortly with everyone's drinks.

# 6

They are on their way to Pizza Express when they bump into Matt in front of Greggs on the high street. He is the last person Steve wants to see, especially since he is full of the party they went to last weekend when Fay was out celebrating Katie's birthday. What Matt is saying is less of an issue than the furtive looks he keeps giving Fay. He's being so weird.

'Did Steve tell you that he even got on the decks?' Matt rotates his hands around on an imaginary turntable. His eyes are half shut and he flaps around a bit on his feet, as if he has been transported back inside the music. He looks ludicrous. In Steve's mind, Matt deserves the same derision he attaches to the two middle-aged men at the skate park he often cycles past, decked out in their fancy protection gear, stringy grey hair hanging out of their helmets, both desperately clinging to a time that has long gone.

'Yeah,' says Matt after Fay shakes her head. 'He had some go in him that night. Didn't you, boy?'

Steve wonders if Matt's matey banter is a front for something more conniving. Whether he is purposefully trying to make trouble since he knows Fay is Katie's confidante. Matt knows that Joni invited Steve to join her in DJing and that Joni is not a girl who Steve wants to discuss here, on the pavement, in the company of his wife.

When Matt says, 'He played some mega tunes,' without an iota of self-consciousness, Steve thinks: no. His theory is far too sophisticated. Matt is benign. He's actually just a bit of a dick.

'I want to go,' says Rose, pulling hard on Steve's hand.

'Yes, sweetheart,' he says, adding curtly, 'Matt, we're in a rush.' Understandably, Rose isn't happy about standing around. They are on their way to her sixth birthday party. She should be the focus of everyone's attention.

'So, you told him about our arrangement,' whispers Fay as they walk away before she shouts, 'Rose! Wait!' Rose is getting further out of sight, skipping in and around the Saturday morning shoppers.

'No, I didn't. He guessed and I didn't want to lie. But if I had told him, I don't think you would have had the right to be upset. You told Katie we'd discussed it, didn't you?' says Steve defensively.

Fay ignores his point about Katie. 'He guessed? Really? I mean, did you even go out with Matt?' She stops to deliver her next question. 'Or did you lie so you could go out with someone else?'

'Of course I didn't lie. Why would I? Anyway, what exactly is your problem?' Steve automatically glances over at Rose as he speaks, noting that she has stopped nearby and is now holding onto a lamp post and pirouetting around, singing to herself. 'That I told Matt? Or that I might have been with someone else?'

'I don't know.' Fay's honesty is like a sedative. He immediately relaxes. Everything is going to be okay. 'I guess a bit of both. Didn't you feel that way about Reuben?'

It's the first time Fay has said Reuben's name aloud since the arrangement began and it makes Steve think of a precious stone, which annoys the hell out of him, because fancy name or not, there is nothing precious about another man screwing his wife.

'I didn't let myself,' he says, half telling the truth. 'Look, if it's making you feel jealous or sad, we can stop this. We can go back to how things were. This instant.' He raises his hand, clicks his fingers. 'Just like that. This arrangement was meant to be freeing.'

'It is. It will be. I'm just processing everything.'

He says, 'Okay, if you say so.'

As they beckon to Rose and walk on briskly, he is thinking about the conversation they've just had, and guesses he must be smiling to himself because Fay says, 'What? What's so amusing?'

'You're too evolved to admit that you might be jealous. My apologies. I can't believe I'd forgotten that about you.'

It's impossible to keep the sarcasm out of his voice, but Fay doesn't take it badly. 'That's alright,' she says, with a small wink. 'You're forgiven.'

/

The night Fay was at Katie's get-together, Matt had badgered Steve into going to the pub for a quick drink and a game of darts. Or at least that had been the idea. When he got there, his heart sank. Ryan, Chris and Ali were grouped awkwardly around a too-small table.

Ryan was the first to get to his feet. 'Alright, Steve.' He straightened the hem of his white shirt and shook Steve's hand. 'How's it going?'

'Didn't expect to see you lot.' Steve spoke in an upbeat, friendly voice. He tried to make it sound like this encounter was a pleasant surprise, but being here without Fay was a new configuration. In fact, it was Fay who had met Katie first and introduced Steve to Matt, and Matt who had insisted he come and play football with the men around this table a few years back. But Steve didn't play football any more and he rarely saw any of them, which suited him. These blokes were decent enough, but he had begun to feel stuck inside the smallness of the chat. He wanted to get more out of the people he spent time with.

Steve shook all of their hands, then pulled his hoodie over his head so he was just wearing his T-shirt. He'd forgotten how sticky and hot the small pubs in town got at the weekend.

Chris pushed a pint towards him. 'Got yours in.'

'Nice one. Thanks.'

'Uh-oh, trouble's back.' Steve glanced over his shoulder at where Ryan was looking and saw that Matt was approaching the table. He mouthed *hello mate* at Steve, then went back to concentrating on carrying a tray of shot glasses.

'Here you go.' He slid the tray onto the table and handed around the glasses. 'Suze's got us into tonight's hot ticket. A private bash at the arts club. A tequila or two should get us in the mood.'

A brunette at Matt's side holding a glass of something with a straw in it smiled at them. This must be the PA that Matt had met online. She was wearing a short dress that barely covered her thighs and she looked much younger than in the photo Matt had sent Steve accompanied by a row of smiling emojis. Steve had replied automatically with something vague and dismissive like, *I'm happy for you.* The text had arrived as he was about to lead a new client meeting and his life and Matt's felt far apart.

'Suze's in event planning, aren't you?' Suze nodded. 'Gets access to great stuff.' Matt sounded so excited that he didn't notice the prospect of partying was making the others react nervously.

Ryan said, 'Cool, great, let me text home, I think it'll be fine.'

Ali mumbled, 'Same.'

Steve didn't need to check with Fay, but that didn't mean he wanted to be part of this. He couldn't remember a time when he'd had a big night without her. He liked doing things separately, but Fay was his best friend and partying without her signified a strange regression, as if he was trying on a former version of himself. Looking at the others digesting the plan, he imagined they were having similar thoughts.

'I'll come but not for long.' Steve wasn't afraid to admit this – he didn't care about pleasing Matt.

After downing a shot and being pressed by Matt to reach

for another, Steve could tell everyone was trying to create a wave of excitement, but it wasn't happening. The wave was tiny, a little lap of foam at their feet. Only Matt looked happy, even smug, as if he was better than them because he had a social life that didn't make him feel uncomfortable.

*Yeah, but I can shag other women and still keep my wife*, Steve said to himself. He expected this thought to amuse him, but actually it made him feel anxious about what everyone would make of him if they knew.

Inside the venue the stairwell was full of people much younger than them. The girls' ages were harder to work out, but some of the blokes didn't look much older than Billy. This made Steve cringe. He had an urge to announce that he was an age-appropriate sort of guy, that he really wasn't chasing his youth. With his eyes averted, he followed the others up the stairs to the second floor.

The bar area was stylish but only half-full. Pretty quickly, Steve peeled away from everyone and followed the house music into a room adjoining the bar. At the far end, a DJ was hovering behind some turntables and although the music was great, only a couple of girls were dancing. If more people had been on the dance floor, Steve might have been tempted to join them. Instead he decided to investigate where the couple drifting through the door near the DJ had come from.

Behind the door was an attractive old staircase which he went up, holding on to the uneven oak banister. The two doors on the first floor were closed, so he kept following the light overhead. On the second floor, he read the scrappy notice stuck next to the light switch advertising a group art exhibition and he wandered in.

Apart from a girl at a table bent over her phone, Steve was alone. Looking at the paintings closest to him, he was impressed. He particularly liked one of children playing in and around a swimming pool, which reminded him very slightly of a David Hockney. The children's fingers were jammed with gold rings and a small gun lay casually on a striped beach towel, elements which he considered to be an excellent moral comment on a warped society. He brought his phone out to photograph it and the artist's name for Fay when the girl called out, 'That's my favourite too.'

Steve turned around. 'Great, isn't it?' He kept walking around the room, but now he was aware of the girl, shifting in her chair, putting her glass down on the table. When he leant in to examine a watercolour of a naked woman on a sofa surrounded by piles of books, she said, 'But the artist is a dick.'

Unsure of how to respond, Steve nodded slowly. It was information that he didn't need to know.

'I'm allowed to say that. We hooked up for a while. He wasn't very nice to me.'

'Sorry to hear that.' Steve kept walking around, but he'd lost interest in the art, so he stopped and turned to look at the girl. Her small, sharp face was framed by a blaze of dark hair which matched her clothes and nail polish. He wondered why she was alone.

'Why wasn't he nice to you?' Steve hadn't known he was going to ask this, but it was just the two of them. He figured he could leave the room if the conversation turned odd.

'Apparently...' she said in a withering voice, '...I wasn't sociable enough. He wanted to go out all the time, but he said I didn't have the right temperament for people. What does that even mean?' Picking at her nails, her eyes widened, as if the notion still baffled her. 'He's uber-talented. I'll give him that.'

'What do you do?' asked Steve. 'Are you also an artist?'

'No, I'm a destination counsellor.'

'A travel agent?'

'Yup.' She smiled for the first time.

Steve shook his head. 'What's with these stupid job titles?'

She shrugged. 'Don't ask me.'

Steve wondered whether it was a generational thing that she showed no interest in what he did, since everyone he knew defined others through their work. It was pretty pathetic to admit it, but he would have liked the chance to tell her that he had his own business. Instead, they lapsed into silence. After a couple of minutes, he was about to make a move downstairs when she said, 'I shaved my hair off for a while.'

Steve ran his hand over his head. He felt the mix of smoothness and the scratch of new growth in places. 'I didn't really have a choice.' He laughed. He had been days off his thirtieth birthday when he noticed the first thin patch. Within months he was thinning all over, until he couldn't cover the gaps, so he shaved it all off. It was shameful to admit it now, but he had cried a couple of times. It made him feel vulnerable. And for a while his sexuality felt so bound up with his hair that he went through a short spell where he didn't even want to have sex.

'Strangers kept asking me if I was having chemotherapy.'

'No way.' Steve was genuinely taken aback by this. 'People are ignorant.' They fell into another silence. 'Why are you up here on your own?'

'I didn't want to come. My flatmate insisted. As you can see, I'm not enriching anyone's evening.'

'Maybe your flatmate didn't want you to sit in on your own on a Saturday night.'

The girl leant forward and said in a vaguely deep, maternal voice, 'Worse things happen.'

Steve nodded. 'True enough.'

Then the girl brought a large black Nike sports bottle out of her bag and unscrewed the lid. 'Do you want some wine? It's warm but drinkable.'

'Sure. Why not?' Steve walked over, thanking her as she splashed a small amount of wine into his glass. Without waiting to be asked, he pulled a chair away from the table and sat down, a good respectable distance from her.

'I'm Joni.' When he raised his eyebrows, she added wearily, 'Yes. After that Joni.'

'That's a good name. I'm Steve.'

'Steve.' Joni filled her own glass and took a sip. 'No one is called Steve any more.'

'Nope. We're a dying breed.'

'It's an honest name.'

'You mean boring.'

She laughed. 'Maybe.' She pointed at his wrist. 'That's a big watch you're wearing there, Steve.'

Steve glanced down at the Ingersoll that he had spent a lot of money on, replacing all the bits and giving it a new heart. 'It was my dad's.' On his dad's birthday last year, he had telephoned his mum and told her that he'd got it repaired. He had stupidly thought they could chat about his dad, that she might even comfort him. Instead, she said dismissively, 'Oh, I hated that watch. Far too big for him, Stephen. He had such tiny wrists. I don't know why he insisted on wearing it.'

'*Was* your dad's?' said Joni.

'He died.' Steve gave the watch face a stroke. 'Eighteen months ago.'

'I'm sorry. That sucks.' Joni had already drained her glass. When she held out the sports bottle again, Steve shook his head. The wine was pretty cheap-tasting.

'My mum is sick.' Joni screwed up her face as if to stop herself crying. 'She has some rare kidney cancer that they can't do anything about.'

'God. I'm sorry.' Steve paused and took a deep breath. 'My dad had cancer too.'

When Joni nodded sadly, Steve realised that this random exchange could probably make them both cry, which was odd given they had been strangers to each other five minutes ago.

'She has a gold chain that I'll wear,' said Joni. 'I've already told my sister that it's mine.'

'That will help.' Steve looked at his watch again. 'Well,

as much as anything does.' When he looked up, Joni was scratching her neck red. 'Are you okay?'

'Yep.' She stopped scratching. 'Who are you with?' she asked.

'A few friends. I didn't want to come either. Aren't we fun?' He laughed and drank the last of his drink.

'So, where's your wife tonight?' Joni was staring at his wedding ring. 'Looking after the kids?' Her voice was light but mocking.

'Actually, she's out for a friend's birthday. A babysitter is home with our daughter.'

'What would your wife say if she knew you were chatting to me?'

Steve said, 'Honestly? She'd be fine with it.' He stared over Joni's shoulder through the large window, at the charcoal-sketched roofs. 'We have an open relationship.' Strangely, the words weren't difficult to say. He wasn't flustered. He didn't feel sick. Joni raised her eyebrows, then alarmingly, crossed her legs, smoothed down her skirt and swivelled her body slightly away from him.

'Joni, I'm not about to make a move on you. I'm about twice your age.'

'I have to be careful with myself.'

'Of course. Let me reassure you. This is just a chat. I'm not interested in anything else.'

'Okay. Cool.' She frowned. 'Is it my braces?'

'Sorry?'

She opened her mouth and pointed. On closer inspection, Steve realised she had light-coloured plastic braces. He shook his head.

'I want straight teeth,' she said.

'Good for you.' Steve couldn't think of what else to say. He sensed the conversation was drying up or would start spraying off into directions that would make him like her less. They'd had their moment.

She drained her glass and stood up, wavering slightly as

she reached for her bag. 'I got roped into DJing. My friend on the decks wants to nip out to another party. Do you want to join me?'

Steve was surprised at what a blast he was having. He could never have imagined a night where he would be DJing while a crowd of people half his age visibly enjoyed the tunes he selected. When he discovered a couple of excellent northern soul records in a crate of vinyl, he handed them to Joni, who was pretty dismissive; her preference was for deep, penetrating drum and bass. But her response was also down to a bartender she knew refilling her sports bottle on the sly – Steve could tell from her loud and runny voice as she argued pointlessly against northern soul that she was drunk. It wasn't a surprise when ten minutes later she announced she was going to be sick. She charged past him, a hand to her mouth. Luckily, the DJ was back and ready to take over, so Steve followed in the direction of the toilet next to the dark staircase.

'Joni, it's Steve. Do you need help?' He heard retching and moaning, then the sound of her throwing up. Eventually, she opened the door before quickly sitting back on the floor and clutching the toilet bowl, pale and shaking like a scared kitten.

'I think I'm okay now,' she said in a quivering voice which Steve rightly suspected was optimistic. A minute later she twisted her body over the toilet. While she threw up and moaned, he bunched her hair above her head like a pineapple. She kept whispering sorry and he knew she was crying because being sick like this was brutal and shaming. He handed her toilet paper to wipe her mouth. 'We've all been there,' he said. 'Don't worry about it.'

After a stint sitting back against the wall, Joni opened her eyes. 'I'm done,' she said. 'I want to go home.' Steve helped her locate her backpack from behind the decks and walked her through the bar to the top of the stairs.

'Thanks for looking after me. I bet you're a great dad.'

The wistful way she said this troubled Steve. 'Do you want some advice?' He was going to suggest that she lay off alcohol whilst her mother was dying.

'No, thanks.' Turning away, she raised her hand in a small wave. He watched her push through all the people still crowding each step and he felt close to this person he hardly knew and would never see again. He too had been involuntarily defiant when his dad was dying. He'd done and said everything he wanted because he felt so cheated by life, so insanely angry. Nothing else had mattered, certainly not whether he was causing offence.

He made his way to a nearby toilet and splashed cold water on his face. It was time for him to go too. It crossed his mind to find the others and let them know, but he couldn't be bothered, so he went down the stairs, thanking the security man who stopped playing Candy Crush to push the door open for him. It was almost two o'clock and the night air was brisk. Steve pulled up his hood. There was no longer a queue, and the street was closed up, as if bad weather was coming.

A little way from the venue, he heard Matt call his name and the pound of footsteps. Steve sighed. For him, the evening was over.

'I've been looking for you,' said Matt when he caught up. 'I saw you DJing, then you disappeared with that girl.'

'She was drunk. I was helping her.'

'Yeah, right.' Matt looked him in the eye. 'Is that what you're going to tell Fay? Come on, we all know why you went off.'

'You're barking up the wrong tree, mate. Nothing happened.' Steve put his hand on Matt's shoulder and pressed down firmly. It was an annoying tactic that he had used a few times on Fay before she told him that she would consider leaving him if he ever tried to rationalise her anger in such a patronising way again.

'Listen, I've been there.' Matt shook his hand off. 'You know what Katie did to me. It was shit.'

Impatiently, Steve made his hands into fists and pushed them into his jeans pockets. 'This isn't the same thing.'

'Yeah, you think Fay would agree?'

'Stop talking about Fay as if you know what you're on about. I'm not cheating on her,' said Steve. 'Let it go.'

Now Matt was pacing around, talking to himself. Steve had undone something in him and he was losing it. 'It's not okay. It's never okay.'

'Did you hear what I said?' asked Steve. 'I'm not cheating on Fay. Nothing happened.'

'It didn't look like nothing when you were up there, having fun behind the decks with her.'

'Matt, you've got it all wrong, mate,' said Steve calmly. 'Just leave it.'

Shaking his head at Steve, Matt was about to say something when he stopped and stepped back. 'Oh my God,' he shouted to the sky, his arms spread open. 'You're doing that open relationship thing.' He pointed a finger at Steve. 'You are, aren't you?'

Steve shook his head. 'Nope,' he said, but before he could say anything else, Matt cut in.

'I knew it. I'm always right about this stuff.'

Steve found this instantly irritating. Matt could be such an annoying human being. 'Okay, maybe we are. But you better keep that to yourself,' Steve said bluntly. 'I don't want you sharing your thoughts with the other lads. Respect our privacy.'

Nodding, Matt kept saying, 'Yeah, yeah, I get it,' as he pulled a pack of tobacco out of his back pocket and rolled himself a cigarette. 'An open relationship.' He said it a couple of times as he licked the cigarette paper. 'How do you do it?'

'Well, I haven't yet.'

Matt lit his roll-up and spoke through a curl of smoke. 'Has Fay?'

'I don't know. Look, Matt, don't take this wrong way, but I don't want to get into it with you.'

But Matt ignored him. 'You don't know?'

'We agreed not to talk about the details.'

'You're mad. Find out everything you can. Trust me, it's the only way you'll sleep at night.' With the roll-up squashed between his fingers, Matt held the bridge of his nose and looked down. When he looked up, he appeared to be on the verge of tears.

'Katie wouldn't tell me a thing about Nathan,' said Matt. 'Said there was no point. But the not knowing kills me. Every fucking day.'

/

In Pizza Express, Fay's dad is sitting alone at their table reading the menu.

'You look nice.' Fay affectionately waggles the knot of Rex's tie through the small opening of his zipped-up beige sports jacket.

'You're late,' he says.

Rex's brusqueness winds Steve up. Nothing is ever right for him. When he comes over for Christmas, Steve has to build in periods throughout the day when he goes upstairs or out, just to change the energy around him. He knows Fay feels the same, but it's complicated for her. The other morning, sitting on the bed doing up her bra, she told Steve that Rex's neighbours of ten years have stopped talking to him. They won't tell Fay what he did or said, but they insisted it was completely unacceptable. Fay suspected that it had something to do with their new Nigerian son-in-law. She remembers neighbours in the street where they grew up giving her and Gerry sweets because they felt sorry for them, having no mum and such a shouty, intolerant dad. There was one neighbour who gave Fay her telephone number and told her to hold on to it. 'Just in case you need it,' she said, folding it into Fay's hands.

'Where's Billy?' asks Fay, looking around. Billy insisted on coming home again, this time on his own, and spent yesterday in the kitchen with Rose, making her an elaborate cake in the shape of Elsa from *Frozen*. 'I hope he hasn't overslept. Steve, can you call him?'

'He'll be here. Relax.'

Now Rex is shouting for Rose to come and see him. His voice is embarrassingly loud and unpleasant, but Steve has no choice but to become part of the instruction. He walks over to Rose and gently leads her back to Rex, so Rex can stare down at her and say, 'Nice of you to come and say hello to your grandad.'

'She's excited, Dad. It's not often she has a sixth birthday party.' Fay and Rose smile at each other.

'And what a lovely six-year-old you are.' Rex runs a hand up and down Rose's face like a flannel.

'Stop that,' says Fay, pulling Rose back.

Rex raises his chin and fondles his tie, a little embarrassed. 'I'm just playing.'

'I've told you before Rose doesn't like it,' says Fay. 'Please respect that.'

'*Respect?* She's a child. What about respecting me?'

Jesus, what an idiot. Steve wants to take Rex outside and tell him a few home truths. Instead, he has to treat him gently, like a burning ember that has fallen out of the fireplace.

'Rex, we all respect you. Come on, let's get into the party spirit.' Steve pats Rex's arm. 'Let's take a breath. Sit yourself down and I'll get you a black coffee.'

Rex sits down. 'Make sure it's hot.'

Fay asks the waitress for a coffee and a bottle of sparkling water, and Steve asks for a beer.

'A beer? Really?' says Fay sharply. 'We've got kids to entertain. I'm going to need your help.'

The waitress stops writing in her pad. As she looks to the ground, Steve swears she's smirking a little. She's been caught in this sort of marital exchange a thousand times.

'A Peroni, if you have one,' he says to her and, once she has walked away, he says snappishly to Fay, 'Of course I'm going to help.' He resents the implication that he'll get drunk and stand around, useless. He always gets stuck in. The kids love him, don't they? Fay will be the one hanging back, chatting. He'll end up making dough balls and pizza bases, his face creased with flour. He's even wearing a metallic paper hat that Rose gave him, with a bushy red streamer coming out of the top and too-tight elastic around his chin. He doesn't see Fay looking stupid to please anyone.

Nodding, Fay touches his cheek. 'Sorry. I know you will.'

'Relax. It's going to be fine.'

She reaches down and squeezes his hand. 'And we're fine, aren't we?' she asks. 'You and me.'

'One hundred per cent,' he says confidently and squeezes her hand back. 'Hey, there's Billy.'

Katie and Billy walk in together, laughing, with Billy holding the cake tin. He goes straight over to the table where Rose is now happily sitting between two girls from her new class, and he makes all the girls laugh, which Rose loves.

Steve would like to go over and say hello to Katie, but Fay has already squirrelled her away from everyone. They are leaning into each other, talking furtively.

Now Matt knows, Fay might be telling Katie about their arrangement. Fay looks animated enough, pausing thoughtfully here and there, and Katie appears engrossed. It also occurs to Steve that Fay could be confiding deeply personal and significant stuff about Reuben, things that Steve has no idea about, and it's the first time in his marriage, as far as he knows, that they have these separate stories which they haven't shared with each other. Steve turns away, feeling anxious, panicked, and very alone with this panic, which makes it even worse.

# 7

Katie is late. This is particularly galling because she invited herself along to the art fair where Emma French has a stall over the weekend, and because she knows how irritated Fay gets about lateness. It isn't respectful to leave someone standing around.

Yet here Fay is, waiting. At least she isn't the only person hanging around outside the church on her own. A couple of feet away, a man wearing a matching grey hoodie and snug jogging bottoms is vaping and talking on his mobile. His face is obscured, the large phone pressed against his cheek, but when he turns his body to her, Fay's eyes land on his crotch. Good God! Steve is well-endowed – or more accurately, he's fine and average and satisfying and he can hold his head up in any gym changing room – but this thing in her vision is a different beast entirely. For a moment, Fay has trouble believing it's even real.

Her instinct is to look away, almost squeamishly, but she lets her gaze linger for a moment. Why not? Hell, she can look where she wants, she can do what she wants. She imagines pressing her business card into this man's hand and the freedom that comes with this thought is so intoxicating that she is filled with adolescent energy and still has an urge to giggle as Katie pulls up in her car: beeping, mouthing her apology through the open window. Of course, she manages to nab a parking spot almost directly in front of the church. Fay had to circle for ages and ended up parking three streets over.

'Sorry, sorry,' Katie shouts out, clicking her key over her shoulder to lock the doors. She hugs Fay and says, 'I know I'm always late, don't hate me, and you look great, love that jacket.' Almost immediately, she adds, 'I was thinking in the car. Are you and Steve asking your lovers to take an STD test?'

Fay pulls back crossly as people walk up the steps alongside them. 'Not now, okay?'

Since Fay confided in her about their new arrangement, Katie has emailed over numerous links to articles about open relationships. This seems a bit pointless to Fay, who is already sold on the idea. Also, still humiliated over the Reuben debacle, she doesn't want to keep talking about it with Katie. To have pushed for a radical move in her marriage and then been unable to go through with the sex seems faintly ridiculous to her now, like she signed up to a life-changing diet but has failed to lose a pound.

At the top of the steps, Katie says, 'Okay. One last thing and I won't mention it again. How about I ask Nathan if he has any suitable friends?'

'Absolutely not. No way.' Fay can hear how anxious simply rejecting the idea makes her sound.

Katie frowns. 'His friends are sweet.'

'I'm sure they are, but I'm not on the open market.' Fay slows down her voice. 'Look, I'm still happily married. This is just something we're discreetly exploring.' To keep Katie from commenting further, she adds, 'Anyway, I'm looking at websites that I can sign up to.'

Actually, she has already decided Tinder and Bumble are decent places to look for disposable, throwaway sex, so the past few days she's been working up her blurb. It needs to be pitch perfect because she can't post a photo publicly in case someone recognises her and suspects she's looking to have an affair; now, that really would be humiliating.

'You still haven't told me Emma's tragic backstory,' says Katie as she pulls back the heavy door to the church foyer. 'You said you would.'

'I will,' says Fay. 'Not now though. It's a long one. Remind me later.'

The set-up in the hall looks exactly as she had imagined from the badly designed Facebook page that Emma had sent her a link to. A dozen or so stalls, some lacklustre bunting and a small crowd of people; an amateurish, low-key event. Fay pays the woman behind a table near the doorway a donation from them both and they start to make their way around.

Whilst Katie mooches along beside her, she searches for Emma. It's pretty easy to make her out. She is tall, a head and shoulders above Fay and, even from here, Fay can see her hold court in a way that she now recalls as familiar. That first year at university, Emma was rarely seen on her own, almost always with an entourage of girls who sat in the back of seminars and contributed nothing except the occasional ripple of distracted laughter over some in-joke.

As they approach Emma, Fay mentally adjusts to her style. Of course, neither of them is going to dress like they did all those years ago, but Emma looks so different. In college she was a sweatshirt-and-jeans type of girl, a really bland dresser, whereas today she is wearing shiny tight black trousers, a white T-shirt under a waistcoat, a straw trilby, and long black feathered earrings. She has also recently dyed the ends of her hair hot pink, which Fay is unsure about. It's too try-hard.

When Emma looks in their direction, she raises both her arms and waves so enthusiastically Fay doesn't imagine the greeting is intended for her. Yet it seems that it is. Emma steps out from behind the stall and rushes to embrace her. 'I'm so pleased you came. Amazing!'

'I said I would,' says Fay, aware of how lacking in exuberance she sounds, but it's not natural for her to show overexcitement. 'Emma, you remember Katie.'

'Of course, the birthday girl. How you doing?'

Katie says, 'Good,' they smile at each other, but then Katie pauses as if she is expecting Emma to say something else.

When it doesn't come, she turns her attention to the stall. 'Nice,' she says quickly and too glibly.

Fay joins her in looking, but makes more of an effort, leaning in to examine the collages. Made up from slithers of different fabrics, paint and snatches of magazines and newspapers, they depict Emma's abstract idea of sea scenes. Standing close to her, Emma provides a running commentary on how she makes them and the different techniques she uses.

'They're lovely,' says Fay, although she would never buy this sort of art for herself.

'Really? You think?' Emma claps her hands together, then dips her head briefly and executes the namaste gesture. 'Thank you for saying that. They look even better with light on them. I did ask for a stall by the window, but I guess I wasn't the only one.'

When Emma vaguely refers to the dog walk that she and Fay went on, Katie interrupts. 'Oh, when was this?'

'Last week,' says Fay. 'We lasted about twenty minutes before the rain came.'

'It was unbelievable, wasn't it?' says Emma. 'Apocalyptic.' Emma talks and talks about the rain and how it came through a back wall in her flat because of some guttering problem, then moves seamlessly back to the subject of the fair, waving at the stall owner opposite, before turning her back on him and saying, 'That guy is outselling everyone. And d'you know what he makes? Cushions and oven mitts out of a print with Chihuahuas all over it. I mean, Chihuahuas,' she whispers. 'Are they even proper dogs?'

While Fay and Emma laugh, Katie remains stony-faced and silent. Fay is irritated with how offhand she is being. So much so, it's a relief when a few minutes later, she says she has to pick up her daughter from football practice and leaves after a flurry of thanks and good lucks to Emma and a peck on Fay's cheek.

When it's just the two of them, Fay buys them tea and cake from the stall run by a pair of giggling teenagers, then they sit on the two camping chairs Emma has set out next to her stall.

'Sorry, won't be a tick.' Emma has been texting since Fay sat down. 'Lewis is with his dad today. He's got asthma and was so wheezy this morning, but typical response from Hamish. *Lewis is fine, Em. You're being OTT.*' Tapping away, Emma shakes her head. As she puts her phone away and glances up and around, she shrieks, 'No!' then leans her whole body into Fay, hiding herself from the room. When she lifts herself away to glance gingerly over her shoulder, Fay feels cold as if the sun has rolled past her, which takes her by surprise.

'Thank God. He didn't see me.'

'Who's he?' asks Fay.

'An ex.' Emma waves her hand. 'I haven't seen him since I caught him in the pub right-swiping girls on Tinder while I was getting the drinks in.'

'No way,' says Fay.

'Yeah.' Emma takes a sip of tea. 'He wasn't always a shit. I know he cared about me. He just wasn't in a good place then.'

'Well, I'm impressed how cool you are about it.' Shaking her head, Fay crosses her arms over her chest. 'He sounds like a cretin to me.'

Emma shrugs. 'It's fine. I'm used to people like him.'

'Well, you shouldn't be,' says Fay, hearing the righteousness in her voice.

Emma smiles. Stealing a glance at Fay from under her hat rim, she says hesitantly, 'Don't take this the wrong way…'

Fay straightens up and sits on her hands, aware that a criticism is about to be lobbed her way. 'Uh-huh.'

'Do you think…' Emma falters. 'Well, I'm guessing that you don't have as much baggage as us?'

*Us.* Such a small word, but Fay feels it cut straight into her. *Us.* The messy people. The people who go around being hurtful and getting hurt. She inhales. There is nothing to feel defensive about, she thinks. Emma hasn't presented it as a fact. She posed it as a question, which, combined with the tilt of her head, suggests she's leaving room for doubt.

'I've offended you, haven't I?' says Emma. 'Me and my big mouth.'

Fay shakes her head. 'Not at all.' Of course, it's better to be the person with less baggage and trauma, with less crazy going on. Fay knows this. And yet, there is something painful about being cast in this role, being considered someone who hasn't had the emotional stuffing ripped out of them yet. In Fay's mind, it's tantamount to Emma saying, I'm guessing you haven't really lived?

Fay takes a sip of her tea. 'Not everything is as it seems, you know,' she says loftily. When Emma's eyes widen with enquiry, Fay half regrets even saying that – for one thing, she knows nothing about Emma and her ability to keep things to herself – but the temptation to alter Emma's perspective of her wins out. Fay simply can't bear to be seen as so straight and tidy. 'As it happens, Steve and I have an open relationship.'

Emma bolts upright in her seat. 'Well, well, well. You *are* a dark horse, Fay Munro. Who'd have thought?'

While Emma breaks off a bit of lemon cake, Fay smiles, a little smugly. Well, that certainly felt good, showing something unexpected about herself. She waits for Emma to ask her more about it, but instead Emma is talking about a woman she met on a yoga retreat who was poly and how great she made it all sound.

Fay gestures a crooked finger towards Emma's face. 'You've got something there. Icing, I think.'

Emma says, 'Oh,' and wipes her mouth with the back of her hand. 'Gone?'

'Nope. Still there.' After Emma rubs a second time with no luck, she says, 'Just get it off me, please. I've got a thing about having food on my face.' Fay leans forward and flicks at the stubborn icing stuck to Emma's downy upper lip, surprised at how soft her skin feels.

'Thank you, Mum.'

'Can't take you anywhere.' Fay meets Emma's warm but intense gaze until it carries on for a fraction longer than expected and Fay must shyly look away.

/

The next afternoon, Fay stands dutifully in a semicircle of family members watching Steve's mum, Patricia, open her pile of birthday gifts. As Fay is trying to remember the last time Patricia came to see them – was it two or three years ago? Patricia insists that she gets carsickness – a phone starts to ring.

'Fay, that's yours,' calls out Steve, pointing at her bag on the rug nearby.

'No, it's not.' She cranes around to look at him, smiling. 'That's not my ringtone.'

'It is.' Steve says her name in a harried voice and snaps his fingers at her to pass him the bag. Then, as he casts a worried glance in his mum's direction, it clicks into place for Fay. Her other phone is ringing. The naughty phone, as she sometimes refers to it in her mind, although Steve gave it to her the morning after she last saw Reuben, so it actually hasn't seen any naughtiness at all.

'Sorry! Excuse me.' Fay rifles through her oversized tote bag as she charges out of the room into the hallway. Who the hell is calling her? It can't be Reuben. He doesn't have this number – not that he'll ever call her again anyway. Their encounter was miserable. A total disconnect that no amount of booze or loneliness could turn into something worth rekindling.

Jesus, she needs a smaller bag, full of less crap. Eventually, she puts her hand on the mobile and pulls it out. The number is not familiar. 'Hello,' she whispers. There is a fuzzy pause, then someone, somewhere in the world, introduces themselves and asks if they can talk to Fay about contents insurance.

'No, you can't. Please take me off your list. Thank you.' Fay turns off the phone and drops it into her bag with trembling hands. With her back against the radiator, she stands there for a few minutes, catching her breath before discreetly threading back into the throng still gathered around Steve's mum.

Billy, who has travelled across London with Caroline to be here for the day at Patricia's insistence, squeezes her shoulder. 'You're an old lady, Mum. They never know their phone is ringing,' he says, adding in an exaggerated voice: 'Do you need help with the buttons, dear?'

Fay laughs along, she elbows him playfully, but her face feels warm. She mustn't panic. A ringing mobile won't whet anyone's curiosity. They wouldn't guess what the phone is for, thank God. She'd be a pariah if they did because they all adore Steve. In their eyes, he can do little wrong, he's the golden boy. Although, to be fair, he doesn't have much competition. His only sibling, Anthony, is unbearably lazy. The last time they went to his house for lunch, they were sitting in the living room when Anthony dropped a bowl of crisps on the rug. Rather than go and get the Hoover, he called for his spaniel to eat up the crisps, then texted his wife who was in the kitchen to bring through more snacks.

'Oh, these mobiles,' says Patricia. 'Why does everyone need to be connected all the time?'

Her comment, which just drags out the situation and makes it even more public, fuels Steve's anger with Fay. She can see he is furious. He's doing that thing where he bites his bottom lip and raises his eyebrows, as if he's trying really hard to contain himself.

'What did I miss, Patricia?' she says. 'Did someone buy you the sports car you've been angling for?'

It amazes Fay that every year before lunch they must go through the same ritual of watching Patricia unwrap all her birthday presents. You're not a child, Fay always wants to calmly suggest. Who cares what you get? Doug, Patricia's partner of over twenty-five years, whom she has proudly never married, stands at the end of the blue patterned sofa like her production manager. He's the one who will have put the gifts by Patricia's side, along with her cup of hot water and lemon, and arranged the cushions behind her. His main job is to ensure everything in her life runs smoothly.

Patricia waves a hand towards Fay for her to grab. In her other hand, she clutches a cerise silk neck scarf. 'Oh, it's beautiful, Fay. I feel very special, thank you.' As she bares her overcrowded teeth and her many crowns and fillings, Fay sends gratitude for the umpteenth time that the kids haven't got her teeth. 'Such generosity,' says Patricia, adding theatrically, as if she is addressing the nation, 'I feel very spoiled.'

Then the doorbell goes, and Patricia stands up, touching the back of her hair. 'Doug, could you get the door, please? That must be Francesca and Elliot.'

'Francesca from your old street?' says Steve in a flustered voice.

'Yes. Marcie from shul said she was back, and then I ran into her in Boots, of all places. Didn't I say?'

'No, you didn't.' When Steve adds, 'Why are they here?' Fay notices that his face is suddenly leached of colour.

'They've just moved back from Spain and they're in a hotel until they can get into their new place next week. It was only right to ask them over for a home-cooked meal.' Without registering Steve's anxious reaction, Patricia adds, 'They've done terribly well for themselves over there, by all accounts.'

Once she leaves the room, most of the family are quick to disperse, making their way towards the French doors into the airy kitchen, past the piano adorned with photographs of Patricia and their black Labrador, and the reading corner where Doug is often found in his wing chair doing a sudoku.

When it is just Fay and Steve, she turns to him and whispers, 'Why do you look so stressed? Is this couple awful? You looked like you were going to be sick when Patricia mentioned that woman's name.'

Shaking his head as he gathers up bits of wrapping paper, Steve doesn't stop to look at her. When they hear voices in the hallway, he stands up straight and pushes back his shoulders.

'So, what's the matter?' she asks snappishly. God, he can be so irritatingly passive-aggressive. 'I'm sorry about the ringing phone, okay?'

'Uh-huh. Look, just go and look after your kids.'

'*My* kids?' Fay leans in close. 'For God's sake, it was an accident. I forgot the phone was in my bag.'

'It was embarrassing,' he hisses in a low voice.

'No, it wasn't. No one else knows what the phone is for.' She pauses, calms her voice. 'I'm sorry. It should have been turned off.'

'It was sloppy,' rasps Steve.

'It wasn't Reuben,' she whispers. 'It wasn't him if that's what this is about. It was a cold-caller wanting to sell me insurance. I'm not taking booty calls whilst I'm with your family. I do have some respect.'

Steve swallows. 'It was sloppy,' he repeats.

This conversation is going nowhere. But looking at him grimacing at her as he closes his fist around a scrap of shiny gold paper, Fay is surprised to find she feels sorry for him.

'Don't take it out on me,' she says quietly. He might be angry with her, but he overreacts to everything when they are in Patricia's company.

'For God's sake, don't start all that,' he says. 'It's not her.'

He'll always deny it, but his mum's presence automatically sounds an internal alarm bell, reminding him that he was never good enough for her. If he had been, she wouldn't have left him and Anthony when they were kids. Fay wishes she could get him to acknowledge, properly acknowledge, Patricia's deep-rooted selfishness.

'Okay then, it's me,' she says in a resigned voice.

But it's not just Steve's personality that changes when they come here; it's his appearance too. His shirt, ironed this morning, is tucked into smart tan-coloured chinos and he is stubble-free, because Patricia is vocal about how she prefers him shaven and in crisp long-sleeve shirts, not the T-shirts he prefers. He is also wearing an expensive leather belt she bought him last Christmas, insisting that a man's outfit is incomplete without one, something Fay and Steve laughed hard about at the time.

God, Fay hates this whole look, the casual wanker-banker look. It's a complete turn-off. With his shaved head and his smooth face, Steve looks like a grumpy, badly dressed cherub.

And so now, with every bit of sympathy for him eroded by irritation, she turns away and walks through to the extension where she briefly stands under the skylight windows, turning her face to the stretch of blue sky. When she looks down, Doug is holding out a glass of champagne. 'Come and meet Francesca and Elliot.'

When Fay feels the phone in her pocket vibrate, she panics briefly until she realises it's her regular phone. 'I will do. Thanks, Doug. Just give me a sec.' She moves towards the garden doors to read the WhatsApp message from Emma, who effusively greets her – *Hello you lovely woman!* – and says that she has a night off the following Wednesday and asks if Fay wants to go with her to a friend's birthday drinks. Fay feels a jolt of pleasure hearing from Emma so soon after seeing her, even if she is slightly put off by the overzealous use of random emojis and exclamation marks. But drinks with Emma and a new set of people sounds perfect. She is quick to respond.

## Fay

Sounds great! Count me in. X

Half-smiling to herself, Fay follows Doug around the table where Steve is standing around awkwardly and smiling at a middle-aged couple passing their jackets to one of Steve's teenage nieces. Steve really doesn't look good, as if panic is running down his insides.

'It has to be twenty-four years,' the woman is saying. 'You were about to go to university.'

'I was.' Steve clears his throat.

'You haven't changed,' she says.

'Less hair.' He laughs nervously. 'But I would never have recognised you, Francesca,' he says honestly. 'Not in a million years.'

The woman slips her hands into the pockets of her navy trousers. 'An improvement, don't you think?'

Steve starts rubbing the back of his neck. He looks so unsure of himself. Fay can't quite figure out what's going on with him.

'I'm just teasing, Steve.' The woman turns to Fay. 'I'm Frankie. You must be Steve's wife.'

Fay nods. 'Yes, I'm Fay. Lovely to meet you.'

'I don't think I've ever called you Frankie,' says Steve.

'Elliot prefers it.' Frankie shrugs like she doesn't know why exactly, but neither does she care. 'It means I get to call him all sorts of things.' She releases a silky, confident laugh.

'How's Hannah?' asks Steve. 'She must be all grown-up now.' He turns to Fay and says, 'Hannah is Frankie's daughter. Elliot's stepdaughter.'

'Oh, she's terrific.' Frankie smiles. 'She's been living in Sydney the past couple of years. She's a set designer at the Sydney Opera House.'

'Wow,' says Steve. 'That's impressive.'

'She is.' Frankie nods proudly. As she turns away to respond to a question Elliot is asking of her, Steve whispers into Fay's hair, 'Can you drive?' Fay raises her eyebrows, as if to say, you're asking me for a favour now? They are still mid-row. Besides, she drove here and they usually each do one leg of the tedious journey.

'Well?' he says urgently. His glass is empty; clearly, he is desperate to refill it.

'Fine.' She watches him fill his glass with champagne and drink, then returns her attention to Frankie, who is telling them about the cottage they've bought.

'Oh, you're not too far from us.' Fay tells her where they live, about a fifteen-minute drive away. 'We're almost neighbours.'

'How lovely.' Frankie's dark eyes are huge and soft, like the centre of sunflowers. 'I don't really know anyone else in Sussex.'

When Frankie smiles, Fay decides she is even more stunning. Early fifties, or thereabouts, tall and slim, with short-clipped dark hair framing a tanned face, which might or might not have had work. Fay can never tell; surgery is so discreet these days. She is classically dressed in a loose white shirt rolled back to the elbows, no other jewellery except one solid, expensive-looking silver bracelet. Fay suspects Frankie doesn't really want anyone to know she has money, but she can tell from the cut of her trousers that she does, probably quite a bit. Fay knows about trousers. It is one of the very few expensive pieces of clothing she thinks are worth every penny.

'Of course, we'll be the only Jews in the village,' interrupts Elliot, scratching his pockmarked cheeks. 'But I think we can handle that.' Elliot is a large man who wears a black leather jacket over a grey shirt that hangs messily over his jeans. Fay doesn't find him remotely physically attractive. He has that unfit, fraying look that older men with money think they can get away with.

'It will be me who has to deal with all the locals,' says Frankie. 'You'll be too busy writing your novels.'

'Elliot's debut crime novel is about to be published. There was an auction,' says Patricia. Everyone says mazel tov, wonderful, how incredible, you're never too old.

'You'll both have to come to the book launch next week. It's being held in a bar near you,' says Frankie while Fay watches Steve nod and refill his glass yet again.

/

Now they are driving home. They never stay over, even though it's a four-hour round trip and there are two impeccably decorated spare bedrooms. Patricia doesn't like overnight guests, which Steve has always put down to an undiagnosed form of OCD. He says she worries about everything being perfect and it's too exhausting for her to sustain these standards when they are all there overnight.

With her eyes on the road, Fay unbuttons her trousers. She always feels so bloated after Patricia and Doug's cooking. They might decorate the table flamboyantly, with candles and flower arrangements and sometimes even place name-cards, but this only serves as a temporary distraction from the food. Today they dished up bowls of fusilli with a lumpy, tasteless tomato and basil-flecked sauce and baskets of dryish garlic bread. Fay could tell Frankie was surprised, that she had associated Patricia with a greater standard of hospitality.

Steve's eyes are closed, his legs are extended. They've barely spoken in hours, so it seems reasonable that Fay resents him trying to catnap next to her while she is negotiating Sunday afternoon traffic.

'Someone was spooked by Frankie,' she says loud enough to stir him. 'What was that about?'

When he grunts, she says, 'Well?'

'Nothing.' He opens his eyes and rubs them.

'It really didn't look like nothing. Tell me.'

'No, not now. I'm not in the mood.'

That bothers Fay. 'Hey, I've driven both ways so you could drown your anxieties. The least you could do is tell me what was wrong.'

Steve sighs. He sits up and rearranges the seat belt, then glances over his shoulder to check Rose is listening to her audiobook through headphones. 'Alright,' he says, but still takes a while to get going. 'So, Francesca… I mean Frankie… she rented the house opposite my mum and Doug when I was about eighteen. I don't know all the details, but she was in the middle of a divorce. She was dating Elliot, but he wasn't living there. I guess she was about twenty-eight, thirty? I don't know, I'm rubbish with ages.'

When he pauses, Fay says, 'And?'

'So she looked very different back then. She was big. I mean…' He glances sideways at Fay. 'Really big. Fat.'

'No way! You'd never know.'

'Well, she was. Anyway, she asked if me and my friend Luke could help her clear her back garden. It was a right state. She offered to pay us, and it was the summer before uni, so we said okay. One day she came out with a plate full of home-made chocolate chip biscuits for us. Said something like here's a little something for you boys to snack on. Anyway…' Steve pauses. 'Luke started making fun of her as she went inside. Laughed about how it was no surprise she was that fat if she thought this was a little snack. I don't remember what he said. I think I've blocked it out. But…' Steve inhales. 'I joined in. I laughed along with Luke. Then I saw that Frankie hadn't gone inside. She was just standing by the patio door and heard everything. She looked so upset. It was awful. I felt like such a shit. I apologised several times. She said it was fine and then she went into the house and closed the patio door on me. I only saw her once after that, when she paid us. She barely said a word.'

'God, that's terrible, Steve,' says Fay.

'Yeah, I know. Thanks for pointing out the obvious,' he snaps.

'Sorry. Of course you do.'

'I knew I shouldn't have told you.'

'Don't be like that,' she says softly.

'Let's forget about it,' he says and shuts his eyes again.

# 8

Steve only expects to know Frankie and Elliot at the book launch, and he can't spot either of them from the door of the bar. By the time he realises Frankie is not there yet and Elliot is too busy to notice him, he's been ushered in, handed a glass of wine and gently, but specifically, encouraged to spend a staggering nineteen pounds on a hardback copy of Elliot's novel, *Tin Eye*. Steve is in awe of anyone who can write a novel, let alone attract a proper publisher, but he forgets about this awe as he taps his debit card against the machine.

After ten minutes of standing around awkwardly without anyone to speak to, his aloneness feels so public that he has taken to poring over *Tin Eye*, pretending to read sections of it in between glimpsing around, particularly in Elliot's direction. Elliot is still surrounded by people and is being well looked after, which he appears pretty comfortable with. Two male servers keep circling him with their trays of canapés and a tall, gangly girl with a single plait down her back has just handed him a glass of water and a couple of pills she has shaken from a bottle. She even watches him, nodding until he downs them.

Eventually, Frankie breezes through the door, looking rather mannish in a grey pinstriped suit over a white T-shirt. Steve watches her until she glances around the room and notices him. When she waves and comes over, he is relieved to have a legitimate reason to move out of his corner.

'Hello! I'm *so* glad you could come.' Her heavy charm

bracelet clunks noisily in his ear as she rests a hand on his shoulder and kisses both his cheeks. 'No Fay?'

'She couldn't make it. She sends her apologies.'

He is still unhappy with Fay for refusing to cancel her friend Emma and come here. At work today he got it into his head that her absence might be construed as rude and he felt like he had a lot of ground to make up with Frankie, so just before he left the house, he asked Fay again to change her plans and come with him. At the time she was sitting cross-legged in front of their long bedroom mirror, brushing on eye shadow. She refused. 'No one will care whether I'm there,' she insisted, which irritated him, so he just muttered goodbye and left, childishly slamming the door. He heard her call out his name, but he didn't go back upstairs.

But Fay was right. Frankie looks completely disinterested in her absence. 'The wine is awful, isn't it? Come and sit at the bar and have a proper drink with me,' she says, adding quietly: 'I could do with some decent company.'

She loops arms with him as they walk across the room, then pulls out two stools secreted away at the far end of the bar where Steve would usually expect the staff to sneakily drink free drinks and check their phones.

'Won't Elliot expect you to socialise?' he asks after they both order mojitos. 'Do the meet-and-greet thing?'

'Probably, but I don't want to,' whispers Frankie. 'He met a lot of these people through a local sailing club. They're not my crowd.'

Elliot's love of water sports is one of the reasons Steve knows they are wealthy. After the lunch at his mum's, Steve and Fay had discussed exactly how wealthy, employing their usual sliding scale of comfortable through to unnecessarily, disgustingly rich. They agreed it was probably near the lower end but still pretty significant. Another giveaway had been when Elliot glossed over a big business deal that had gone horribly wrong the year before. He had quickly stopped himself sounding hard done by, as if he knew they still had too much water in their well to moan about being thirsty.

Frankie glances around to make sure no one else is listening. 'They are all so bloody dull.'

Steve laughs as the bartender delivers their drinks.

'Cheers to interesting people,' she says as they raise their glasses.

He grins. 'You're nothing like how I remember.'

Frankie doesn't miss a beat. 'How so? Because I'm not fat any more or because you didn't think I had a sense of humour?' Still smiling, she takes another sip of her drink. 'Hmm… delicious, isn't it?'

Steve puts down his glass and knits his hands together, nervously sandwiching them between his thighs.

'What you overheard that day was unforgivable. I'm genuinely sorry. I couldn't be sorrier.'

'Oh, it doesn't matter.' But the look that comes over her face tells him that quite possibly she wants to hear him fall on his sword, that she is not nearly as breezy about this memory as she likes to make out.

'Yes, it does. It was totally out of order. In fact,' he reaches for his glass, 'I've thought many times over the years about finding you and apologising. I acted like such an insensitive twat. I really am sorry…'

'Enough self-flagellation,' she says. 'Let's move on to more exciting topics. I promise I'm fine. It was a long time ago. I won't bring it up again.'

Steve nods. 'Okay,' he says, and looks past her shoulder as Elliot and a well-dressed middle-aged couple rearrange themselves for a photo. Elliot smooths his hair under his baseball cap, then pulls the visor down his forehead. When he moves in between the couple, hanging his big arms over their shoulders, Steve notices the woman with the blonde plait step far outside the frame of the picture. After the photo is taken, she returns to Elliot's side, says something just to him and they laugh, then he touches her shoulder lightly but intimately.

'Is that Hannah?' Steve asks aloud, wondering if that is Frankie's daughter from her first marriage. Frankie had mentioned that she was in England at the moment and, age-wise, it would be about right; the last time he saw Hannah, she was a sad-looking six-year-old who played hopscotch alone on the pavement while Frankie watched her from the upstairs window.

Frankie swivels around to look over her shoulder, then turns back and says, 'The blonde? No. That's Amy. Elliot's girlfriend.'

'Girlfriend? Elliot has a girlfriend?'

'He does. And guess what?' she says, adding in a staged whisper: 'I have a boyfriend.' Steve must look shocked because she laughs as she gently squeezes his knee. 'Now I'm really not who you remember, huh?'

Steve joins in with her uneasy laughter as he brings his glass to his mouth for something to do. After he puts it down, he plants a forearm on the bar to steady himself. 'Actually, Fay and I have just started opening up our marriage.'

It's still a bit odd hearing this said aloud, as if he is talking about a separate part of himself, but if Frankie is surprised, she does a good job hiding it.

'We're a growing breed.' She claps her hands excitedly. 'We're taking over.'

This is entirely possible. It feels to Steve that something might have happened to the world while he was mining his own small life, sure that he had everything he needed and wanted. There has been a shift, a move to a parallel universe where relationships have altered so much in their arrangement he is completely out of step.

'You mustn't say a word of this to Mum,' warns Steve.

'Oh my God, you think I'm going to tell Pat? Don't be silly.'

Now the bartender is in earshot, Frankie leans across the bar and asks for two more mojitos, then says, 'Do you have a girlfriend?'

'Nope. I've only had one sort of date. It's taken me a while to get going.' Steve thinks back to his coffee with Debbie, a woman who described herself in her dating profile as a lively, playful kitten, which in hindsight should have been an immediate deterrent. 'It was pretty painful.'

'That's a shame. Where did you meet her?'

'On a polyamorous dating site.'

Frankie frowns. 'Oh dear. I don't go near them any more.'

'I'm not sure I will again.' He runs his hand over his head. 'It wasn't just her fault though. I didn't know what I was doing.'

The date had started badly. Debbie had arrived after him and as she approached the table, overtaken with fear, he suddenly found himself questioning whether to get up or stay seated, shake her hand or kiss her cheek. In the end he had half stood up in an uncomfortable, contorted position, the edge of the table pressed against his thigh. All the time saying to himself, *Debbie doesn't have to be the one. She can be your try-it-out person. You're not being unfaithful; Fay wants you to do this.*

'She was decent enough,' he says to Frankie. 'Just not for me.' Steve knew he wouldn't sleep with Debbie from the moment she removed her Cuban revolutionist beret and lacy fingerless gloves and flattened down her fine hair. He couldn't locate any sexual attraction for her as he watched her unravelling one cotton neck scarf, then another. Folding them both carefully. Putting them in her bag. Taking off her jacket. Turning up the cuffs of her cardigan. All the time she was folding and arranging and rearranging, she didn't look at him or say a word. Eventually, he said, 'You alright there? Shall I come back in half an hour?'

To her credit, Debbie had laughed, but by then, he was already feeling nostalgic for the walk over to the café, for the hopeful moments that had occasionally surfaced through his anxieties and allowed him to think, *hey, maybe meeting Debbie will be great. Maybe it will be amazing and erotic and blow my mind.*

'Was she pretty?' Steve notices how Frankie lengthens and strokes her neck as she asks. Fay would do this. She would be thinking of herself and her own level of attractiveness when asking about another woman.

'She was fine. Nice.' Debbie was neither remarkable nor off-putting. Probably more like the sort of woman Steve would have ended up with if he hadn't raised his game by marrying Fay.

'I dated one man from a poly site.' Frankie holds up a finger threateningly. 'Just one. He kept asking me these stupid questions. If you could be a book, what book would you be? If you could be an animal...' Frankie bangs her fist unexpectedly on the bar. 'I hate artificial conversation. What happened to old-fashioned awkwardness? Is it so bad if we stumble through a few pauses or talk over each other?'

Steve nods. 'Agreed. Those sorts of questions would kill it for me.' He takes a handful of wasabi peas from the tray on the bar and tosses a couple into his mouth. He's really warming to this conversation. In fact, he can't quite believe he is sitting here, neutrally discussing his extramarital date with a married woman who has a boyfriend.

He gestures in the vague direction of Elliot and Amy. 'So, why do you do it?' he asks.

Frankie shrugs. 'Why not?'

'That's not really an answer.'

'Okay, well.' She pauses. 'It was something we discussed early on. Whether we were monogamous because we really believed in it or whether it was by default. We agreed on the latter. Then it just happened.'

'Do you mind me asking if your marriage was in a bad place when you decided?'

'No, it wasn't,' says Frankie impatiently, as if she has been asked this question so many times it now bores her. 'It's such a misconception that the marriage must be failing. If anything, it's the opposite. A couple needs to have a lot of trust and confidence between them to open it up.'

Steve agrees with this rationale. In his uncertain moments, when the voices in his head buzz around being negative or scared about the new set-up, he quietens them down by insisting his marriage is strong and filled with love.

'Were you both into the idea straight away?' he asks. This thought isn't as easy to silence. He might be on board, but the whole non-monogamy thing isn't his idea and never has been.

'Honestly? No. I was closed at first. Elliot convinced me to try and then it became our normal.'

'It's sort of the same for us. Fay instigated it.'

'Oh, really... so, why are *you* doing it?'

Steve takes a few seconds to consider his answer. 'I guess once I got used to the idea, I could see the benefit in having no-strings-attached fun with new people, away from our marriage.' He shrugs his shoulders. 'And you know, bring that energy back into our sex life. I mean, don't get me wrong, I've never been dissatisfied with Fay, but I get what she was saying about doing something totally different and outside of our comfort zone. We've been together over two decades.' Thinking about it, Steve shakes his head. It is *such* a long time. 'But then, if I'm being honest, sometimes I think... more partners, more rules... it all seems so complicated. It could really get out of hand.'

'Listen, just do it the way you,' Frankie leans out and touches his chest, 'want to do it. That's what it's about. Personal freedom on your terms.'

Steve reaches for more wasabi peas, although the inside of his mouth is already burning. It annoys him how sensitive he is to spicy foods. 'Yeah, put like that, it sounds good.'

'Is Fay with someone?'

'I don't know. There was one guy, but I think that's over.' When Frankie raises her eyebrows, he adds, 'We agreed that we wouldn't discuss the details.'

'Really? I couldn't do that.' Frankie shakes her head. 'I'd feel too insecure.'

Steve nods. She is right, Matt is right – it seems so obvious now. Yes, he thinks, watching Amy rearrange a few of Elliot's books on the table near the door. This is something he and Fay need to discuss. 'Doesn't it bother you, Amy being here? Doing the things that maybe you should be doing?'

Frankie glances over her shoulder again. 'What, like

collecting glasses? Sorting out Elliot's books? What exactly am I missing?'

'Yeah. I need to get a grip,' says Steve, cross at himself.

Frankie leans forward and places a hand on his knee. 'You just need to relax and have fun with it,' she says in a soft voice, without lifting her hand away.

'I do,' he replies, enjoying how close their faces are as he meets her eyes. 'I really do.'

/

Steve walks home fast, feeling excitement opening up inside him. Speaking to Frankie did him the world of good. Inside the house, before he's even hung up his jacket, he calls out to Fay from the hallway. Remembering Rose is in bed, he calls out more softly the next time. Fay still doesn't respond and in the dark living room he is deflated to find the babysitter, Kyla, on the sofa, looking gaunt and shadowy in the light off her phone. She pauses the show she was watching, stands up and straightens her jumper.

'Hi. Fay called. She asked me to stay on another hour.'

'No problem.' Steve smiles to show he's fine with that as he turns on a sidelight and draws the curtains. It's not her fault that his wife hasn't bothered to communicate her lateness to him. He wonders if this suggests what kind of evening Fay is having, that she might have met a man in the pub. Steve tries not to get trapped in the anxiety rising inside him; instead, he draws on his conversation with Frankie. He tells himself it would be okay if Fay had met a man. He would try and be pleased for her.

Kyla picks up her bag and puts her phone away. After she pops a couple of tabs of chewing gum in her mouth, she says, 'Oh, yeah. Rose was in a really bad mood at bedtime. Like really bad. I almost called you.'

Steve looks at her, surprised. Kyla is much more a girl than a young woman, despite being twenty-two and through university. She and Rose are great pals. She always comes over with her vanity case and lets Rose paint her nails and put on a ridiculous amount of make-up, then they spend ages mucking around on Snapchat.

'Do you know why?' he asks.

When she shakes her head, Steve apologises and tells her he'll speak to Rose. Then he overpays her by a couple of pounds but insists she keep the change, because it's too awkward asking for it back. It sounds like she's earned it and it's such a small amount to him, far less than it is to her.

After she leaves, Steve drifts around the messy kitchen. He wipes surfaces and stacks the dishwasher. He brought mud in with his trainers, which he sweeps up, then he mops the floor. He jangles with energy, which feels driven by all the thinking he is doing. This, combined with blasts of excitement, makes him feel he's had a breakthrough in himself. *Where are you*, he texts Fay. He needs to share this with her. After a while he calls her, but it rings to voicemail.

When she eventually walks in, he has just turned off the kitchen light. He turns it back on. She looks all mussed up, drunk.

'I'm not, before you say anything.' She drops her bag on the table. 'Don't look at me like that. I'm really not.' She pulls out a chair nearest her bag and sits across from him. 'Ended up going to A & E with Emma. Her son got taken in.' Steve exclaims in response, but without looking at him, Fay says, 'No, he's going to be fine, I think. But the night didn't turn out as I expected. Anyway. Rose okay?'

Steve repeats what Kyla told him, and Fay makes a face. 'Really? I thought we were out of that stage.'

'Me too. We'll talk to her tomorrow,' he says, adding in a fake upbeat voice: 'I had a good night too, thanks for asking.'

Fay doesn't register his sarcasm. Does she even realise he'd spoken? Her head is turned to her phone, which has just chimed three times in a row; WhatsApp messages are coming through fast.

When she glances back at him, her look is completely blank,

as if she is thinking of something else entirely. He stands up. It wouldn't kill her to also notice that he's cleaned the kitchen. God knows she likes to be appreciated for everything she does. This morning, she spent a couple of minutes forcing the sideboard out of its corner to sweep up dust balls and crumpled tissues and lost pennies and she told him about it straight away. Of course, he thanked her. Quite possibly, he thanked her twice. Sometimes Fay's need to be recognised is strangely disproportionate to his, which he puts down to one of the small but annoying things that he can usually tolerate about her. Tonight, however, it frustrates the hell out of him.

'Hello,' he says loudly, holding on to the back of his chair and shaking it. 'I'm right here. I've got stuff I need to talk about.'

'Sorry,' she says. 'I was miles away.'

'You think?' Some wet seeps through his socks on the walk over to the fridge. He takes out two bottles of beer and removes the lids before giving one to Fay.

'I'm sorry,' she says. 'Really. Talk to me.'

'The book launch was interesting.'

'Of course! The launch. Why interesting?'

'Well... drum roll... *big* news of the night... Frankie and Elliot have an open relationship.'

Fay looks shocked. 'No way.'

Well, that got her attention. 'Yes, way,' he says, over the sound of another message notification. 'Who's texting you at this time?'

'Emma. She's in a state. Don't look like that; you know her history. Seeing her son in the hospital freaked her out. Let me just text her back. Sign off for the night.'

While Steve sits down on their old sofa under the skylight, Fay taps away at her phone, then tosses it into her bag and comes to sit next to him.

'Frankie and Elliot.' Shaking her head, she pulls off her trainers and folds her legs beneath her, then takes a sip of beer and puts it on the floor. 'I don't want to imagine him having sex with anyone,' she adds with a fake shudder. 'He's nowhere near as charming as he thinks he is.'

Smiling, Steve crosses his stretched-out legs at the ankles. 'It was fun to talk to Frankie.' He stares down at the bottle in his hand and idly picks at the label, trying not to let the muted ping of yet another WhatsApp message put him on edge. 'We had a good night.'

Fay lightly squeezes his shoulder. 'That's great.'

'But it's made me think.' He turns his whole body to face her. 'I want to be upfront about the people we hook up with. Talk about it.'

Fay says okay slowly, as if she is moving this new information around in her mind. 'Well, that's a different tack.'

'Yes, but it's what I want,' he says firmly. 'I've always told you everything. I don't want to stop now. And not knowing what's happening isn't bringing us closer together, is it? It feels like we've got secrets. Is that what you want?'

'Of course not.' Fay moves her legs from out beneath her and pulls them to her chest.

'I'm really into this new rule, Fay.' He puts a hand on her thigh. 'I don't need to hear every sexual detail. I just want to talk about what's going on for us. Some honesty. I don't think it will make me more jealous. I think it will help.'

'Good,' she says.

He studies her face. 'I can't work out whether you mean that or not?'

'If it's what you want, then I'm up for it.'

Steve thinks she doesn't sound sure, but he's also not going to push it. It's what he wants, and Fay will just have to go along with it this time, regardless of whether it's the approach she would choose for herself. He has just leant in and kissed her when he hears more pinging from her bag.

'That woman needs some other friends,' he says as Fay whispers 'Yeah' in a vague voice, her attention shifting away from him, her head turned towards her phone once again.

# 9

When Fay returns to the hospital the next morning, Hamish has just left, and Emma is on her phone pacing around. Her surprised expression at Fay's impromptu decision to come back uninvited makes Fay cringe and think, this is a mistake. *Sorry*, she mouths, then turns and points back the way she came.

Emma shakes her head and gestures towards the free chair under the window, next to a pile of her stuff: trainers, her vintage Nike tracksuit top and a full Lidl plastic bag. So Fay sits down, holds her handbag on her lap and shuts her eyes as the soft yolk of sunlight breaks over her. It is barely nine thirty in the morning and she is already stiff with exhaustion. Hours spent tossing and turning, overthinking and pushing Steve away so she could rehash the evening's events without his breath breezing through her hair. Today will be a write-off. Not a jot of quality work will be done.

Now Emma has edged closer, kicking her socked toe at the floor as she talks. From what Fay can glean, she seems to have trouble convincing her mum that Lewis is going to be fine, and her mum doesn't need to get a train down.

'He's much better this morning,' she says. 'Honestly, Ma. Why would I lie?' Every now and again she looks over and smiles at Fay, although Fay thinks the smile appears a little opaque, almost dishonest.

'He's sleeping.' Emma's hand keeps opening and flexing. '*Sleeping*. The connection is terrible. Yes... Promise. Yep. Absolutely. And we'll see you in a couple of days.'

Emma gets off the phone, moves her stuff onto the floor and slumps down next to Fay. Up close, she also looks tired. Ambushed.

'Sorry. My mum is in a state. Lewis is the apple of her eye.'

'I got your text,' says Fay. 'It's brilliant they're going to let him come home.'

Emma nods. 'Fingers crossed. I'm just waiting for the doctor.' She smiles at Fay. 'I didn't expect you to come back. You did more than enough last night.'

'I hope I'm not being invasive,' says Fay anxiously. 'I won't be offended if you want me to go. I was just worried about you.'

'It's great that you're here.' As Emma rests her head against the wall behind her and closes her eyes, Fay stares at her profile, wondering if she is aware that Fay is looking at her. Without opening her eyes, Emma murmurs, 'I guess you also want to talk about what happened last night?'

Breath catches in Fay's throat. 'Yes, please,' she says, trying not to sound nervous.

/

Fay was on her way to meet Emma in the pub when Emma called. At first Fay wasn't entirely sure it was Emma talking; her voice sounded so distorted. She was saying that her son, Lewis, had got drunk and taken a bad party drug. 'He's overdosed,' she screamed. His friends had freaked over his comatose state and called an ambulance. Now he was intubated in ITU. Emma kept crying and saying, 'I knew something like this would happen one day. He's not going to be alright. He's not going to get through this.'

Fay's gut instinct was that this was not the case, that Lewis's death was far from inevitable, but Emma had experience with unexpected tragedy, so she was careful not to foist empty, placatory comments on her. She mustn't be trite. In fact, she said nothing except, 'I'm on my way. I'll be twenty minutes.'

Once inside the hospital, Fay got lost navigating the corridors of the old, sprawling building, half of which was being rebuilt and covered in sheets of plastic. She tried to keep calm, but she was shot through with a terrible sense of urgency. Emma's fear had been contagious, and Fay felt it as if it was her own.

Eventually, a nurse directed her to a side room near ITU where Emma was shouting at a slight, trim man in a short-sleeved shirt who kept stepping back from her voice. Tears had mingled with Emma's eyeliner and a dark streak ran down the side of both cheeks. Her nose was wet and red, and her lipstick was smudged because she kept wiping her mouth with the back of her hand. She looked clownish, tragic.

Emma didn't stop shouting to acknowledge Fay, she just brought her into the discussion. 'Hamish didn't know Lewis was going to the party, Fay. He was supposed to be looking after him. *He didn't know where he was.*'

'For God's sake, Em. Stop being so naive,' said Hamish. 'He's fifteen. You can't monitor his every move.'

'I can. It's called parenting,' screamed Emma.

'That's bullshit. I do parent him. You know I do.'

Fay didn't know what to say. She didn't want to take sides. 'Lewis is in the best place,' she said gently.

'Exactly.' Hamish dropped his arms to his side. He sounded relieved to have Fay's support. 'The doctors have already said they're not too concerned. They've intubated him as a precaution, so he doesn't inhale his vomit if he's sick.'

'Let's hope so,' shouted Emma.

'I'm going to wait outside,' said Fay.

'Don't,' said Emma. 'I want you to stay.'

'Your friend doesn't want to watch us go at each other,' said Hamish in a hard voice. 'Who the hell would?'

As Fay sat down on a chair in the corridor, a woman nearby started acting like someone out of the movies, slamming her fist on the side of a vending machine and demanding to know where her Frazzles were. Fay edged two seats over.

The movement was involuntary. Ten years ago, an ill-looking man had held a penknife in front of her face at a cashpoint in Farringdon. Fay's radar was fine-tuned for a stranger's accidental, and non-accidental, flashes of anger.

'Can you believe this piece of shit?' the woman said furiously. Fay maintained a neutral smile. She didn't engage, she didn't offer advice. It was too easy to become part of someone else's problems when they were out of control.

The crisps eventually dropped and, as the woman tore open the packet and moved down the corridor, Fay relaxed a little. Still, she wished she hadn't offered to come. After all, she had never met Lewis, and Emma wasn't a close friend. A feeling of awkwardness around being here began to preoccupy her. She was about to text Emma and slip away without saying goodbye in person when a doctor, or at least someone official-looking in scrubs, stifled a yawn and knocked on the door where Emma and Hamish were. Fay decided to wait until she heard what he'd said.

'Lewis is going to be fine,' Hamish said to Fay when they all came out. 'They're going to keep him in overnight. It's just a question of waiting for it to wear off and waking him tomorrow.'

'They think he's going to be fine,' added Emma sharply. '*Think.*'

'That's brilliant.' Fay understood that Emma didn't mean to be so contrary, that for her hope was not always possible to access.

'Unfortunately, only one of you can stay with him,' said the doctor, who really did look tired.

'I will,' said Emma.

'It's my night with him,' said Hamish.

'I'm his mother.'

'You're very upset,' said Hamish more gently. 'You know that stresses Lewis out.'

'Of course I'm upset!'

'Em, honestly. Go home. All Lewis will do is sleep. Come

back in the morning. I promise I won't leave his side. I'll text you updates.'

'I can get you home,' said Fay.

Emma considered this, then nodded. 'Let me just get my things.'

After she went back into the room, Hamish turned to Fay. 'Make sure you keep an eye on her,' he said. 'Em goes to a really bad place with all this stuff.'

'It's alright,' said Fay, adding, 'I was at college with her.'

'So you know,' said Hamish, looking relieved. 'Good.'


In the taxi, Emma stared out of the window. She seemed to have spun herself out. 'The ward was boiling,' she said eventually. 'Lewis hates being too hot. It makes him feel sick.' She was tracing the rain splats on the other side of the window with her finger. When the taxi stopped at a set of traffic lights, she turned her head and said to Fay, 'That doctor was cute.'

'Do you think?' said Fay.

'Yeah. You should have got his number.'

Fay turned to her window without replying. She had only just got Katie to back off. She hoped Emma wouldn't start suggesting possible matches for her. But if she did, Fay only had herself to blame for telling Emma about what she and Steve had agreed.

'This is me.' Emma spoke directly to the taxi driver. 'Thanks, lovely.' The street was treeless but wide. If Fay was honest, it was far nicer than she had expected. Emma reached into her coat pocket for money, but Fay blocked her.

'I've got this,' she said, and Emma didn't resist.

In her second-floor flat, Emma went around turning on all the lights.

'This is great,' said Fay, and she meant it. Very pretty, very boho. The living room windows were old and draughty but apparently afforded a sea view if you leant dangerously far out. There were healthy, interesting plants everywhere, colourful throws on the sofas and framed photos and prints covering most of one wall. At one end of the galley kitchen, near to the long window, a couple of papier mâché puppet figures dangled in between a spray of cheese-plant leaves. When Fay exclaimed her delight, Emma said in a tired voice that she had run a puppet theatre company for a while.

'Which one?' After Emma told her the name, Fay said, 'Oh, I used to take Rose to their shows. That's very cool.'

'Well, I guess I didn't run it exactly.' Emma handed Fay the cup of tea she had asked for. 'I was regularly employed by them for a while. We were great friends.'

Fay was still wandering around examining everything when she realised Emma had disappeared. She went to look for her and found her sitting cross-legged on Lewis's bed with his dark blue striped duvet hung over her shoulders. Seeing Fay in the doorway, she lifted her head hesitantly and said in a trembling voice, 'What if he dies?'

This massive dip in Emma's mood was sudden but not unreasonable. Fay could imagine walking into Billy's room while he was in the hospital, having dodged a serious overdose, and not wanting to do anything but wrap herself in his duvet – even if that was the sort of thing you did when someone was gone, properly gone, and not when they were temporarily absent.

'Shall we sit in the front room?' Fay asked. 'It might make you feel better.'

Emma shook her head.

'Shall I go home? Do you want to be alone?'

When Emma shook her head again, Fay sat down on the edge of the bed. Now she said nothing; thoughtful silence seemed appropriate. But a few minutes in, the silence seemed to make things worse as if she was leaving Emma to stew in her own dark, extreme thoughts, which felt horrible. She needed to make a difference to the situation somehow.

'Let's think about what we know for certain. About what

that doctor said. Not what your brain is letting you think.' Fay rattled off all the positive signs about Lewis's current condition. 'Emma, there is no evidence whatsoever that Lewis is going to die.'

And yet, as she produced those words in a kindly voice, Fay understood it was futile. Who was she to talk to Emma about evidence? If she was Emma, she too would be able to convince herself that it was possible to leave her son recovering in hospital, only to get a call to say he was no longer alive. In Emma's world, anything was possible.

Fay inched up. She took one of Emma's hands and held it in hers and reverted back to silence.

'I shouldn't have been a mother,' said Emma, about to cry again. 'I can't handle it. Hamish is right. I'm too anxious. I try to control everything to do with Lewis.'

Fay nods. 'Honestly. I get it.'

'You know, I wanted an abortion,' wept Emma. 'But I was too far along when I found out I was pregnant.'

'Oh, Emma. That makes me sad.'

'I always knew that if I had a child, I'd live in permanent fear that they'd be in danger.'

'We all feel that.'

'Not like this. Your fears are normal. Me, I feel like I could be punished at any time.'

'That won't happen.'

'Fay, get real. I killed someone,' shouted Emma. 'I killed someone. Eye for an eye and all that.'

Fay felt goosebumps hearing those words. 'You didn't kill them intentionally. It was an accident.'

'Tell that to Richard Drake's mother. I still think about her all the time, do you know that? Every single day she comes into my head. I even got the courage up to write to her and her husband a couple of years ago, but they never replied.' Emma pulled her hand out of Fay's and tugged the duvet even tighter around her shoulders. 'I deserve something bad to happen to me. But it should happen to me, not Lewis.'

'It was an accident,' repeated Fay. 'You weren't speeding. You weren't drunk. Her son stepped out in front of your car without looking. Everyone knows that. The newspapers said it, the police said it. And there were witnesses.'

'Richard is dead, Fay. A sixteen-year-old boy died because of me. A boy not much older than Lewis.'

Fay knew that whatever she said, Emma would counter. She took Emma's hand again and, as she turned it over, she saw a small, straight scar on her wrist. Emma noticed her looking and yanked her hand away.

'I'm so sorry,' said Fay. 'I can't imagine living with that inside you all this time. You're amazing.'

'I'm not. I'm anything but.'

'You could have given up. You've kept going.'

Emma wiped her eyes. 'Sometimes I think, I can live with this. I can find some peace. And then something like this happens and wham, I'm face down in shit again.' She sat up straight and seemed to shake herself. 'It's just a shock. I'll be alright. I know Lewis will be too. Thank you, Fay. I'm lucky to have met you again.'

'I haven't done anything. I wish I could do more.'

Emma shook her head. 'You've tried to understand.'

'Well, you're a victim too,' said Fay softly.

Nodding, Emma started crying again and said, 'Thank you for saying that. It means a lot to me.' She held the side of Fay's face. 'You're a beautiful woman. Inside and out.'

'Oh, stop that bollocks or I'll cry too.' Fay rolled her eyes, trying not to well up again.

They were both laughing in a slightly heightened, almost manic way when it happened. There was no tricky pause or build-up, they just moved from emotional, intimate laughter to this: Emma leaning forward and kissing Fay on the lips. And Fay, after making a small noise in her throat and feeling her face crinkle slightly in surprise, parting her lips to let Emma's tongue touch hers.

Rose's after-school swimming club has a race every term, like a mini gala, for family and friends. Fay arrives just as Rose slides into the water and pulls her goggles over her eyes. Rose doesn't look happy. Swimming isn't really her thing – she only comes because Steve insists. He couldn't swim until he went to university, and he still feels ashamed of not being able to do something so fundamental to childhood.

A sense of unease attaches itself to Fay when she spots Steve and edges along the row of parents towards him. To avoid him asking her about her day, she starts shouting in support of Rose immediately after kissing him hello. She doesn't even sit down. Her arms are raised above her head, and she is clapping so hard her shirt rides up her back.

Rose doesn't win. She comes fourth. Fay still continues to clap hard. Unlike some of the other mothers, she doesn't care about her child winning. She's seen Rose so unhappy in the past; she just cares about her feeling good about herself.

'This isn't going to improve Rose's mood,' says Steve out of the corner of his mouth. They both wave and grin and Fay sticks up both thumbs as Rose slouches away with barely a look in their direction.

When they sit back down, Steve puts his hand on Fay's leg. 'Thanks for last night,' he whispers.

'I enjoyed it,' she says, which is not wholly true. She had knelt on the kitchen floor and given Steve head for other reasons than to enjoy herself. He had been so excited by his chat with Frankie, whilst she had sat there feeling guilty; she knew she should tell him about kissing Emma, but she wasn't ready to, despite the new rule.

But giving Steve a blow job had only made her feel worse. It would shock Steve, like it shocked her, to know how absent she had been throughout. Her mouth moved as normal, yet her mind was somewhere else completely. This isn't like her. She is not someone who does anything sexual unless she feels like it. She has friends who regularly give in to get their partners off their back – literally – but she has always refused to barter with her body. Until last night, that is.

*I've actually kissed a woman*, Fay kept thinking as she worked on Steve, amazed by the swift change in her circumstances. Her hands had raked through a woman's long thick hair. She had tasted the faint sweetness of lipstick. It was the first time anything like this had happened with a woman. It was all astonishing and new, yet entirely familiar and comfortable. Almost as soon as it started, they had rushed into the living room where the kissing escalated. What surprised them both was that Fay had taken the lead. She had asked Emma to take off her T-shirt and bra so she could see her naked from the waist up. Yet she couldn't touch her. By then, the evening had leaked so much electricity and emotion Fay had to leave in a hurry. She had to get out into the night air and find herself again.

'I might repay the favour tonight if you play your cards right,' Steve whispers in her ear.

'Great,' says Fay, although she suspects she'll find an excuse. She is too tired, too distracted.

'There's Katie.' Steve points to the other side of the pool and they both wave. Then Fay feels her phone buzzing in her pocket. As she pulls it out and reads the message, Steve asks, 'How's Emma's son?'

'This isn't from her,' she says too quickly.

He shrugs like he doesn't understand her response. 'How is he?'

'Fine, I think.'

Fay acts like she doesn't know, when in fact she drove both Emma and Lewis home from the hospital today. She couldn't not. Emma had looked drained, so Fay had offered. She parked outside their building and Lewis went ahead while Fay and Emma sat in the car. All Fay wanted to do was talk – their conversation had been aborted in the hospital by the doctor arriving for his morning rounds – yet instead they had kissed. Another kiss that was almost surreal in its intensity. Fay knows she shouldn't have done that, not before she'd told Steve about Emma. At least she'd managed to explain the rules to Emma, who didn't seem remotely bothered by them. She was too busy trying to unbutton Fay's shirt in broad daylight, which panicked Fay into pushing away her hands.

Rose appears at the end of the row in her towelling robe. Now that other parents are out of their seats and mingling, it's easy for her to push through. Fay sweeps her up into her arms. 'You did so well, darling.'

'Fantastic swimming,' says Steve.

'I didn't win,' says Rose, putting her thumb in her mouth briefly before Fay gently moves it out.

'That's okay,' says Fay.

'No, it's not! Stop lying.' Fay sighs. Rose was in a terrible mood this morning before school and now, after a big swim, her slight body will be tired, and she will be even worse.

'Well, I think you did brilliantly.'

'I don't care what you think.'

'Hey,' says Steve. 'Don't talk to your mother like that. We all need to have a chat when we get home. I don't like the way you're treating everyone.'

'Leave me alone.' Rose kneels up onto the ledge behind them and stares out of the window as Katie appears.

'Congrats, Rose, you did great,' Katie calls out. 'Edie's in the changing room. She's got a Crunchie for you.' Rose doesn't even turn around. Edie is three years older than Rose and at a different school. Although they're not really friends, Edie always makes an effort with Rose, something Fay would like her daughter to reciprocate.

'Sorry,' says Fay as Steve turns away to chat with another dad who Fay vaguely recognises but doesn't know.

Katie gestures with her hands like it's nothing. 'Don't you look radiant?' she whispers to Fay. 'Who is he?'

Fay thinks of Emma's hair sloping over her bare shoulders and chest. 'There is no he.'

# 10

After Rose has finished her cereal and goes upstairs to brush her teeth, Steve says to Fay in a deliberately casual voice, 'What do you think about Frankie?' When Fay raises her eyebrows, he adds, 'As someone. You know, for me.'

'Oh.' A flash of surprise comes over her face which she disguises by averting her eyes back to the article she is reading on the iPad. 'I see.'

'Sorry,' he says. 'Silly time to bring it up.'

'Don't be sorry.' Is Fay finding it difficult to smile or is he imagining it? 'You just caught me off guard. Well, I think Frankie is really nice.'

'She is. And she's fun,' says Steve. 'I like her.'

'So do I,' says Fay.

He still can't really tell whether she means it – she hasn't been as vocal as usual about anything these past few days. Not that he's pushed her on it because neither of them like to be interrogated when they feel like retreating for a bit. Besides, he doesn't really know what he'd say. She's still been loving and attentive. Running a bath for him the other night; organising Katie to pick up Rose so they could have an impromptu afternoon cycle ride across the Downs; the unexpected love note she left in one of his trainers. And of course, there was that unexpected blow job in the kitchen after he got home from the book launch. It's all been great, and he's appreciated everything she's done for him.

'And I know you've met her, but it's not like she's one of

our mutual friends, is it? I mean, she's not really a friend of mine at all. I don't think I've broken any rules, do you agree?'

When Fay nods, he says, 'And you're fine with this?'

'Absolutely fine.' She nods again as she stands up. 'Has something happened between you?'

Steve is sure that he's red in the face. 'No, not yet.' It would have made far more sense if he'd come to the conversation with something real to report, because really, what does he have? Yes, he felt Frankie was flirting with him a little at the launch. And yes, he has been thinking about her and he hopes that she has also been preoccupied with thoughts of him. Quietly, he took it as a promising sign when she texted an invitation to lunch and didn't ask him to bring Fay along. 'She's making me lunch today.'

'Ah. Right.' Surprisingly, Fay puts down the cereal bowls she has stacked up and moves behind him. Bending down, she hangs her arms around his neck. He clasps them, enjoying her warm weight on his back.

'Frankie will be lucky to get to spend time with you,' she says, adding: 'And I'm lucky to have you.' This is such a generous and unexpectedly nice thing to hear that it almost brings tears to Steve's eyes.

He loosens her arms and stands up, turning around to face her. 'Yes, you are,' he says, smiling. 'Bloody lucky.'

As Fay kisses him, her hand moves under his T-shirt, tugging his chest hair a little roughly but not too roughly, exactly how he likes it. She's acting as if she's properly turned on by the idea that he might be about to take a lover. He enjoys the attention, although if he's honest, he's slightly wounded that she's not more unnerved at the prospect.

*Stephen*, he admonishes himself. *Get the fuck over it.* This is Fay, this is who she is. He has to accept that he's far more likely to be weirded out by this stuff than her. He realised this the other night when he was filling the car with petrol, thinking about Frankie, and he was struck by this sudden visceral feeling that he was putting his marriage in irreversible danger. His hand was shaking so hard he could barely squeeze the petrol pump.

He can't imagine that happening to his self-assured wife. It's not about strength, he has come to realise – he's a pretty solid sort of guy, a guy for a crisis as Fay likes to tell him. It's more that Fay has tighter control over herself and her interactions with the world. She might fall apart when things go wrong, but she never leaches out for long. Whereas when things get really hard for him, he knows he irritates her by lying around punctured for ages, not always sure how to find a way through.

'What about you?' he asks as she pulls her hand out of his shirt and moves away. 'Anything cooking?'

'Maybe,' she says quietly.

'D'ya wanna share it with me? Dem da rules,' he says, pretending to sound light-hearted, but he doesn't pull it off. He sounds weird.

'I know the rules,' she says in a tired voice. 'When I have something to share, I will. Promise.' She bends down to pick a spoon off the floor that Rose had dropped. 'Just think about yourself today, babe. Have a fun lunch.'

Steve feels an immediate flutter in his chest. *Babe*. An endearment they despise and have always refused to use, yet apparently now said by Fay without any irony. Without even noticing! Steve watches her as she opens the dishwasher. He wonders exactly what they are letting in, what else might change.


Steve stands on the gravel driveway admiring the wide, traditional cottage. He wants to stand there a while. He appreciates old places where history seeps out, but conscious that Frankie might be by a window watching him scrutinise her house, he walks toward the door.

His nerves feel raw again. This morning he was so busy at work that he felt fine, but now he has to pause, reset himself.

He mustn't let the nerves take hold – or maybe it's guilt, he's not sure, only that he feels uncomfortable – because if he does, he might end up turning around and heading back down the confusing countryside lanes.

After he rings the bell, he doesn't hear a thing until the door flings open and Frankie leans weightlessly against the door frame in a black tunic top and wide-legged, floaty black trousers. She is barefoot.

'You found us.' She stands back and gestures for him to come inside. 'Welcome.'

Steve's glad that she is also casually dressed, otherwise he might have felt out of place in his unbuttoned flannel shirt, vintage T-shirt with crappy beer logo across the front, jeans and red Puma trainers. In fact, only Frankie's carefully made-up face suggests that she is expecting company. Heavy around her big eyes, a brush of pink on her high cheekbones. Her hair is flyaway, shiny. He suspects it's freshly dyed as he remembers many more grey strands shining under the wine-bar lights.

'Sorry I'm late. I got a bit lost on the way from the station.'

'You didn't cycle?'

'Decided against it. The chain was broken,' he lies. 'I didn't have time to sort it.' It would have been a forty-five-minute journey from his office, a hard cycle, and Steve realised he cared too much about arriving in Lycra with sweat coming off him. 'And I fancied a drink,' he admitted as Frankie shut the door behind him. He holds out the carrier bag containing a bottle of white wine and four beers.

'Bring them through,' she says without thanking him.

To get to the kitchen they walk across a living room where the furniture is surprisingly masculine. A massive flat-screen TV is mounted over one wall and there are two beige sofas and a long glass and chrome coffee table. Steve doesn't like how the cottage interior has been gutted and transformed – it's dispiritingly contemporary. It feels dishonest.

And the kitchen is even more modern. All granite surfaces

and stark white cupboard doors. Not a bit of soft, natural wood anywhere. Well, the island top might be wood, he can't see – it's almost entirely covered with foods from Waitrose. In fact, glancing around, most of the countertops are strewn with produce, shopping bags and a couple of cardboard boxes with a French wine supplier's logo on the side. It's an upmarket mess and Steve feels slightly disappointed by this. He doesn't want to be. He doesn't want Frankie to be able to afford so much that all her possessions are a blur to her. She takes his bag of booze and dumps it in front of a blender. He wonders if she'll even remember that he brought it.

'Red or white or beer? I also have spirits.'

'Beer, please.'

Frankie gets him a beer, pours herself a glass of white wine, then boils a saucepan of water for the new potatoes. They chat about their weeks, the weather, his off-road cycling routes. They agree on the brilliance of *Curb Your Enthusiasm* and laugh over their favourite episodes. The conversation flows, it's easy, and he feels good about coming over now he knows that their relationship can move beyond that one illuminating chat at the book launch.

Somehow, they get on to the subject of Frankie's tattoos. She was forty-eight when she had her first, then another half a dozen over the next few years. This is daring to her, he can tell, coming late to something that is commonplace to so many.

She lifts her trouser leg to show him her first – he likes the sight of her delicate, tanned ankle, but the crudely inked flower does nothing for him. 'You don't like it.' She drops her leg.

'I do, it's pretty. I'm just not massively into tattoos,' he admits.

'Are you not?' She doesn't sound like she cares, which he appreciates. 'That runs in the family then,' she says as she takes an iceberg lettuce out of the fridge, then rummages through a bag of shopping. 'I can't remember how it came up after you left, but your mum was appalled to hear I had some.

She made a point of saying that neither of her children would ever have tattoos because she forbids it.'

Steve has to take a breath. They are dropping into tricky emotional territory. 'Yep, that sounds like something she'd say.'

Steve knows his mum thinks her opinion is the only opinion that matters, that she has a breathtaking sense of self-importance. After enough alcohol, in the right mood, he can admit that she is a narcissist and her leaving is not his fault, but for reasons no one can ever help him unpick, he always ends up justifying her behaviour somehow – his parents' marriage wasn't good, her own mother died in childbirth, he and Anthony were a handful. Deep down, Steve knows he's too scared of losing his mum again to stay upset or angry with her for long.

'I'm sorry. I've spoken out of turn, haven't I?' Frankie must have seen something rise in him, a familiar sadness that he would rather not have to feel here, in conversation with a woman who has beautiful ankles.

He shakes his head and his beer at her. 'Not at all. It's fine.'

'I never met your dad, what was he like?' she asks, glancing curiously at him.

Steve stands up and takes his second beer bottle from her as she continues to walk around the kitchen, finding vegetables, chopping them. 'You'd have liked him. Everyone did.'

He's staring at the microwave for somewhere to focus his thoughts and stop the emotion flooding him, but it's the wrong place to look. Now he can see lots of post and documents haphazardly stacked up next to it. His father had piles of papers everywhere in the tiny office behind the kitchen in the café. He was not a natural businessman. Far too interested in cooking and not enough attention to admin. He never opened letters from the tax office, he failed to keep proper receipts. But he was always smiling, thinks Steve, feeling a twinge of loss. Always. Steve doesn't know anyone else who could tap into such simple joyfulness.

'I hope I didn't say too much at the launch,' carries on Frankie and there is a different quality in her voice, a hesitancy that was not there before. 'I can be too pushy.' She makes her voice raspy. 'You must think this! Do that!' She pauses. 'It drives Elliot mad.'

'No, it was great. And because of you, Fay and I have agreed to tell each other what we're up to.'

'Yeh! That's terrific news.' Frankie picks up her phone. 'We need some music.'

She decides on a female Cuban musician whom Steve hasn't heard of before, but he likes – it even spurs him on to dance a little and encourage Frankie to stop chopping and join in for a couple of minutes, which is fun. He keeps trying to understand what's going on between them – on the one hand, he doesn't want to get ahead of himself, on the other he's pretty sure that she is attracted to him. But when his stomach growls and he starts to feel slightly spacey, he realises it's futile to analyse their dynamic after three beers and nothing to eat since breakfast.

One more beer later, Frankie puts a bowl of salad on the table. She slaps sea bass fillets into a hot capery butter in a frying pan, then presents him with the fish and new potatoes.

Steve eats everything quickly. 'This is delicious,' he says, meaning it. While he helps himself to more salad, Frankie pushes her mostly full plate away, which seems both wasteful and antisocial. He doesn't want to be sitting here eating alone. She must pick up on his disapproval, for she pulls her plate back and picks at the salad leaves, if somewhat half-heartedly.

'You're a good listener,' she says after he takes an interest in her eleven-year stint in Spain and the story of her two cancerous moles which have been cut away, but which made her and Elliot decide the harsh sunny climate was not for them any more. 'I appreciate that in someone,' she adds, taking their plates to the sink.

As Steve sits and looks out at the garden, he feels good about himself. Why shouldn't he? As far as he can tell, he hasn't put a foot wrong yet. And whatever their connection was before lunch, Frankie has stepped it up with regular, loaded looks in his direction that have awoken his groin and confirmed that the attraction is neither one-way nor a by-product of his imagination.

'I don't have pudding,' Frankie says and hands him another beer. 'But' – she holds out a fancy-looking pipe and lighter – 'voila! I do have some weed. It's very giggly stuff.'

'Oh-oh. This could be dangerous.' Steve's relationship with weed has not always been successful. Prone to behaving immaturely and emerging afterwards full of regrets, he doesn't smoke often and almost never in the daytime without a bed nearby to slump into. And yet this isn't enough to stop him. If anything, this makes him want it even more.

'Damn, you're right,' he says fifteen minutes later. 'This stuff is perfection.' Light and smooth, not a flicker of paranoia. Before long they are sitting comfortably next to each other on a leather sofa laughing at the length of Frankie's second toe on her left foot. It's bewilderingly long.

'Does it fit into a sock?' he asks.

'Of course!' she says witheringly. 'Is that a joke?' Steve shakes his head, but then they both laugh and keep laughing. After Frankie calms down, she takes another hit from the pipe, then hands it to him. About to light up, the front door opens and shuts. Even that noise is startling, prompting Steve into concealing the pipe at his side and sitting up straight. When Elliot strides in smiling, Steve's heart thuds in his chest. Getting up, he stammers out a greeting while Frankie doesn't move an inch. She appears completely relaxed.

'Well, look at you kids.' Elliot pushes the visor of his baseball cap up his forehead. He is unshaven and his patchy stubble is near-white, making him look older than Steve remembers. Holding a phone, a newspaper and a couple of large brown envelopes, he jams the phone into his front jeans pocket to free up a hand for Steve to shake. 'Nice to see you again.'

'Yeah, you too,' stammers Steve, hyperconscious of being

stoned and how unfazed Elliot is to find him in his living room with his wife.

'Do you want some food?' asks Frankie without moving.

'No, I ate already. I need to go make some calls. Excuse me, guys.'

Only after Steve is sure that Elliot is in his upstairs office does he sit back down. His mind is spinning out. He has no idea how much of that is down to the weed. 'Jesus. That was awkward.'

'Was it?' Frankie looks surprised. 'Why?'

'I had no idea I'd see him.' Steve holds his hands out in front of him. 'See, I'm trembling.' Looking sideways at Frankie, he says, 'Doesn't he mind me being here with you like this?'

'Not at all. We've talked about it. About you.'

'It feels odd.'

'It's fine. Really. He's not bothered.' She yawns and briefly presses her hand on his back. 'Promise.'

Steve feels better. 'Okay,' he whispers.

Frankie struggles to her feet. 'I want to play you something.'

'What?'

'Wait.' She pads through to the kitchen and returns, scrolling through her phone. Satisfied, she sits back down, eyes closed. When a woman's voice starts up, Steve turns and says to her, 'Maria Callas.'

Frankie opens her eyes. 'Yes.' She sounds surprised. 'Which opera?'

He shrugs. 'No idea.'

'*Norma* by Bellini. "Casta Diva".' Her lids lower again. 'Divine.'

Callas's voice soars through speakers, filling the room with a bleak beauty. It is unbearably moving, but by God it is also really loud.

'Won't it disturb Elliot?' Steve asks in a raised voice.

Frankie shrugs. 'Don't worry about him. Sit back and enjoy it.'

Following her instruction, Steve sits back. He closes his eyes, lets his shoulders drop. Pretty quickly the music runs over his thoughts. When Frankie says, 'Wasn't that something?' her voice startles him. He had almost dropped off.

Turning her face close to his, she runs her tongue over her bottom lip. 'I like you.'

'And I like you,' he says, although the words are not easy to say. He has half a mind on the chair wheels rolling soft across the carpet overhead, followed by the blare of someone's voice through a hand-free phone before Elliot picks it up. Now snatches of Elliot's muffled voice is enough of a reminder of how wrong it is for Steve to be sitting here enjoying Elliot's wife, unconscionably wrong. And still – still! – his body responds to Frankie.

Frankie puts a hand on Steve and lightly feels his hardness before lifting her hand away. 'It's true,' she says. 'You do like me.'

He smiles. 'What about your boyfriend?'

'He moved. Took a yoga residency in the Lake District,' she says. 'So I have a vacancy.'

'Excellent,' says Steve. 'Can I apply? Or is there stiff competition?' He starts laughing, confident that he is being amusing, and she quickly joins in.

'I love Fay,' he blurts out.

'I love Elliot.'

'I'm not looking for anything… more than, well, you know…' Steve stops. He has literally no idea how to say he just wants to fuck without sounding like precisely the sort of man he never thought he'd be.

'Wonderful,' she says. 'Nor am I.'

He has an urge to touch her face, but the urge is also frozen in him. As he wonders what she wants him to do, a last shot of afternoon light suddenly finds its way into the room.

'Too bright.' She frowns. 'I fare better in the gloom.'

'Nonsense.'

'Not nonsense. I'm old.'

'Frankie, you look sensational in any light. Now, how about another beer and a dance in the kitchen to that Cuban singer?'

Around five, Steve takes the train home, sure he is smiling throughout the entire journey. Now he can see what Fay meant. Such a tantalising feeling would be impossible to recreate at this point in their relationship.

When he gets back, Fay, already dressed in her workout gear, is in the kitchen by the dishwasher. This is where he left her this morning, only now she is unloading clean dishes.

'I bloody hate the dishwasher,' he says. 'It makes me go nuts thinking of all the times I'm going to load and unload that thing before I die.'

Fay laughs. 'Er, I'm the one doing it.' As she reaches up to put a couple of mugs in the overhead cupboard, Steve snakes his arm around her waist from behind. 'You know what I mean.' He has to bend to kiss her head; he could stand tall when cuddling Frankie goodbye and still meet her eyes.

'So, someone had fun.' Fay covers his hand with one of hers. Turning her head slightly, she says, 'I told you it feels good.'

'You did.' Steve leans into her. 'We smoked a lot of weed. I was pretty funny, as it goes.'

'I'm sure you were.' Fay turns around and touches the tip of his nose. 'You are funny.'

'Nothing happened, just so you know. Not yet.' He and Frankie had danced and laughed in the kitchen for a while, then she pleaded exhaustion and they went and sat back on the sofa. She had played Maria Callas on repeat and said that not everything erotic is found in sex. He had agreed although he also suggested that a tragic opera wasn't exactly a turn-on and she had laughed and said touché. Eventually, not long after he heard Elliot take a shower, Steve got up to leave – he hated not seeing Rose before she went to bed – and Frankie had said, 'You're so much better than the yoga teacher.' At the door he tried to kiss her gently on the lips, but she refused and said, 'No, next time.'

Fay twists away from him. 'I have to go. I'll be late for boxing. Are you going to be alright with Rose? She's in another fierce mood.'

Steve staggers back a little, opens the bread bin and takes out a slice of rye bread. 'She'll be putty in my hands.'

'More like you'll be putty in Rose's hands.' Fay pulls on her hoodie, zips it up to her neck. 'Don't let her stay up late.'

'Nope.' Inertia floods through him as he slots the bread into the toaster. It would have been nice to come back home and relax. Wallow in the most original day he's had in a long time. Instead, he is being left to sort Rose. Either she'll still be in a mood and ignore him or she'll expect him to get stuck into serious play with her toys and won't accept any lapse in his attention.

'I need a wee, then I'm off.'

When Fay leaves the room to head upstairs, Steve pours himself a glass of water and roots around in a drawer for Nurofen. His head already feels sore. As he sits down at the kitchen table and swallows a couple of pills, he hears a message come through on Fay's mobile. It is lying in his line of vision, half out of her bag that is slopped over the table. Drinking his water, hearing the toast pop up behind him, Steve leans in – fatally, he will come to think later – towards the phone.

### Emma

What a crap motorway journey back! Good to be home. How was your day? Xxx

It is the next message that arrives before Steve has even finished reading this one that makes him feel as if the water is not going down, as if his throat is closed over.

## Emma

Forgot what you said about using the other phone.
I'll text you there. xxxx

And then, in slow motion, as a chill runs through him, knowing he shouldn't be doing this, of course, that it is completely unacceptable, he reaches into Fay's bag and takes out her other phone as it pings.

## Emma

Me again. Thought about you a lot on the way back. Miss you, babe.
I'll show you how much when I see you. 😜😜😜 xxxx

# 11

Fay needs to gather courage before she goes into Steve's office. Last night's row is still fresh in her mind – if you could even call it a row. That would imply there was an exchange of words when Steve did all the talking. The moment she came home from her boxing class, with Rose asleep, he turned on her, shouting about her breaking the rules so quickly. 'What does it say about you if you can't be honest early on? It doesn't really inspire me to continue. Do you get that? Do you?' He didn't really want to hear her apology, which is all she wanted to offer, and it was impossible to have a conversation with a man who kept walking out of every room she entered.

Fay knocks briefly and pushes open the door. 'Hello,' she says warmly.

Steve looks shocked but catches himself. 'Hi there,' he says in a crisp, professional voice. He won't appreciate her turning up at his office uninvited, but neither will he make a scene in front of the others.

'So nice to see you, Mrs Ariti.' Laura is at her desk doing whatever an intern does.

'Call me Fay.'

Laura nods. 'Okay,' she says, adding shyly, 'My mum's name is Fay.'

'Is it?' Fay smiles. She literally has no idea how else to answer this.

Fay glances at Steve sitting at the long white IKEA table near the window. It had been a hell of a job for them to put the table together but fun all the same. BBC Radio 6 Music had played through Steve's laptop, Billy put the small desks together and Rose sat in a new office chair, asking repeatedly to be spun around. They were a good family that day. A sense of joy ran through everything they did, and they laughed and worked well together as if they were the wave pushing Steve away from his corporate marketing job into going it alone. Fay remembers giving a sentimental toast and Billy rolling his eyes at her cracking voice.

With deliberate casualness, Steve puts a foot on the chair next to him. 'To what do I owe this honour?' he says, as if he doesn't know. His laptop sits in front of him, surrounded by papers, and he is looking in that direction, picking up a document, putting it down, concentrating on everything but Fay.

Fay calls out a greeting to Lizzy, the twenty-four-year-old graphics and computer whizz-kid hunched over a laptop across the table from Steve with her back to Fay.

'Hey, Fay.' Lizzy turns her head slightly, Fay can see her slight smile, but that's about it. At her interview Lizzy had told Steve that she had problems maintaining eye contact and was uncomfortable talking on the telephone.

Fay holds up a box and gently shakes it. 'I bought macaroons for everyone.'

Laura claps her hands. 'Awesome. I love macaroons!'

Fay puts a few on a serviette she took from the bakery. 'I thought we could take ours to the beach,' she says to Steve.

'Nice idea but no can do.' He doesn't look at her. He gets up and walks his laptop back to his desk in the corner. 'We're on a deadline.'

'I can finish off,' says Lizzy. 'We're pretty much there.'

'Great.' Fay walks over to Steve's desk. 'Come on, you. Let's get some fresh air.'

She says this in a friendly, knowing way, as if only she, the wife, can gently close the boss's laptop, daring him to refuse her in front of others. Steve makes eye contact with her. *Stop it*, he mouths. *No*, she mouths crossly. He sighs.

'Guys, I won't be long. Lizzy, call me with anything. Okay?'

On the street, Steve doesn't reach for her hand like he usually does. Instead, he stuffs his fists in the front pocket of his hoodie. He walks ahead of her, fast.

When she catches up, he says in a voice that suggests he is either seething or he loathes her, or quite possibly both, 'I really resent you coming to my work. Couldn't this have waited until I got home?'

'I want to sort this out. I've already said I was completely out of order.' More than once, she thinks. In fact, she had apologised repeatedly again this morning and insisted that he was right, she should have told him about Emma.

Steve keeps walking, ignoring her once more. He doesn't seem to want her to repent, he wants her to stay feeling bad, which makes her lose her patience and feel hard-hearted towards him.

They separate to let an elderly couple walk between them, but the moment they are out of earshot, Steve says, 'So you're not worried that I might say fuck it? Let's end all this, go back to how we were?'

'No.' Actually, she is – even this conversation triggers a wave of panic. What if Steve did insist that she put a stop to things? Would she graciously concede? She's not sure she can, not when she feels such an undercurrent of excitement. Not when things have barely got going.

They cross the main road to the beach in silence. The warm wind is up, and Fay hasn't bought a clip, so her hair tumbles across her cheeks. Down the steps to the beach, the pebbles press against the thin, rubbery soles of her ballet pumps. Steve strides along a bit from the steps, then stops and squats with his back to the wall, checking his watch impatiently in the minute or so it takes Fay to catch up and sit down next to him.

'Steve, how many times can I say I was wrong and I'm sorry before you believe me?'

'You kissed her and didn't tell me. Why would you do that?'

Fay pauses. 'It was a big surprise to me. I wanted to sit with it a while before saying something.'

Steve picks up a stone and throws it across the near-empty beach. 'I hope that's true,' he says, looking sideways at her for the first time. 'Because you don't usually lie.'

Above them, as the sun sprays out gently from behind the one dense cloud, Fay takes her sunglasses out of her bag and puts them on. 'Really? I thought I was a born liar. One of the many delightful things you said to me last night.'

'I was upset.' Steve presses his tense forearms on his thighs and knits his hands together. 'What about boundaries? You broke the rules.'

'Can you stop talking about rules?'

'Why? Because it's getting in the way of all your fun?'

Fay looks out to the clear horizon. 'I really didn't mean to disrespect you.'

Steve drops both of his hands to his sides and rakes them through the pebbles. 'Okay.' Fay is relieved for the breakthrough. She closes her eyes and enjoys the warmth on her face.

'This friction starting up between us,' he says. 'It worries me.'

Fay opens her eyes and looks at him. 'Did you think that when you were getting stoned and drunk with Frankie?'

At least he has the grace to say, 'No, I guess not.'

'I think we're fine.'

'Think?' he says with a nervous laugh.

'We are fine,' she says quickly and firmly.

'Yeah, well, you don't sound so sure.'

'I am.' Yet exactly *how* sure, Fay can't say. She squeezes Steve's hand. Her current feelings are new and unpredictable; she doesn't know what she's thinking. The silence continues, but when Steve does speak, he sounds okay. Not happy, but not harsh. 'So, are you a lesbian now?'

Knowing Steve as she does, such black-and-white thinking is not a surprise. 'Noooo. Of course not.' With her hand still on his, she thinks of how sometimes in the mornings she props herself up on her elbows and watches him come through naked from the shower, with his strong buttocks and tough legs from years of cycling, and she'll either make him laugh by patting the bed next to her or wolf-whistling. Her attraction to men, to Steve, is very real; she can't imagine giving that up anytime soon. But whilst she is physically drawn to Emma, she suspects that the attraction is just as much about feeling like a teenager in Emma's company. It's pretty exhilarating to be around someone who lives in the moment.

'Really?' Steve looks at her with such uncertainty. 'You can move between us that easily? I can't get my head around that.'

Fay shrugs. 'I guess I can.'

'Have you ever thought about being with a woman before? When you've been with me?'

'Never,' she says. They sit silently again looking at the two young girls being shown how to skim stones. Fay wonders if Steve is thinking about how Billy used to love that, how he would beg daily to be brought to the beach.

'Please respect the rules, Fay,' he says, looking at her.

'I will,' she says, looking ahead. 'Promise.' She tells herself that she isn't lying, she is starting afresh from now. It makes absolutely no sense to tell Steve what happened after he left for work that morning.

/

When the doorbell rang about ten o'clock, Fay swore at the interruption. She had been engrossed in writing copy for a new dog charity's website. With numerous drafts under her belt, she was now finessing the sentences, reading each paragraph aloud, slashing surplus words. This was her favourite bit, although she had to be careful. Her tendency at this point was to strip away too much until the rhythm was lost and it fell a bit flat.

Hurrying down the stairs from the attic, she heard a workman next door, the sound of a drill. In the gardens backing on to theirs, a child was crying out for his mother. Two dogs were barking at each other over a fence.

'Coming,' she shouted out as her slippers clipped against the floorboards. Delivery people seemed to come and go so quickly, as if they hoped not to find anyone at home.

When she pulled back the door, Emma was standing up close. There was almost no distance between them. 'Oh hi,' said Fay. 'Hi.' She wanted to say something more, but she could taste the sourness in her mouth. She hadn't eaten breakfast or brushed her teeth, only drunk two cups of tea.

Emma started laughing. 'Your face is a total picture. Is it a bad time? I've got three shifts in a row starting tonight, so I thought I'd pop by on the off-chance.'

Still paranoid about her breath, Fay stepped back, smiling. 'I was working.' She really needed to say, I'm on a deadline, I've got a team of dog lovers waiting for my copy. But in truth, she was more alarmed at the state of herself. She hadn't showered. Her hair was scraped back. Determined to get one more day out of her beloved green velour tracksuit, she had rescued it from the washing basket this morning after Steve had scooped it off their bedroom floor. By contrast, Emma looked dramatically better. She was fully made-up, and her black denim jacket went well with her tight grey jeans and chunky black ankle boots.

'I thought you might be,' said Emma, without embarrassment. 'Anyway, I just really wanted to give you these.' She put her hand into a bag she was holding and with the strings caught up between her fingers, she pulled out a couple of puppets by their necks – an old, wizened man in a three-piece suit and a young girl in a shiny blue dress with a long red plait down her back. 'I've been storing these at my mum's since I move around so much. I thought Rose would like them.'

'That's so kind of you.' Fay was genuinely touched. Also, it was now impossible to refuse Emma entry. When she gestured for her to come in, Emma walked in straight away and with such confidence it briefly crossed Fay's mind that she hadn't expected to be turned away.

'You can see I dressed for company,' said Fay.

'You look great. Don't worry about that.'

Fay spotted a blotch of tomato soup near the zip of her top. 'No, let me change. Have a seat in here.' She pushed open the door to the living room. 'I won't be a minute.'

In her bedroom, Fay quickly rubbed a make-up wipe under both arms and between her legs, then changed into a new bra and a flattering red vintage dress over black leggings. As she brushed on mascara and some rouge, she kept thinking: *Emma shouldn't be here. Steve would go mad.*

When she returned downstairs, Emma wasn't in the living room. The bag with the puppets was on the floor along with her handbag and denim jacket, and the doors leading to the garden had been unlocked and opened. Emma was out there, crouched down by their smoke tree.

'This tree is sick,' she said, looking up at Fay.

'What do you mean, sick?'

'I'm sure it has verticillium wilt.' Emma straightened up. 'A fungal disease in the soil which gets into the roots, then spreads through the tree. These leaves are a giveaway. See how scorched they are?' She sounded so authoritative and convincing.

'Oh God. It's not dead, is it? It's Steve's favourite tree.'

'Hard to say. It's not looking good.' Emma talked in detail about the leaves and the bark and even bent down again to take earth in her hand and pull out a few of the weeds around the trunk, just because their presence was annoying to her.

'You should be a gardener,' said Fay. 'I'd hire you.'

'Done that. Got the T-shirt.'

'Really? When?'

'Oh, a while ago now. I worked for a landscape gardener for nearly two years. I loved it. But he was a pig when I left. He wouldn't give me a reference. Said I had been trying to pinch his clients. I could hardly afford to buy my own trowel at the time! I wasn't going to set up in business. But I couldn't get another job in the industry without a reference so…'

As Fay tutted and shook her head sympathetically, she did also wonder why so many jobs never worked out for Emma. There was a definite pattern. This boss was misogynistic. That company was exploiting her. A less competent colleague was taking all the credit. While Fay believed the situations were very real, she wondered if it was also to do with Emma's perspective. It seemed unlikely that Emma was always right and everyone else was wrong.

'Anyway, I won't work for a set-up like that again,' said Emma. 'Tiny companies run by cocky, entitled men.'

Fay wondered if her face openly conveyed that she was thinking of Steve because Emma added in a hurry, 'They're not all like that, obviously. I bet Steve's a great boss.'

As they walked back towards the house, Fay said, 'Why let a reference get in the way? You could start a business up without it. There are loads of ways in.'

'Sure are, if you have money. Or a nice husband to help you out.'

Emma didn't say this meanly, but neither did she attempt to save Fay's feelings. As she said it, Fay blanched and mumbled, 'True.' If Emma was gently cutting her down to size, she probably deserved it. She was too glib. She did have more than Emma and that would likely always be the case. Even after the brutal years of infertility or having parents who had never lived up to expectations, her life didn't have a terrible tragedy running through it like a river.

'Now, tea or coffee?'

'Black coffee, please.'

In the kitchen, Fay turned on the kettle and checked the mugs were clean. She could hear Emma moving around and looking at photos. Fay had spooned ground coffee into the cafetière, then filled it with boiled water, when Emma appeared behind her again.

'Your house is nothing like I expected.'

'Oh really? Why?'

'I thought it would be… more done-up. Fancier.'

Fay laughed as she plunged then poured coffee into both mugs and handed one to Emma. 'Nope. Never.' It wasn't the first time this comment had been levelled at her. She must give off the air of someone who took these things seriously, yet she found the sort of perfection that interior design relied on to be ludicrous. She had no interest in it. All those photos in magazines of perfectly curated interiors were just junk. Fay made mistakes and didn't correct them. She bought what she liked. If this lamp didn't go with that rug, well, too bad.

'Steve is a good-looking guy,' said Emma, adding, 'That's a bit of a surprise too. I thought he'd be kind of nondescript.'

'Really? Thanks,' said Fay dryly.

Emma burst out laughing. 'That sounds awful. What I mean is that you've opened up your relationship. I guessed you weren't attracted to each other any more.'

'We have sex,' said Fay. 'Good sex.' She felt brave saying it, but it was the truth, and she was sure that Emma could take hearing it.

'How good?'

'Good.' Fay shrugged. She couldn't tell from Emma's expression if she was being laughed at. They stood opposite each other, leaning back against cupboards, sipping their coffee.

'I don't know how I feel about that,' said Emma, frowning as she put her mug down behind her.

'I never said we didn't have sex.' Fay could hear how highly strung and defensive she sounded.

'I know.' Emma edged forward and rested her hands on the counter on either side of Fay. 'I mean, I'm not sure I like the sex being good. I guess I'll have to be better.' Her voice took on a low, manufactured timbre, then she grinned. Despite the strangeness of the moment and the intensity of being this close to her, Fay managed to smile.

But Emma didn't touch Fay. They stared at each other and neither of them moved for what seemed like ages but was probably only seconds. Fay could smell Emma's peachy, light scent. It wasn't one she had smelt on her before. Fay found it fascinating that Emma had different smells; she would not have considered doing this herself. It was enough remembering to spray on the one perfume that she had.

'Are you going to give me a tour?' Emma circled her finger towards the ceiling, one eyebrow raised. 'See for myself where you have *good* sex.'

Fay shook her head. 'We're not going upstairs. You really shouldn't be here. I agreed with Steve that the house was off limits. Our bedroom certainly is.'

Fay didn't quite push Emma away, she couldn't bear to do that, but she straightened up, reaching over Emma's arm for her mug.

Emma's expression lost its dreaminess. She stood back and crossed her arms protectively against her chest. 'Well, that's a bit dull.'

Fay felt sick. She swallowed. 'I think it's fair enough. It's Steve's home too.' She expected she might have to justify her actions again, but Emma smiled and tried to laugh it off.

'Don't go all serious on me, Fay Munro. I'm just playing with you. I get it. I swear I won't show up here again.'

'Okay,' said Fay, breathing more easily. 'Great.'

'But since I am here...' Emma rested the tip of her finger on Fay's bottom lip, then she leant forward and kissed her. Fay felt the countertop press into the small of her back, heard the slow drip of the tap they had never got round to fixing. Emma's hands were now under the soft fabric of her dress, moving into the waistband of her leggings.

'I can't.' Fay put her hands over Emma's hands. 'Not in the house.'

Emma pulled her hands free and tugged Fay's leggings down her hips, just enough to be able to push Fay's legs apart and move her fingers into Fay's underwear and into Fay. 'Are you sure about that...'

Fay gasped. Her body felt as if it was swimming away from her. 'We mustn't.'

'We're not upstairs,' whispered Emma in an equally thick voice. 'We're not in your bed.'

Fay took a deep breath. 'We can never do this here again,' she said as she unbuttoned Emma's top. Seeing that Emma wasn't wearing a bra, she boiled up inside. 'Okay?' she said. 'Okay?'

/

Fay rushes from Steve's office to pick Rose up from school. Once they get home, they hole up in Rose's bedroom, sorting through the clothes in Rose's chest of drawers and discarding those that no longer fit since her recent growth spurt. But Rose, who sits on the rug near her, playing with the puppets that Fay said she got from a charity shop, is making the easy, mindless task complicated; she insists on challenging Fay over every item Fay wants to get rid of.

But Fay puts up with this. She even lets Rose play some game on her phone, because it gives her the space to keep running over the scene that took place in the kitchen only hours earlier. She can't remember the last time she had been filled with such intense sexual desire. Afterwards, Emma had tried to cajole her into the living room, talking up how lovely it would be to lie naked together on the sofa. Fay had wanted to, of course, but couldn't. She thought of Steve and insisted Emma had to leave.

When Steve comes in from work, he greets and kisses them both. Then he sits down close to Rose, watching her move a couple of puppets around and talk to them whilst he tells Fay about a potential new client. A small but successful vegan burger chain is launching a new breakfast menu and has asked Steve to tender for the digital marketing campaign.

The conversation is so light and pleasant, such a relief after their row, Fay has the urge to accompany it with a glass of wine. She is about to suggest this when Rose says in an angry voice, 'You're annoying me, you weirdo. I'm going to cast a spell on you,' and smashes the puppets' heads together.

'Hey. *Hey.* Stop that.' Steve pulls them out of her hands. 'You'll break them.'

Fay watches, slightly dazed. 'What's going on, Rose?'

'Is someone being mean to you at school?' asks Steve quietly. 'You can tell us.'

Rose shakes her head.

'Is it to do with your hair?' asks Fay.

'Her hair?' Steve looks up at Fay, frowning.

'Tell Daddy what you told me.'

When Rose refuses, Fay says, 'One of the girls told her that she can't be a princess because they never have brown curls.' This was the first thing Rose had told Fay when they came out of school, and at the time, Rose was looking over her shoulder as if she could see the child who said it. Fay followed her gaze, but all she could see was a swarm of children and parents, most of whom are still unfamiliar to her after four weeks at this new school.

'Well, that's complete rubbish. Don't listen to whoever said it,' says Steve. 'We'll show you some photos of real-life princesses. You'll see how different they all are.'

Rose doesn't reply. Her sullen, disappearing look is so familiar Fay's chest feels stretched thin. A coldness runs down to her bones. Convinced of Rose's new happiness, she had forgotten to worry about her for a while. She had needed, and allowed herself, a break.

She bends down to sit next to them on the rug and exchanges a glance with Steve, who nods. He understands. He feels it too. The weightiness of Rose has returned.

# 12

Steve is sitting in Frankie's living room, flicking disinterestedly through one of Elliot's photography magazines. He hasn't taken his jacket off yet. Waiting down here is a bit of a mood killer, but Frankie had insisted on heading upstairs first. 'A girl needs to freshen up,' she said, pulling out of his arms with an old-fashioned coyness.

She calls for him eventually, just as he is about to shout up and remind her that he is still sitting here on his own. He follows the faint trail of light up to the spare room and when he enters, it's pretty obvious why Frankie needed time. The room has been dressed, set up for a production. Nicely, if a tad predictably, half a dozen fat, lit candles are arranged around the place. Less predictably, as the smell of sandalwood incense rushes at him, Steve feels both pleasure and a certain melancholy; he is quickly transported back to Bali where he, Fay and Billy visited after a third miscarriage had taken much of Fay's goodwill with it.

Frankie is lying on her back, knees bent, slightly propped up by a pillow. He can tell that she has glossed her lips. From the little he can see, he thinks she might be naked, or as near as, beneath the light grey duvet.

'Hello,' he says, not wanting to smell the incense or think about Fay, about romantic walks on black-sand beaches, about anything to do with his other life. His real life.

'Hi.' Frankie's smile is uncertain, almost fearful.

'You doing alright over there?' Steve hangs his jacket on

the door. As she nods, he walks to the end of the bed. 'Don't go all shy on me now.'

She smooths the duvet with her palms. 'I'm not young.'

'Nor am I.' He wants to tell her he is also nervous. Air is collecting in his throat, making him want to cough it away.

'Oh, come on. Don't do that.' She frowns. 'You're younger than me.'

'I don't care about all that.' Holding on to the wooden curve of the bedstead, Steve leans forward and takes in her large, deep eyes, the sharp edge of her cheekbones. 'You're gorgeous. In fact, I don't know why I'm still standing here debating it.'

With comedic speed, he yanks his T-shirt and sweatshirt over his head and hurls them across the room, then almost topples over pulling down his trousers. Giggling, Frankie forgets to pin the duvet across her. As he moves onto the bed, she glances at his hardness and the look that passes over her face makes him feel great about himself. Lying next to her on his side, raised up on his elbow, he peels the duvet gently away from her. She has almost no breasts, her arms are skinny, her stomach is raised and soft, but he doesn't see these things as good or bad, only different, another body. He touches the line of her hip and her thigh. She touches his chest.

'I'm hairy,' he says, apologetically.

'I like it.' She grows bolder, moving her fingers roughly over him. 'It turns me on. Elliot doesn't have a damn hair on his chest.'

When they start kissing, he loves the taste of her. It astonishes him how easily he can get used to another woman – he's not nearly as overwhelmed as he was even five minutes ago. And the truth is that with every stroke, every long and delicious kiss, a fog slowly rolls over his mental image of Fay until Frankie moves on top of him and Fay disappears completely out of sight.

Ten minutes later, Steve sits on the edge of the bed, looking down at the beige carpet in a daze of self-loathing. Frankie has tried to be funny and kind. She has even offered to get them bowls of ice cream and put on a film.

'Like you would with a kid,' he says miserably.

Her hand touches his back. 'Steve, it was great.'

'Please, don't,' he says over his shoulder. 'It was a disaster.'

She sighs as if he's wrong but how else to describe ejaculating within seconds of moving inside her? Her expression told him how startled she was. He could hear her thinking *wow* and not in a good way. He had felt like wailing. 'Maybe it was the condom,' she says.

He shakes his head – it's not that. It's never been a problem before.

'Lie down. Come on.'

On his back, next to her, Steve closes his eyes. He feels exhausted, as though he has run along the seafront in the bracing wind, which should be a good feeling, yet it's far from that. This has never happened to him before, not even as a gauche teen. He has always taken a shy, secret pride in being able to control himself.

He gently strokes Frankie's arm. 'I'm better than that, I promise.'

'I loved it.'

'Stop saying that. It wasn't something to love.'

'I came, didn't I?' she says.

As soon as he had pulled out of her, in a desperate bid to mitigate the disaster, he had scrambled down and worked hard until he was sure of her tiny cry and felt her body relax under his hands.

'Not in the way I wanted.' He stares at the ceiling. 'It was like it was my first time.'

She runs a hand over his head. 'I suppose it was in some ways.'

A short while later, they try again. This time is even worse. Steve stays soft. It's almost a relief that Frankie also recognises that their evening has come to a strange and sad close and she doesn't stop him from going.

While she sits and watches him get changed, he keeps saying, 'I don't get it.'

'Steve, it doesn't matter.'

After Steve has put on his T-shirt, he says, 'Fay's with a woman. Maybe that's it.'

When Frankie looks at him quizzically, he adds, 'Well, perhaps it's got into my head somehow.'

It's not completely impossible. The fact Fay has chosen a woman for a lover yet insisted it has never been something she'd thought about before did send some negative messages to his brain. She said she is only trying out Emma for fun, but what if she ends up preferring women? The idea of Fay with Emma does makes him feel slightly doomed, both self-conscious of his manliness whilst also feeling emasculated. It a bit of a no-win.

'That's so interesting. Would you feel better if she was with a guy twenty years younger who—' Frankie stops abruptly.

'Who was rock hard?' says Steve, zipping up his flies.

'I didn't mean that. I just mean, everyone new brings a certain threat.' Frankie takes a tube of cream off the bedside table and squeezes some into the palm of her hand. 'I've been with women. Three, in fact,' she says as she massages the cream into her hands and wrists. 'It's not a big deal. Women have got less hang-ups about trying it out with the same sex.' She smiles at him. 'Don't fret, Steve. I've had a lovely night. Truly.'

Despite her kindness, Steve is glad when he eventually gets home. He sits in the unlit living room, feeling the heaviness of failure spread through him. It seems irrelevant now that he made Frankie laugh and held her interest all night – what matters is the sex, the limp and pathetic sex. After all, it's at the heart of his offering to her. Before he goes to bed, he decides to take a shower. He takes off his watch and puts it next to his brown leather wallet and phone on the window ledge. When he gets out of the shower, he sees that Frankie has already texted him to say how much she is looking forward to seeing him again, but he doesn't reply and say it back. He isn't there yet. All he can think of saying is sorry, it wasn't you, it was me, see you soon. Tomorrow he might want to try again with Frankie, but tonight he wants only to be married, to have his small and safe life.

Rubbing himself dry, he stares through the window. The moon casts a soft halo over the top of the smoke tree. He stops rubbing and holds the towel in his hands. Two days earlier, a local tree surgeon, a friend of their neighbour, had visited and confirmed that their smoke tree was probably beyond help and might need removing. He pruned some of it back and cut away a few of the branches, then said either he or an arborist he worked with would return in a few months to check on its progress. This deepens Steve's despair tonight. How did he not notice? The tree had been there long before they moved in. Why haven't they taken better care of it?

He can't stand how neglectful it makes him feel. He really can't stand it.

/

When he wakes late the next morning, the house is empty, so he lies in bed for a while reading the news on his phone. Then he changes into his cycle gear and heads out to the Downs for some serious off-road cycling. When he gets back a few hours later, Fay is home. Taking off his helmet, he is cheered by the smell of fried chicken, before remembering it is Rex's favourite; his father-in-law has come over for supper.

Steve finds Rex at the kitchen table and Fay by the oven, batting away smoke. 'Hi,' she calls out, leaning over the sink to open the window.

'Alright, Steve.' Rex puts his folded copy of the *Daily Mail* down on the table and lays his pen on the top of the half-filled-out crossword. He is smirking at Steve, clearly amused by his Lycra cycling outfit. 'Hope it's not cutting off the blood supply down there,' he says with a wink. When Steve smiles, Rex adds, 'I don't get it.'

'Don't get what, Rex?'

'How you can go out like that.' Rex sits up in his chair, warming to the subject. He flaps his hands around. 'Like a girl.' He smiles. No, actually, he grins.

'I think it's a good look,' says Steve evenly. 'Since I'm a homosexual.'

Roaring, Rex points a finger at him and says, 'Spot on.'

Steve hates how Rex finds humour in belittling others. Of course, Steve could shatter his laughter in a heartbeat by telling him Fay has his permission to have sex with Emma. Who would Rex hate more? Fay for wanting to have sex with a woman or Steve for letting her?

'You could always join me for a cycle ride one day,' says Steve.

'Not on your life. I work hard to keep my figure.' Rex knits his hands over his expansive stomach.

'You should be keeping fit at your age,' says Steve.

'I dare say I should. But I won't go changing now.' Rex raises his empty can. 'Talking of which. If you don't mind, sir.'

Steve nods and makes his way across the kitchen to the fridge. He hands a beer to Rex, then sidles up to Fay and asks how her day was.

'Fine.' She stands back from the hob as fat frizzles and bursts in the frying pan. 'You got in late last night,' she says. 'Fun night with Frankie?'

He nods, not ready to discuss it – will he ever be? He doesn't think so. He can't stand the idea of Fay feeling sorry for him. 'Thanks for giving me the day off.'

'Sure, we had a nice day. Until a strange thing happened.' Fay lowers her voice even more. 'You know Rose was meant to go to Olivia's after school on Monday? The mum texted and cancelled. No reason. I texted back, saying hope everything is okay between the girls? Not a word.'

Steve shrugs. 'I wouldn't read anything into it.'

'I'm not, but it's weird. No?'

'Her mum might have some personal stuff going on. Who knows?' Steve takes a large mouthful of his beer. 'Have you told Rose?'

'Yeah. She was really angry, then upset.' Fay sighs as she tongs a strip of breaded chicken out of the frying pan onto a plate lined with a sheet of kitchen roll. 'I get it. She was excited. First play date at her new school.'

Steve nods. He knows Fay needs to talk this out and, understandably, she always expects him to jump into discussions about Rose with a keen level of interest and concern. After all, her instinct is better than his – she was the one who insisted Rose was being bullied weeks before Rose would admit it, a claim that Steve batted away dismissively until Rose broke down one day and told them everything.

But right now it's hard for him to muster any proper interest in this conversation because all he can think about are his own shortcomings.

'Do you want me to talk to her?' he asks.

'No. She's upstairs calming down. I gave her extra time on the iPad. We'll call her for supper.'

'Okay. Good job.' Steve kisses her neck, sniffs, then sniffs again. 'Is that a new perfume?'

Fay looks back at the hob. 'Uh-huh.'

'Nice,' he says. 'Suits you.'


After Rex leaves, Fay shuts the door and puts the chain on. Steve is sprawled out on the sofa. His other phone has just pinged inside his rucksack, but he doesn't feel like engaging with Frankie tonight. He's pretty drunk – he drank quite a lot over dinner in a useless attempt to dull Rex's unpalatable opinions – and he's stressed. When he went looking for Rose to tell her supper was ready, he found her in the bathroom hacking at a curl with nail scissors. She has so much hair it won't be noticeable, but it put the fear into them. She won't talk about the cancelled play date, but stuff is brewing. Now that they've put her to bed and checked she's asleep, he's almost ready to call it a day himself. He watches Fay dim the lights and mess with her phone until music plays through the speakers. Then she sits down, pulls her legs beneath her and sips from her mug.

'Do you think we should take Rose to a child psychologist?' she asks.

'I don't know,' he says, trying not to yawn.

'I just think—'

He cuts in. 'Can we not do this? Do you mind? Let's give ourselves the night off Rose.' For the past hour, he's been constantly worried that somehow Rose is picking up on the change in his and Fay's relationship. If he tells Fay, she'll want to analyse the life out of it, and he can't face it. Not now. 'I promise we'll talk about it properly tomorrow.'

'Didn't you have a good time with Frankie?' she asks quietly.

'I did. But I don't want to talk about that either.'

'Anything else off limits?'

Detecting the slight edge in her voice, he says, 'Sorry. Just not in the mood for conversation.' Closing his eyes, he feels the cushions shift around as Fay shifts with them. He hopes she can get comfortable and just sit here with him listening to music or watching TV because that's all he's got in him tonight.

'Well, are you in the mood for this?'

He opens his eyes to see that Fay has removed her shirt. He smiles through the voice in his head that is fast to chime in and insist that he's way too tired. Fay doesn't like being rejected. 'I could be.' He reaches out and touches her bra's lace cup. 'New?' When she nods, he says, 'Is it for me? Or for her?'

Fay smiles. 'For me.'

As he leans over to kiss her, she wraps her arms around his neck and kisses him back. Her mouth moves in ways he understands, and he knows she'll plant kisses along his jawline and then she'll put her lips on his earlobe until something in him melts and stiffens at the same time.

Yep. He hardens against her. Actually, this might be a good idea. If he can just push through the tiredness, he'll go the distance and feel like himself again. They kiss as they slowly undress and after they are naked, he holds her body close to his, loving her so much, feeling almost joined to her. In that moment, he wonders if this is what Fay meant; everything they are doing apart could change them together for the better.

Then, as he tries to sit up so she can straddle him, she says wait and reaches to the floor to pick up a grey patterned scarf.

'Blindfold me,' she orders.

He doesn't know whether to be confused or stirred. They tried it once years ago and she felt claustrophobic, even scared.

'Come on.'

He does what he is told. He bends her head, so her hair, the colour of tea, dips on to his cheeks. He ties the scarf over her eyes and pulls it tight, and then she gets back on top of him, and they have furious, exciting sex and she shouts hard as she collapses onto him, moments before he comes. She stays there, kissing him, then whispers, 'Wow, that was amazing.'

And yet. Watching her peel away the scarf, Steve feels an unpleasant tightness in his chest. It might be his imagination, but something is off, a bit strange. What if Fay likes the blindfold because she doesn't want to see him, she wants to imagine someone else?

# 13

Rose's teacher, Miss Floss, scrapes a small plastic chair away from one of the children's tables and gestures for them to sit down opposite. 'Please.'

She follows this up with something bland about the lovely, warm days – 'Summer is almost here,' she says twice – but Fay can see the panic in her eyes. This is Miranda Floss's first teaching job. Her faltering voice on the telephone implied this is also the first time she has needed to ask a parent to come in after school to discuss a serious matter that cannot wait another day. Fay pulls out a chair. In the corridor, a couple of pupils are talking at the top of their voices, no one around to tell them not to.

Miss Floss stares at her hands, taking a moment for herself. Her mouth moves, as if she is running through her lines.

Fay knows this is going to be bad. 'Why don't you go ahead and tell us why we're here?' She unbuttons her blazer as she talks.

'Miss Floss is coming to that,' says Steve. Fay shoots him a look. *Please don't do that. Don't rein me in.*

Miss Floss's permanently flushed cheeks flame a bit more. 'Of course.' She pauses. 'We have received an allegation about Rose. I'm afraid to say she has been bullying another child.'

'No,' gasps Fay, clutching her jaw.

'Bullying? Rose? No way.' When Steve speaks quickly and harshly, Fay knows he is also petrified by those words.

'It's true. The allegation has been corroborated. Rose has also owned up to certain behaviours.'

Miss Floss sets out the charges. When Rose joined the class, she and Olivia hit it off, but Anne, Olivia's best friend, felt excluded. Apparently, she wasn't very kind to Rose, but this has quickly morphed into something more serious. Rose has encouraged Olivia and some other girls to be mean to Anne. To leave her out, say cruel things. Yesterday Rose pushed Anne over in the playground and laughed when Anne cried. This morning, Anne's mother made a formal complaint to the head.

Fay listens numbly. Now it makes sense why Michelle, Olivia's mum, cancelled the play date. Why Carmen's mother hasn't even bothered to reply to Fay's text inviting Carmen for tea.

'Although Rose took the lead, we are speaking to all the girls involved. We have some strong personalities in this class,' says Miss Floss. 'And there have been problems with Anne before.' She stops abruptly and chews on her bottom lip. This mention of Anne is a rookie error, Fay realises with a degree of compassion. Later, when Miss Floss picks over their conversation, this will be the moment she feels sick about. Fay wants to reach out and tell her not to worry. We won't repeat it, no one will know.

'Anne picked on Rose first?' Steve leans awkwardly over the small desk. 'Yes? That's how it started?' Miss Floss nods. 'So why didn't you call us in then? Especially after Rose's experience at her other school.'

'I'm sorry.' Miss Floss swallows. 'I wish I had.'

'I've never even heard of Anne,' says Fay quietly.

This admission sounds so feeble, so damning. But it's too much to take in. What is worse – her own enormous failings, for not having a clue about any of this? Or being told that you have an unkind child?

'Well, something has been going on with Rose,' says Steve. Turning his face to Fay, he looks old or sad or both. She can't decide. 'She's been very moody the past couple of weeks. We thought there was a chance she was being bullied again. We didn't for a moment think... Oh, God.'

149

He sits back uncomfortably and rubs the back of his neck. 'We'll get to the bottom of this. It's not the Rose I know. You were thinking along the right lines,' he says to Fay, adding, 'Fay said the other night maybe Rose should see someone. A therapist. The bullying she went through might have damaged her more than we realise.'

Miss Floss nods. 'Yes, yes,' she says. She presses her hands together. An excellent idea to get Rose some support. She outlines how the school will monitor Rose's behaviour and encourage friendships between the girls; twice she mentions the school's zero-bullying policy. Now her voice is different. Stronger, freed from panic. I've survived this, she is thinking. Fay imagines that she'll go home and post an online photo of herself stroking her cute cat, saying what a tonic he is after the day she had. She probably thinks they are terrible parents.

Fay gets up without saying anything further and follows Miss Floss and Steve to the door and down the corridor. When her phone pings, she brings it out of her bag and takes a look.

## Emma

Can't wait to see you tonight. Bar Renegade from 7.30ish. I'm ready for a night off!
I'll be the one wearing the face glitter. 😎😎 X

Fay returns the phone to her bag as Miss Floss leans into the heavy door to push it open for them. 'Thank you,' says Fay. 'I'm so sorry. I'm devastated about this. We will sort it out.'

Steve nods and says over his shoulder, 'She's a good kid. She is.'

Miss Floss nods vaguely and smiles. She wants them gone. The door slams as they walk away. 'What the hell?' says Steve. 'What are we going to do?'

Fay rakes her hands through her hair. 'I don't know.'

Trudging slowly and sadly across the quiet playground

towards the reception area where they will collect Rose from the after-school art club, Fay lifts out her phone again and taps out a swift reply.

## Fay

I can't come. I'm really sorry. Something horrible has come up. I'll fill you in later.
XXX

When Steve glances crossly at her texting, Fay quickly sends the message and puts the phone away. Inside the reception area, they stand there mutely amongst the other chatty parents. When they spot Rose, she is walking at the thinning end of the group, looking small and remote. Seeing them both waiting for her, Fay watches the emotion change on her face from childish pleasure to worry. She knows.

'Miss Floss asked to see us,' says Steve when they leave reception and are halfway up the path to the street. 'I'm sure you know why. We'll talk about it when we get home.' Rose doesn't reply as she slides a hand into each of theirs and squeezes tight. With the radio on loud during the drive back, the news plasters over the disturbance between them all. Minutes before they are home, Fay hears a couple of WhatsApp notifications, so when they are out of the car and Steve has his back to her, she sneaks a look.

## Emma

Lord, what's happened?
You'll be missed.
XXX

## Emma

Me again. Sorry. Could you transfer the £20 I laid out for drinks last week before I go out tonight? Sorry to ask, I'm skint. 🍸 🍸 Xx

Fay texts back straight away.

## Fay

Of course. Totally forgot. Will do it in a bit. Xx

In the kitchen, they all sit around the table. Rose had started chatting about her lunch and how greasy the school pizza is, but now she just sits on her hands without saying anything. As Steve repeats what Miss Floss told them, Rose looks at them with her usual intense expression. She doesn't seem afraid to meet their eye.

'Is it true?' asks Fay.

'I don't like Anne.'

'Have you been mean to her?' asks Steve. 'Like the girls at your old school were mean to you?'

'Maybe.' Then, as if she feels tired all of a sudden, Rose rests her head on her hands.

'So, you know how bad it feels but you do it to someone else,' says Fay. 'And encourage other girls to do it too?'

'Fay, calm down.' Steve puts a hand on her back. 'Getting angry isn't going to help.'

Fay ignores him. 'Why didn't you talk to us about Anne? Well?'

'Fay, let's take a breather. You,' he points a finger at Rose, 'go upstairs. No screen, no iPad. Spend some time thinking about what you've done. Your mum and I are going to talk about how we're going to deal with this. With you.'

Rose slides off her chair. 'Will I go to a different school?'

'No,' they say in unison.

'I want to.'

Fay says wearily, 'There is nowhere else. We're out of schools.'

Besides, Fay knows it won't make a difference. The private truth that she almost never allows herself to dwell on is that children don't easily gravitate towards Rose. Friendships are scarce and fleeting. Play dates are almost non-existent. Visits to the local playground end with them sitting on the sidelines after Rose tires of climbing and running on her own.

It is why Rose wants to be sent to yet another school, to have another go at friendships, to keep trying at something that doesn't come naturally to her. Fay wants to weep. But she has done her best, hasn't she? She has tried hard to help Rose fit in, to find life easier. Fay wants Billy back from London. He was so popular; the house was always filled with his nice friends. And yet, he never cared about learning, not like Rose does. He never tried at school; he only ever wanted to be the class clown. At fourteen, he even got caught by a teacher with cigarettes and a mini bottle of whiskey. Fay had to beg the head not to expel him. She sighs. Yes, Billy was hard work in a different way. The parenting part of her personal history is strange; it's so easy to forget or distort bits.

Noting Rose's lowered head as she walks away, Fay feels awful for her ungenerous thoughts, her quiet comparisons. *I adore you*, she thinks. *I'd take a bullet for you.* Unquestionably, caring for her kids has been her greatest joy. But after all the hell of trying to get pregnant and stay pregnant, Fay could do with a reprieve from having to worry so much about Rose. The worry hollows her out.

'Rose.' Fay calls her back. When Rose stands in front of her, Fay drops to her knees and hugs her hard. 'We love you, Rose. We'll always be your friends.'

/

Fay sits on the end of her bed. After barely saying a word since she went up to her bedroom, Rose has read herself to sleep. Fay imagines Steve is sitting, waiting for her. If she doesn't go down soon, he will come looking for her, worried that she has fallen asleep with Rose.

Fay thinks about her few dates with Emma this past fortnight and her favourite, a walk in Fulking followed by a Guinness and furtive, urgent kissing in a secluded area in a local pub. When they got back to Emma's, they had lain in bed for hours, their mouths all over each other until Emma had fallen into a brief post-orgasm doze, her body spent. Fay had watched her, willing her to stir so they could do it all over again, which they did before Fay had to reluctantly come home.

Fay stands up and goes to her wardrobe. She swaps jeans for black tights and a black dress. She is downstairs pulling on her denim jacket when Steve comes out into the hallway.

'What are you doing?'

'I need to get out.'

'You what? We've got a massive problem on our hands.'

Fay tugs out her crooked jacket collar. 'Which isn't going anywhere,' she says calmly. 'We can talk about it tomorrow.'

'You've got to be kidding.'

'I need to blow off steam.'

'Un-fucking-believable.' Steve flicks a hand unpleasantly at her as he storms into the living room and slams the door.

Fay moves towards it. She curls her fingers around the handle, then hesitates. It's not in her nature to leave things on bad terms, but the only way to appease Steve is to stay and she won't. She can't. She opens the door, then pushes her head into the gap so he can hear her without seeing her face. 'I'm sorry. I know I'm being awful.'

She shuts the door on any response and leaves the house, walking fast in the direction of town.

/

Bar Renegade is a dive. No wonder Fay has never heard of it. Dirty walls and a slippery floor. Dim lighting to hide the flaws and the cheap furniture. Yet the place is heaving, and Fay has to keep saying excuse me as she pushes through to find Emma and her friends. Although, strictly speaking, it is only a bar, Fay eventually spots them dancing around the end of their table, unconcerned about getting in people's way.

Emma is sashaying close to a petite girl with black hair pulled back so tight into a knot it looks sprayed on. They are twirling their hands above their heads in intended synchronicity, oblivious to anyone else. Fay's stomach knots until Emma spots her waving and, to Fay's relief, she looks delighted. She rushes over, kisses Fay on the lips and says, 'Yeh!' in a celebratory voice. 'What was so terrible? What happened?'

Fay is about to run through events when Emma greets a woman edging past.

'Don't worry,' says Fay when Emma focuses on her again. 'I'll tell you another time. I'm better off forgetting about it tonight.'

'Sure?' says Emma.

'I'm sure. Do you want a drink?'

Emma puts her hands on her hips. 'Do you even need to ask?'

Fay smiles. 'A large gin and tonic? And a sneaky vodka shot?'

'You're so naughty! I love it.' Emma's voice flashes with pleasure. 'Yes, please, to both.'

This is Fay's first trip of many to the bar. She needs to drink a lot tonight. Her day has deflated her and the average age of everyone in this place makes her feel old, something that doesn't seem to bother Emma. She is too busy laughing and whooping around with her friends, the sort of group that Fay used to notice in a bar and quietly covet: the fun party people, with their eye-catching clothes and statement jewellery, whose sole mission is to enjoy their evening.

Yet now she's been invited in, Fay can see that she isn't a good fit. She is too self-conscious, too private. Or too uptight, as Emma insinuated when they were crammed into the toilet so she could glitter Fay's eyelids and cheeks. 'You could just let yourself go and not care,' Emma had said curtly when Fay suggested that she dial back the amount of glitter she was using. Afterwards, Fay had stared at her over-the-top new self in the mirror and forced herself to say, 'Hell yeah, you rock, lady,' which sounded totally fake to her, but had made Emma laugh and hug her from behind and say, 'Maybe later we'll come back in here for you-know-what.'

For a while, Fay stands quietly drinking by Emma's side, while others flutter around, wanting her attention. Fay joins in here and there, she tries to get stuck in, but she finds she has little to say. She is happier listening to Emma chat whilst Emma strokes her hair or touches the back of her neck.

Then Emma wants to dance again. She tries to drag Fay with her, but Fay refuses. Even after three gins and a vodka shot, she can't dance to this shit, some tinny nineties pop. Instead, she perches on a chair at the end of the table, watching.

When the girl next to Fay pulls on her sleeve and shouts in her ear, 'Would you?' Fay turns and smiles.

'Sorry, I wasn't listening.'

'Iris just asked me if I'd drink my own urine.' The girl gestures towards an impish-looking girl next to her leaning on her elbow in a drunken, sloppy way. 'Well, would you?'

'God, no. Never.' Fay tries hard to conceal her horror.

Iris laughs. 'Well, I do. It's got loads of health benefits.'

'Is that right?' Was that a trick question? If it was, Fay has failed. She wishes she could think of an interesting reply, but she has nothing to add. She has no interest in learning about the health benefits. She will never, ever drink her own urine. But that brief exchange confirms what she has already started to think, that her time here is up. After a visit to the loo, she's going to head home.

In the damp, smelly corridor outside the two occupied unisex toilets, she is thinking about Rose, about whether she will be able to get an appointment with a decent psychologist anytime soon, when Emma appears behind her.

'I wondered where you got to. What's up? Don't you like my friends?'

'Of course I do.' Fay puts as much pretence as she can muster into her voice. 'They're lovely.'

'You don't seem to want to be here.'

'Sorry. I thought I was hiding it. Just feeling a bit crap.' She hopes Emma will ask her what happened, now they are alone and she's ready to talk about it.

'Still? Oh no.' Emma runs a fingertip gently down Fay's cheek. 'Maybe you shouldn't have come out.'

Fay is taken aback. Then she feels a rush of panic.

'I mean, if it's not making you feel better.'

Fay nods. She tells herself, *Emma's right, she is*. There is no point being here, dampening her fun. 'If I'm honest, I probably just wanted to see you on your own.'

Emma smiles. 'Which I love, as you know. But tonight…' She waves towards the busy bar on the other side of the door.

'I think I'll go,' says Fay.

'Sure,' says Emma. 'Don't worry. I get it.'

Fay's breath starts doing odd things again. After two jabbering girls emerge from the toilet, sniffing as they pass by, she pulls Emma in and kisses her deeply. 'Or you could take me home and get me acquainted with that dildo.'

The last time they saw each other, Emma had come into the living room holding a large purple penis-shaped vibrator. 'I've always wanted to use this on another woman,' she declared. Fay was turned on, but she was already dressed and late getting home, so she had to promise that she'd be up for it another time soon.

'I've been thinking about it tonight,' says Fay. 'It's made me really horny.' She slips her hands between Emma's legs.

'I can't. It's Mia's birthday,' says Emma.

'But I really want you to fuck me with it,' says Fay.

Emma groans and makes a noise in Fay's hair. 'You're very persuasive,' she says. 'Okay. Let's go.'

After a twenty-minute drunken walk, they reach Emma's flat and go straight to the bedroom where they swiftly undress.

Then Emma gets the vibrator out of her chest of drawers and starts to ease it in and out of Fay, kissing her at the same time. Lewis is with Hamish, so they can be unrestrained and noisy, which they embrace; Emma swears and gasps and Fay is so aroused, she feels so free in her body, she forgets about everything and moans loudly through her orgasm.

Afterwards Emma collapses next to her and Fay touches her soft, slightly damp cheeks.

'You're so good for me,' she whispers and strokes her hand.

'Thank you, honey,' Emma says and shuts her eyes.

# 14

The sun is bright, and the motorway is crowded, even though it's Saturday and not yet nine in the morning.

'Road trip!' says Steve, glancing at Rose in the rear mirror.

'Yeah,' she replies with a degree of disinterest, wiping her greasy hands on her leggings. Bacon sarnies for breakfast in the car like a pair of old truckers is how Steve sold her on this impromptu trip to meet his mum and Doug. That and the promise he'll play her favourite songs on Spotify the entire drive back.

An hour and a half later, at the sight of the bare Japanese cherry blossom trees along the park's main walkway, Steve forgets about the long car drive and his sore lower back and being irritated with all the people in shorts and sandals getting in his way, especially when he's wearing a long-sleeve shirt tucked into his jeans. His dad had adored cherry blossoms – so much so he'd visited Japan in spring on an organised tour with a small group of Greek pensioners, to see all the trees bursting into life. Steve feels the loss of his dad so viscerally he picks up a protesting Rose and burrows himself into her for some sort of support.

Rose asks to be put down the instant she sees his mum. 'Grandma,' she shouts, racing towards her. Steve waves. He likes the look of his mum from here, in her pale blue coat and matching pillbox handbag. With her slow walk and quiet manner, she has the air of a gentle, well-turned-out woman who makes an effort to greet every day with a smile. He almost wants time to freeze, because he knows he will find her easier to love from this distance.

When they meet on the path, she calls Steve darling and offers him her heavily powdered cheek while Doug puts out his hand for him to shake, then bends down and whispers something into Rose's ear as he rummages through his jacket pockets, pretending to unsuccessfully locate something for her.

Steve is doing his best to act normally so his mum won't guess that he still feels a little cool towards her. The night before, he'd called on a whim and announced that he and Rose would make a flying visit around lunchtime, for a sandwich and a catch-up. Foolishly – always foolishly! – he had expected her to respond positively, yet she immediately said no. Her cleaner was due this morning. What was the point in her spending hours doing a deep clean for visitors to spoil it? Of course, Steve's feelings were hurt; he was bringing her granddaughter, not a car full of lice-ridden strangers, but thankfully, Doug stepped in and rescued the call. He took the phone off Patricia and arranged to meet them here. It will be perfect, he had said with typical Doug enthusiasm. Rose will feed the animals and the café does a splendid Welsh rarebit. Far better than anything they can dish up.

'They've bought me a game,' Rose says to Steve with happy eyes. She shows him the box. 'Pocket snakes and ladders.'

'Guys, you shouldn't have.' What he means is, why have you done this? You know what's been happening with Rose. He makes a what-the-hell face to his mum.

'Oh, come now,' says Patricia. 'Don't look like that.'

'She doesn't need gifts.'

'It's just a little game. Let her enjoy it. Rose, say thank you to Grandma.'

While Rose thanks her, Steve pushes the resentment down inside him as they fall into step on the path. He tells himself that he has enough on his plate, he doesn't need to make a thing of this. Ahead of them, Doug pretends to race Rose to the petting area. For a seventy-year-old man who has mostly sat behind a desk in his professional life, he is surprisingly fit.

'He's great with Rose,' says Steve.

'Yes, he is,' says his mum in a slightly put-out voice. 'Tell me, why does Fay need to work at the weekend?'

'Oh, some website relaunch. Big deadline. She sends her love,' he lies.

Steve didn't invite Fay to come along, and Fay didn't ask. He hasn't wanted to be around her much since she left him the other night to go and see Emma. Good God, he was disgusted with her, properly disgusted. The next morning, he couldn't look at her. It didn't matter that she apologised and cried and said it was completely wrong of her to leave, she just felt so overwhelmed. He refused to feel bad for her. He had his own feelings to look after.

'At the weekend?' she persists.

'She lost a bit of time this week with the Rose stuff,' he says.

'Ah yes, that.'

'I'm really disappointed in Rose,' he says with unexpected candour as several dogs pull on their owners' leads, straining towards a squirrel rushing across the path. He hadn't planned to discuss it with his mum, he knew there would be no point, but still the words just came out.

'Oh, don't be. Children are children.'

'Mum, she was bullying another kid. Do you know how concerned we are?' He feels hot, a tightness in his chest. The shame of Rose's behaviour is always hovering, ready to press on him. 'I want her to be kind.'

'Of course you do, what an obvious thing to say. Oh, look, there's Morris who lives two doors down. Morris... hello there!' She waves at the elderly man in a suit walking slowly in the opposite direction.

'Don't criticise me,' says Steve, in a voice that is too high to gain her respect – or his, for that matter.

She doesn't even look at him. 'Oh, you're like a little boy, Stephen. So touchy.'

'I'm not. I'm just saying… oh, forget it.' Even without Fay beside him, providing witness, Steve knows he has caved far too easily. But really, he can't be bothered, not when he knows his mum will exercise her mean streak if cornered. He still remembers her rowing with his dad, how much more energy she had for insult-slinging. One time, she even followed him from room to room, ranting at him while banging on a saucepan for a bit of a beat.

Christ, Steve is tired of the women around him. A mother who smiles beautifully as she slaps him down, a bullying daughter and a wife who slips away to her lover at a time of crisis. At certain points in his life, he's felt like he's won the lottery. This is certainly not one of them.

Now they have fallen into silence, he decides against telling his mum how he has been pragmatically addressing the situation with Rose, which might have made for good conversation if she'd shown any interest. He could have told her that he brought home pieces of A3 white card and thick marker pens and all three of them had written up statements that they expected Rose to live by. *Be respectful. Be kind! Always include other kids. Don't leave anyone out - remember how bad it made you feel? We will not be mean to others even when we're hurting. Everyone's feelings matter - including yours!*

Steve had hung the sheets over a wall by the kitchen table. He gets choked up thinking about Rose eating her cereal, her eyes passing from one sign to another, taking it all in. Or not. Steve has no idea if their approach is correct, if they are tapping into where her negative behaviour has come from. He hopes they'll find out when they see the psychologist next week.

'Did Billy tell you I sent him some money?' When Steve shakes his head, his mum frowns and says, 'He wanted to buy a new frying pan.'

'Yeah, he's also been badgering us to transfer some cash.' He hopes she doesn't expect him to thank her – he's prepared to tell her she's touchy if she asks. Steve doesn't mind Billy hitting him up for money. After his week, he was grateful to have one child who was happy and solid in himself, who only needed his help to buy a particular type of non-stick Teflon cookware.

At the petting area, Rose is feeding a donkey peeled carrots through the wire, laughing at how he nuzzles her bare hand for more.

'By the way,' Steve says casually. 'I went to Elliot's book launch.'

His mum frowns again. 'We never got an invite.'

Steve shrugs. 'Well, you're in London. And it wasn't a big event.'

'I did call Frankie to see if they had settled in. She hasn't telephoned back.'

That's because she's shagging him. 'She's really nice,' he says.

His mum nods. 'It's good to see her settled. After the terrible time she had with that ex-husband. He was a real piece of work, let me tell you.'

'What did he do?' Steve knows it isn't appropriate, pushing to have a conversation about a woman he's been sleeping with who is not his wife and is also a friend of his mum's, but it is too late. He and his mum are leaning conspiratorially towards each other.

'He became very religious during the marriage, even studied with rabbis in Israel and then when she refused to become as religious as him, he wouldn't give her a divorce. And he demanded full custody of Hannah. He put all his money into fighting Frankie in court. Oh, it was horrific. When she moved in opposite, I thought she'd had a nervous breakdown. She was in a terrible state. No wonder she was the size of a house.' His mum tightens her hands on her handbag and presses it against her thighs.

Steve shakes his head. 'I had no idea.'

'He was a monster, Stephen, and I do not use that word lightly. What he put her through, well.' His mum shakes her head. 'Thank goodness for Elliot.'

'Why Elliot?'

'Because he helped her fight, and he paid her legal bills. Without him, Frankie could have lost Hannah.'

Steve murmurs something sympathetic, but inside he's feeling like a bit of an asshole. What has he done? He hates knowing this information. He despises it. He might not have been able to figure Frankie out, she might be perplexing, but this isn't the way to piece her together. She made the choice to keep him away from her past.

Pretending his trainer laces need retying, Steve drops to the ground. He places his hands on the gravel and looks down as he takes a few deep breaths before standing up and nodding at whatever his mum is now saying.

/

Steve last saw Frankie the day before everything went wrong at home. She opened the door in a skimpy top and jeans holding a large glass of red wine. It was barely one o'clock in the afternoon, but he wondered if it was her first.

'Beer? Wine?' she asked him in the kitchen.

'Water for now, thanks.' He smiled to show he wasn't being judgemental – in fact, he was quite worried about her drinking. It seemed excessive. He didn't want to think she drank because she was sad or unhappy. She handed him a glass of water and pressed a palm against his chest.

'Hello,' she said, kissing him.

'Hello,' he said, kissing her back.

He put his arm around her waist and pulled her in. On the other two occasions they had sex, he'd managed to stay hard for a while. He liked to joke that it wasn't quite tantric but at least he didn't feel any self-loathing. And it gave him the confidence to touch her how he wanted.

They stood there kissing for a few minutes. He liked kissing her more than almost anything else. She was good at it and, secretly, he knew he was too. When she eventually broke away, she said, 'Let's sit in the garden,' then fully pushed back the bifold doors and stepped onto the patio. On a red metal table was a pile of magazines, a bottle of wine and two small bottles of nail polish; Steve liked to imagine her sitting out here, waiting for him to arrive. She ushered him over to the metal bench next to the table where she had settled several cushions, and he sat down and looked around. The garden was vibrant and interesting. Lots of plants he didn't recognise and an old, stately tree. He sniffed. Something was surprisingly fragrant.

'It's honeysuckle. On the trellis behind you. Lovely, isn't it?' She joined him on the bench. 'How are things at home?'

Steve laced his hands behind his head; Frankie's direct questioning made him feel uncomfortable and unsure of how to respond. Last week he told her that he'd learnt about Emma from her texts to Fay. He was obviously still cross about it, but he hadn't meant to bad-mouth Fay. Afterwards, it had made him feel lousy, like a man trying to get sympathy from his mistress. It wasn't appropriate.

'About that. I shouldn't have discussed Fay with you.'

'I don't mind. It's not like either of us is a secret.'

The way Frankie presented this fact suggested that she and Fay were equal, when this was nowhere near the truth.

'I know,' he said. 'But it doesn't sit well with me.'

'Sure,' Frankie said and drank from her glass. He wanted to go and refill his glass of water, but he couldn't leave. In the silence, he wondered again if he was cut out for this. Perhaps a different sort of man could walk through Frankie's door and easily separate himself from his wife, but he couldn't. He was a straightforward bloke, and this was not a straightforward set-up.

'Okay. I understand. No more Fay talk.' Frankie leant towards him, quick to adapt to the moment. 'I dreamt I deep throated you last night.'

'Did you now?' Steve guessed she only said it to move things along. He didn't think for a moment it was true.

'I think I'll try my dream out,' she said in a silly voice, about to extend her hand towards his groin.

'Hey.' He smiled and stroked her arms. He couldn't say why, but something wasn't right.

She looked at him, her cap of shiny hair obscuring one of her beautiful eyes. 'What?'

'You don't need to do this.'

'Don't I? Why not?' She reached down for her glass, then sat back. When she realised the glass was empty, she stood up and refilled it.

'I guess…' He tried to find more appropriate words this time. 'I worry that you're doing this for me.' He didn't speak again until she had sat down opposite him. 'Not for you.'

She stared at him, clearly trying to formulate what to say. Before she managed to conceal it, she looked exposed, a little crumpled – he had touched a nerve. That didn't last long. 'Don't patronise me,' she snapped. She was no longer soft to look at.

Immediately, he felt the fear rise in him. Once again, he had put his words and thoughts together badly and he couldn't pull them back. 'I'm sorry. I'm… Oh God.' He rubbed his damp palms on his scalp. 'I worry, okay… you drink a lot when you see me.'

Frankie looked at him with narrowed eyes. 'And?'

'I don't know. I just…' He wasn't entirely sure how to articulate that he found her sexual communication with him confusing. Oddly artificial, in fact. Almost every day he received a text from her laden with explicit sex talk, things she wanted to do to him. Every now and again, as if worried even that wasn't enough, she would describe at length the erotic dream she'd had in which he starred.

Yet in bed, during the actual act, she was a totally different person. So quiet and passive he sometimes felt like he was disturbing her. He was convinced she was happier when sex was over and they were lying there, holding each other, chatting.

'I like a drink,' she said. 'And?'

'I'm not judging you.'

'Yes, you are. I used to be fat. Now I'm a drunk.'

He blushed. 'I didn't say that.'

'Then what exactly are you saying?'

'I want to make sure you really want sex with me. That you don't need to be drunk to get through it.' He attempted a self-deprecating laugh, but it came out weirdly.

'How much stroking does your ego need, Steve?'

'That's not fair. I'm thinking about you.'

Frankie stared down at the patio for a while, then back at him. 'I've been through the menopause. Things change. This,' she gestured up and down her body, 'doesn't always rev up the way it did.'

He didn't want to feel confused, but he was. 'So, you don't really want sex?'

'No, I do.' She brought a bent knee to her chest as if she needed to hide herself. 'It's complicated. I think about sex, but my libido feels sluggish. Like it's always lagging behind. Booze helps. So does weed.' She shrugged. 'So, there you go.'

He smiled, awkwardly. 'Frankie, we don't always have to have sex.'

'Oh no?'' she said archly. 'Are you just going to come over and hold my hand?' Although he nodded, she said, 'Exactly,' and took another sip. When she smiled sadly at him, her teeth and tongue were darkened, as if she was bleeding into her mouth. And now it was clear to him why she hoped he'd open up to her; she needed him to want her in other ways.

/

Doug was right, the Welsh rarebit is delicious. After Rose has had a run around the playground and finished a double scoop of mint chocolate chip ice cream, they all hug and part ways.

It is late afternoon when they arrive home. When Rose bangs her fist against the door, Fay shouts out, 'Coming.' She and Steve speak nicely but minimally to each other in front of Rose. From experience, this will be the way until they have it out and resolve things.

As he hangs up their jackets and bags and empties snack wrappers from Rose's pockets, Steve watches Fay drop to her knees to hug Rose as if she hasn't seen her in days. He inwardly rolls his eyes. Her theatrics don't win any points with him, but Rose loves the attention.

'Oh my God,' exclaims Fay when Rose tells her in a rush about the donkey and his big teeth and how heavy his jaw felt in her palm. 'That's so cool.'

After they all troop into the kitchen, Steve is irritated that it is calm and tidy. Clearly, Fay hasn't spent any time preparing supper for them. Sighing, he opens the fridge and closes it when he sees nothing that takes his interest.

'I'm starving. Who fancies a takeaway?'

They agree on Thai and as he places the order over the telephone and arranges to pick it up in thirty minutes, he listens to Rose and Fay excitedly discuss putting on face masks, bringing down Rose's duvet and watching a film while they wait for him. Rose is jumping around saying, 'Yes, yes, yes.' She loves any chance to do grown-up girl stuff with Fay.

Whilst he flicks through the local newspaper, he hears them laughing in the bathroom. Then they come down and dance around showing him their grey-green masks. He pretends to be scared of Rose, who is now in her onesie and lion slippers and rearranging her cuddly toys around her on the sofa. As he picks up his keys, Fay finds a film about octopuses that Rose wants to watch. When he leaves, they are tickling each other under the duvet.

When he returns forty minutes later, after a rush on orders meant a delay, Rose is in the living room alone. She is still wearing her face mask, only now it looks hard and dry and pale grey and is cracking all over her cheeks and forehead. Her mouth is smeared with chocolate. The film is still on, but she has the iPad on her lap and is simultaneously watching YouTube.

'Turn that off.' He gestures to the iPad. 'You know you're not allowed YouTube unless we're in the room. Where's Mum?'

'She had to go to the toilet. She's been ages.'

Rage mounts in Steve as he quickly dumps the bags of food on the kitchen table. He knows he should pause, calm himself down. Instead, he takes the stairs two at a time. Blood is thumping in his ears like a club anthem. Noticing the light escape under the near-closed bathroom door, he opens the door fast. Fay is sitting on the closed toilet, texting. She startles and stands up with a gasp.

'You didn't even hear me come back, did you? You're so engrossed.'

'I just needed five minutes,' she says. 'That's all.'

'You can't even spend half an hour with your daughter,' he hisses. 'What the hell is going on with you?'

As Fay says something that he doesn't hear, he grabs the phone out of her hands.

'I've had enough of this,' he shouts and smashes it on the edge of the bath. He smashes it several times, feeling the exaggerated movement of his arm going up and down as Fay shrieks and pulls on his shoulder. When he eventually stops, he is panting, a little dizzy. As he stands back, Fay drops to her knees. She picks up the phone and puts it to her ear, swearing and crying, then searching around desperately for the tiny shards of glass, which she gathers pointlessly into a pile.

A fizzing rises up in Steve's throat as he backs away to the door. He has never behaved like this before, ever. 'Fay—' he starts to say.

'Go away,' she shouts, staring at the phone, the glass. 'Just go away.'

# 15

Fay feels cold now Emma has left the bed. 'Come back,' she says, patting the duvet. After they have sex, she expects the wanting to wane, but it's remarkable how quickly it makes its way to the surface again.

'Not enough time.' Emma tilts her naked body to one side as she brushes her swing of hair. 'We have to go soon.' She is childishly excited about joining Fay at one of her regular boxing classes.

'I suppose.' Propped up on her elbows, Fay sits up. She's grown familiar with Emma's favourite records, and she recognises Fela Kuti's 'Lady' come through the big, old-fashioned speakers. 'Well, do a little dance for me instead.'

Emma doesn't need much encouragement. 'You got it,' she says and laughs, strutting back and forth in front of her wardrobe, then dragging down the Moroccan shawl that is permanently draped over the door, hiding the bashed-up wood. As she twirls it around and across parts of her body, Fay can't take her eyes off her. Emma's body is far from perfect – her thighs are wide, criss-crossed with silvery stretch marks, her upper arms slightly loose – and yet she totally inhabits her body in a way that Fay adores.

'Mum.' Lewis pounds on the door, startling Fay. They'd been stuck in the bedroom for so long she'd forgotten about anyone else beyond these walls. 'Turn it down. I'm revising, remember?'

'Uh-oh. Sorry, love,' Emma calls out.

With the music on low, Fay can hear her phone on the bedside table beep. She bends back awkwardly to reach for it, reads the text and sighs. Another mum in Rose's class making fake-sounding excuses why their daughter can't come over to play. Fay puts the phone down carefully. After all, it's the only one she's got.

'When is our replacement phone coming?' asks Emma.

'Not sure.' Fay chose not to mention what really happened; she said the phone fell out of her jeans back pocket into the loo. It feels too much to lay on Emma, too heavy and personal – and frankly, deeply unattractive. What could she say? Steve smashed my phone to bits. Oh, actually he was smashing *you*.

Christ, it's good to get away from home. She and Steve still haven't recovered from that incident, and she doesn't think they will anytime soon. It was pretty shocking to them both, the sort of moment that they've not experienced before. And they don't really know what to do with it. There's no exhausting tension, no argument waiting to be had. Just a permanent chill, as if a big pocket of winter air has opened up between them.

When the door buzzes, and they hear Lewis greeting someone, Emma looks confused, then relaxes. 'Oh, that must be Hamish. I completely forgot he was coming round.' She picks her kimono off the floor and puts it on.

'Hamish?' Fay gets out of bed and starts searching for her underwear.

'He's dropping something off for me,' says Emma over her shoulder as she opens the door, then pulls it tight, quick to seal Fay back in.

Fay dresses ridiculously fast in the clean gym wear that she has brought over in her backpack. It doesn't feel good, being closed away on her own, hearing them all chat and laugh. After swiftly retouching her make-up, she ventures into the living room, then finds herself feeling pretty shy.

Hamish and Lewis are wrestling each other on the sofa,

reminding Fay how boisterous Steve and Billy could be when they sat watching football together.

'Enough,' Hamish says, laughing as he pushes Lewis back with his hands. Hamish is more attractive than Fay remembers, but those hospital lights are unforgiving. His eyes are kind and bright and he has a great smile.

'Hi,' she says shyly.

'Oh hi, Fay isn't it… from the hospital.' He nods, his eyes passing between Fay and Emma, as if he understands why Fay has wandered through from Emma's bedroom and at the same time isn't at all surprised. 'Where Em was a total delight to me,' he adds.

Emma enjoys that. In fact, seemingly unembarrassed by the memory, she laughs. 'I'm not apologising.'

'Yeah, why change the habit of a lifetime?' says Lewis from where he now lies sprawled out on the sofa, his face hidden by his huge hoodie. Has Fay seen his whole face yet? She thinks not.

Conscious of being outside of their bubble of easy banter, Fay sits down on the free sofa.

'Fay, you need to have one of these,' says Emma dramatically from where she sits at the table. 'Hamish brought them.' She holds up a paper bag in one hand while biting into layers of flaky pastry. 'God almighty, it's divine.' She licks cream off her upper lip.

Fay puts up a hand. 'I don't eat before boxing.'

Emma pauses. 'Boxing, I forgot.' She shrugs. 'Oh well, if I throw up, I throw up.'

Hamish laughs. 'Nice visual, Em.'

Watching Emma devour the pastry, Fay thinks, *I wish you were devouring me*, followed by, *that is the most ridiculous thing you've ever thought, Fay Munro. Get a grip*.

After Hamish tells Lewis that his new manager can get them tickets to the local football team's big home game in a couple of weeks, Emma turns to Fay and tells her that Hamish is in software security. He tries to keep the hackers out.

When she pretends to snore, Hamish good-naturedly chuckles. 'Yeah, you mock it, but I can make my rent. Which reminds me.' He stands up, walks over to Emma, takes out folded notes from his wallet and puts them on the table.

'I'm only joking.' Emma says to Fay. 'Hamish has a good job. He's worked hard for it.' Her eyes move back to the notes on the table, which she scoops up and presses into her kimono pocket.

'I need it back quicker than the last loan,' says Hamish. 'I'm helping my sister out this month too.'

Emma nods. 'I really will try. Honestly, thanks a lot, Hamish. You know I appreciate it.'

When Fay catches her eye and looks at her, Emma says, 'I've been a bit behind on rent the past couple of months. But…' She tips her head towards Hamish. 'He's sorted me.'

'You know you can always ask me if you're short,' says Fay.

'Oh, that's sweet of you.' Emma takes another bite of her pastry. 'But it's fine.'

'No, really. Especially if Hamish wants to help his sister out. I don't need it back in a big hurry.'

Hamish says, 'Well, that's very kind, Fay. I'll bite your hand off, if I might, on Em's behalf.'

Fay smiles. 'That's sorted then. We'll go to the cashpoint. How much do you need?'

Emma thinks for a second. 'About three hundred?'

'No problem.' Fay hopes she has managed to conceal her surprise, but Emma's idea of being a bit short differs from hers. It's still doable, Fay has enough in her savings account to cover it, but she will have to take it out of their joint account, then transfer her own money back in tonight. Her mind is working fast. In the unlikely event Steve asks, she'll say she needs to pay for her new prescription glasses in advance. This isn't strictly true, she pays for them on collection, but it could be true, which Fay convinces herself is good enough for now.

At the top of the narrow dead-end alley which houses the boxing studio, Emma reaches for Fay's hand. Fay realises this is the first time they have held hands in public, which, even without anyone around, feels both daring and slightly anxiety provoking.

'So, did you?' asks Emma.

'Sorry, what?' Fay is still distracted, feeling Emma's long fingers knit with hers.

'I asked if you'd had a chance to look at my website.' When Fay nods, Emma adds, 'Well? And don't bullshit me. I know I'm not great with words.'

'You are! You're really good.'

'Oh, please.' Emma only half-smiles. 'Don't tell me what you think I want to hear. Tell me the truth.'

The sharpness in her voice is a jolt. 'Well, it's fine. Honestly it is,' says Fay. 'But I think with a bit of work you could really improve it. Just checking the spellings would help.'

Actually, the number of errors was pretty shocking. The home page alone was littered with several of Fay's pet peeves: their (not there), your (not you're), bare (not bear). If the website had been anyone else's, Fay would have sent a screen grab to Steve or Katie, accompanied by a note saying, *who are these people?*

Nodding, Emma says, 'I'm slightly dyslexic.'

'Oh, I didn't know that. Even more reason to get someone to check the writing.' Fay winces at how frank she sounds. 'And it's not quite… grabby enough. Too much copy, perhaps? People just want a few lines of text, lots of visuals and an easy way to buy your stuff. You'd be better off filming yourself talking about your art.'

'Oooh, top idea.' Emma pulls on Fay's arm to slow her to

a stop and kiss her. 'You're a dreamboat, Ms Munro. Can you help me sort it out, pleeeeease?'

Immediately, Steve comes into Fay's mind. She imagines him catching her at her desk, lost in reworking Emma's website while he is waiting for her to bathe Rose or watch a film with him.

'Sure,' she says. 'I'd love to.' She pushes the studio door open. She's not really doing anything wrong, just helping Emma. Steve won't find out. She'll call the document something else, she'll cover her tracks.

She and Emma end up sparring with different partners. George, a new substitute teacher, is running both classes that evening and he has decided Fay is a better fit with a young, mumbling girl around her height and Emma should partner with a tall redhead who always came along with her wife before they split up.

Fay's partner is relentlessly apologetic about her lack of experience and strength, even the rain of sweat coming off her with every move. 'It doesn't matter,' Fay keeps saying automatically, 'we all have to start somewhere,' but it's a disastrous workout. Worse still, Fay can see how compatible Emma and her partner are, even laughing as they take turns pounding each other's pads.

Afterwards, in the changing area, some women dash in and out while a few others hang around to use one of the two showers. As Emma waits her turn, she recounts what she's picked up, she shows Fay this move and that. She speaks loudly and freely, uninterested in who might overhear. When a shower becomes available, she takes in her towel and body wash while Fay waits on the bench, trying not to get in the way of the people arriving for the next class who need to hang up jackets and bags.

A minute later Emma opens the door and sticks out her head and bare shoulder. She calls Fay's name and shouts for her to come over.

Fay stands up, but then she can't move. Her feet feel stuck

in concrete. Olivia's mum is standing there, her eyes moving with intense interest between Fay and Emma.

'Babe, come on. Don't be shy,' calls out Emma. 'Nothing that you haven't seen before.'

'Michelle.' Her name comes out like a gasp. 'Hi there.' Fay clears her throat. 'Hi.' Her pulse is thudding around her body. 'I didn't know you were a member here.'

'I'm not. I'm doing George's class. He's a friend.' Michelle has three girls under eight but still looks incredibly fit.

'Fay,' Emma calls out again.

'One minute,' says Fay, attempting to playfully bat her hands in Emma's direction until Emma shuts the door again. But really, Fay has no idea what she's doing; her body is thrumming with tension.

Michelle puts her duffel bag on the bench. After a quick rummage, she brings out her long pink boxing wraps.

'Michelle.' Fay is talking to her back, to Michelle's long black ponytail, which is likely an expensive clip-on. 'I'm devastated about what happened between Rose and Olivia and Anne... well, all the girls. Rose's behaviour is totally unacceptable. I don't know if you know, but she was bullied at her old school. I think it's left some scars.'

'Don't worry.' Michelle twists around to face Fay as she glides a wrap in and around her fingers and wrist. 'We're all keeping an eye on it.'

Her voice is brisk and dislikeable. Presumably, the 'we' is all the other mums. Fay knows, she just knows, that a WhatsApp group has been set up for the mums of those girls involved. A place to go to share their outrage over Rose, about how she must be brought to justice. Staring at Michelle's closed and superior expression, Fay wants to take one of her tired arms that has just punched the hell out of the drippy dental receptionist and hit Michelle instead.

'Steve and I are dealing with it,' she says quietly. 'With Rose.'

'Sure.' Now Michelle is wrapping her other hand.

Fay takes a deep breath, smiles. 'I know you texted back to say Olivia's busy, but we'd love if it she could come over for a play.' When Michelle turns away slightly as Fay is talking, Fay genuinely wonders if she can do this, if she can stretch her pride so thin. Then she thinks of Rose. 'It would be great for Rose's friendship with the girls if she could have time with them out of school.'

'We're busy for now,' says Michelle over her shoulder.

'Of course,' says Fay. 'Just let me know when Olivia is free. I could take them to the park or soft-play. Whatever.'

'Not the best shower. The water ran cold.' Emma startles her by coming up behind and standing so close Fay can see her open pores, the tiny mole on the edge of her eyelid. 'Hiya,' she says to Michelle in her warm, friendly manner.

'Emma, this is Michelle. Her daughter Olivia and Rose are in the same class at Rose's new school.' Fay knows that she should say nothing else, that what she is about to add is self-destructive, but she can't stop herself; she is a runaway train. 'The girls hit it off right away, didn't they, Michelle?'

*Go on*, she thinks. *Contradict me.*

Michelle says, 'Hmm,' as she tightens the band around her ponytail. 'Class is about to start.'

'Oh sure,' says Fay, almost giddily. 'Enjoy. Nice to see you.' And even while Michelle stares at Emma putting one arm around Fay's waist, moving her aside like a chess piece as she tries to get to her clothes, Fay holds her smile. Because in this moment, she is free-falling, she is beyond judgement. Of course Michelle knows. There can be no doubt. Fay can already picture her in her car after class, frantically texting the group.

You'll never guess who's got a girlfriend? That poor kid. No wonder she's trouble.

When Michelle leaves, Fay slumps back down on the bench. Emma is already dressed, head positioned under the wall-mounted hairdryer.

'You okay?' she calls out over the noise of the dryer when they're alone.

Fay nods. 'I'm fine.' Shaking so hard as she pulls on her clothes, it seems to take forever to navigate the simple process of dressing. Emma is ready to go long before her. 'Come on, Fay, I'm dying for a roll-up.'

'Go. I'll meet you outside.'

As soon as Emma leaves, Fay takes her phone into the toilet cubicle.

'Hello,' says Steve formally when he picks up. 'Everything alright?'

'Yes, just…' Fay had been desperate to tell him about her interaction with Michelle, but now she thinks, *how can I?* If she admits Michelle knows about Emma, Steve will freak out, terrified that being gossiped about will end up affecting Rose. He might even make Fay stop seeing Emma. 'I just wanted to see how Rose was doing.'

There is a pause. He must suspect something is wrong; her slight voice will be a giveaway. He is probably trying to work out whether to push her for the truth. 'She's good. I'm just about to put her to bed.'

'Give her a big kiss from me. How's your sore throat?' She had overheard him explaining to Rose why he was gargling with salt water.

'Fine,' he says.

Fay has an urge to ask him for reassurance that Rose is going to be okay. But she can't ask him anything tonight. There isn't enough goodwill between them. She wipes her forearm across her eyes and says, 'Okay, great, well, see you later then.'

/

Fay feels obliged to explain to Emma why she's feeling quiet, but she doesn't want to, so she's relieved when Emma cuts her off almost straight away by saying, 'Fay, don't let that woman get to you. She's bad news. I bet she's got form for making others feel bad about themselves.'

Fay feels better after this. She even begins to enjoy their walk to the seafront to buy chips from Emma's favourite fish and chip shop, before they make their way slowly down quiet, dimly lit side streets back into the centre of town. When they see a taxi rank, Fay says she is going to treat herself to a taxi home and she will pay for Emma to take one too. As they take their place at the end of the longish queue, she spies the back of a familiar-looking leather jacket, then realises that Katie is a couple of people in front. *Oh God*, she thinks. She's not feeling up to Katie tonight. Not after that scene with Michelle. She is in two minds about whether to make an excuse and pull Emma away, but then she thinks, no. Let's just get this over with.

She steps out of the line and calls out, 'Katie,' a couple of times until Katie turns around and shouts excitedly.

'Fay! Emma!' When she comes over and joins them, Fay is relieved that she is also a bit flappy, that Fay's not the only one feeling uncomfortable. 'Nathan, this is Fay and Emma.'

Everyone says, 'Hello, nice to meet you,' and Nathan offers both of them his hand to shake. He is nothing like Fay expected. Short with high, sprayed dark hair, big cheeks and jeans that are slashed around the knees, he looks like an ex-member of a boy band. Still smiling, Katie is eyeing Emma up. When Fay told her about Emma, after her initial surprise, all she said was Emma was attractive and charismatic. She didn't seem to have anything else to add. Occasionally, she asks Fay how it's going, but they almost always end up discussing Nathan. Fay suspects Katie is mildly put out that Fay has access to an experience that Katie hasn't had first, even if Katie would never see that about herself.

Emma glances down the queue. 'This is going to take forever. I really don't mind getting a bus,' she says to Fay.

'I'm sure it will go down quickly,' says Fay.

'My dad was a bus driver,' says Nathan. 'Nowt wrong with a bus.'

'Oh, respect. It's a real skill, getting those buses around corners,' says Emma enthusiastically.

'Too right,' agrees Nathan. 'Not anyone can drive one.'

Nathan and Emma's interaction is small and meaningless, but Fay can see Katie's smile begin to fade.

Now Emma is talking about a bus driver she knows who used to be a Hollywood stuntman. It's a typical Emma story, brilliantly coloured and unusual. Whilst he is listening, Nathan dips into the full Tesco bag that he is carrying and takes out a large packet of Maltesers, which he offers around. Emma takes a few, throws one up in the air, then catches it in her open mouth. She does this successfully three times and, whilst they all clap, Fay can tell that Emma's playfulness irritates Katie.

Once the fun of the game wears off and conversation between them all starts to dwindle, Emma looks around as if searching for something to squash her boredom.

'Hey, guys, let's see how flexible you are,' she says and leapfrogs over a shiny black post on the pavement nearby. She bounces high, her legs split apart. It's impossibly easy for her. 'Come on,' she shouts to Fay, who runs to the post laughing and just about manages to do it, glad for the stupidity of the moment. It lightens her mood. Emma beckons enthusiastically to Katie, who shakes her head and smiles. 'My jeans are too tight.'

They both watch Nathan attempt to do it comically. He runs at the post and splats against it while Emma cheers him on.

'She's not shy, is she?' says Katie sharply.

'Katie.' Fay touches her arm. 'I told you about Emma's past. She deals with it by being the life and soul of the party. That's all this is.'

Katie doesn't respond until Nathan attempts to moon-walk back and forth while Emma laughs and claps. Then she moves away from Fay and shouts, 'Nathan. The queue's moving. Nathan!'

# 16

Steve is shutting the wardrobe door when Fay comes in eating an apple. 'Fancy-schmancy,' she says. 'Where you off to?'

'Frankie's birthday meal.'

*Formal dress* and *supper party*. Two sets of words destined to turn Steve off the moment he read the invitation on the heavy cream-coloured card that Frankie had sent him by post. So unnecessary, almost pompous; why not just call it dinner and let your guests decide how to dress? Steve had thought about making an excuse, but that felt like a big statement. He might routinely ignore his own birthday, but he understood it meant something to most people.

'Who's that?' asks Fay.

Now he's aware that he's left his laptop open on the bed, he leans over and closes it. It isn't necessary for Fay to examine the full-screen photo of some girl from a non-monogamy website that he's traded a couple of bland messages with. Before Fay came in, he had stood staring at her photo, trying to gauge if he got any feeling from looking at it. 'No one,' he says.

From the way Fay frowns as he puts the closed laptop on the dressing table, Steve recognises that quite possibly he has caught her off guard and he recalls their rules. 'I'm not sure it's working out with Frankie.' He hasn't admitted this to anyone else yet, including Frankie.

'Oh… shame.' Neither of them knows what to say next. Is it his imagination or does she seem worried? 'Are you interested in someone else?'

After he says no and puts on his dad's Ingersoll, Fay says, 'I can help you look if you want.'

'You're going to help me find a lover?' he says incredulously. 'Is that what we've come to?'

Fay laughs and shakes her head in a nervous, skittish way. 'Of course not. I don't know why I said that.'

Now she is near enough to him, he catches her elbow. 'We haven't had sex in weeks.' Without waiting for her response, he says, 'I feel like we're never going to have sex again.'

'Of course we are. You know, a certain someone has got in the way.' Fay points aggressively towards the door where, downstairs, Rose is lying under a blanket in front of the television after a tough swimming lesson.

'That hasn't stopped you and Emma,' he says.

Fay considers this. Before she can say something that he doesn't want to hear, he says, 'I thought this arrangement was going to be great for us. Where's all the thrilling sex you promised me?'

'I promised you?' She yanks her arm away.

Now he feels embarrassed. 'I didn't mean that. I mean, what is this doing for us? For our marriage?' When Fay falls silent, Steve senses his power, which he doesn't really care for. He's tired of the push and pull.

'It hasn't brought us closer. It hasn't set our sex life on fire. And what about the rule over how many times we see someone else?' He tugs at his shirt cuffs as he speaks. 'You must have reached the limit with Emma by now,' he says, adding a little meanly, 'Maybe I can help you find another lover.'

Fay is looking away, so he can't see her expression. She puts the apple on the dressing table and wipes her hands on the front of her grey sweatshirt, then turns around and looks straight at him. 'Right, take off your trousers.' When he doesn't immediately act, confused by this turn of events, she snaps her fingers. 'Come on, I thought you wanted it.'

'Not like this.'

'Oh, please.' She lifts her sweatshirt over her head and stands in her bra and tracksuit bottoms. 'Like you're really going to say no?' Once she removes the band from her stumpy ponytail, her hair falls into a pleasing, sexy mess around her face.

He stares at her bra. 'You're so fucking arrogant sometimes.'

'Fine. Forget it.'

'Not so fast,' he says. 'Take off your pants.'

'No, I'll go down on you. I haven't showered.'

'I don't care.'

'I do.' As she goes to lock the door, he sits on the edge of the bed watching her, thinking not just about the sterility of their exchange, but about Rose downstairs and Louise Webber, the child psychologist they saw a couple of days earlier. 'Should we be doing this?' he says over his shoulder. 'With Rose awake?'

Fay doesn't answer him. She is back, smiling and shrugging as if to say take it or leave it, and he badly wants to leave it. He doesn't want to do this. No, he doesn't want it *like* this. But his mind and body are disconnected. The sight of Fay in that red lacy bra has turned over a stone inside him. Now he's all desire and no self-respect.

He lies back on the bed, his hands behind his head. 'Go on then.'

Fay drags his trousers and his underpants down without touching him, but even that makes him feel emotional. Christ, he's tearing up. What's that about? He tries to relax, but almost immediately he hears Fay swear and jump away.

Then he too can hear Rose crying out, 'Mum, Mum, Mum.' She always signals her arrival well in advance, screaming from wherever she is in the house, something that usually annoys the hell out of Steve, but that he is now grateful for as he springs to his feet, pushing himself painfully into his pants, then zipping up his trousers.

'For God's sake, relax.' Fay pulls on her top. 'You look terrified.'

She unlocks the door and they both pounce on Rose, who is

taken aback yet not at all displeased by this unexpected shower of attention. But he can tell Fay is on edge too, firing far too many questions at Rose about the television programme she was watching. It's not just them scaring each other any more; he knows Fay also sees Louise Webber everywhere, assessing Rose, assessing them.

/

From early on in yesterday's appointment, Steve could tell Louise found Fay more interesting than him. He tracked her eyes, which regularly drifted back to Fay even though he was the one trying to curry favour – complimenting Louise on the friendly room, with the colourful furniture and shelves crowded with toys and stuffed animals, even marvelling over her earrings in the shape of watermelon slices – whilst Fay didn't say a thing. Although really, Louise should have been the one complimenting them given what she charges. Going private annoyed Steve far more than Fay; he thought about the troubled kids whose families had to wait months for an NHS child psychotherapist and he was ashamed of himself for making the system even more unfair. 'But not so principled that you refuse to see her,' Fay had pointed out as she buckled up in the car, a comment that had seen him drive there in moody silence.

Shortly after they sat down, Louise told them a bit about herself and the protocol. After this initial consultation, she expected to see Rose for about six sessions. They could check in with her whenever they needed, but what Rose said during those sessions was confidential. As soon as she told them this, Steve knew, without looking at Fay, this was a red-rag-to-a-bull moment.

'Christ, she's only six,' said Fay predictably. He didn't disagree.

'I understand.' Louise nodded. 'Would you like to reconsider?'

Steve watched Fay turn her gaze to the window and the large leafy tree filling the glass. She shook her head.

'Okay. So, tell me something about your family.'

Steve mapped out their history for Louise. Where they'd met, their marriage, about Billy and their longing for a second child. He was good at this bit of their story; he had it down pat – he'd told enough fertility doctors over the years.

'Rose sounds like a very loved and wanted child.' Louise smiled. Then she asked them, 'Why now? What's been going on that I can help with?' and Steve leant forward and told her.

'How hard was it to hear Rose has been bullying?' Louise readjusted her large red glasses and crossed her legs.

'Difficult,' admitted Steve.

'Horrendous.' Fay removed her small handbag that was hanging diagonally across her chest. The chain clattered as she put it on the small table between them. She was wearing a lilac shirt she usually saved for client meetings because it was a very expensive brand, even though she had found it on the sale rail at TK Maxx.

'You've mentioned Rose's experience of being bullied at her old school. What else has been going on that might be a trigger? Any upheavals? Bereavements?'

Steve pressed his fingernails into the soft arm of his bucket chair. 'My dad died eighteen months ago. I guess he and Rose were close. He wasn't much of a talker, but he loved spending time with her.' It choked him up thinking of his dad sitting on their sofa in his ill-fitting three-piece suit, always confused but bewitched by Rose's running commentary on everything.

'You alright?' said Fay softly.

He nodded. 'Rose occasionally mentions him, doesn't she? But I don't think his death has anything to do with this.'

'I've been thinking about my dad,' said Fay quietly. 'Wondering whether there's a connection... I mean, he can be a bit of a bully.'

'Yeah,' said Steve. 'But mostly he's just an asshole.'

Fay barked out an abrupt laugh, then looked at the floor

and played with her wedding ring. Watching Louise take her in, Steve hoped she was carefully considering whatever she said next. Fay was the sort of person who would reward you if you challenged her, but only if you got it right. She had no time for fools.

'Is that difficult to hear?' asked Louise.

Fay nodded sadly, which made Steve immediately apologise for his remark. 'It's fine,' she said, but slumped back in the chair as if air had leaked out of her. Fay always faced difficult truths head-on. Wasn't that one of the reasons he'd been drawn to her? He knew that he might need that in a partner, that he might not always find it easy to do it for himself. Although lately, things had shifted. He was the one to stick a pitchfork in the truth.

'No, I shouldn't have said that,' he said. 'It was bang out of order.'

'It's okay.' She looked sideways at him. 'I get it.'

'But I really don't think there's a connection between your dad and Rose's behaviour,' he said gently, repeating 'okay' until she nodded. 'Or my mum's, come to think of it.' When Louise looked at him enquiringly, Steve found himself tired of discussing their parents when it didn't feel like they were the problem. 'My mum is tricky, but this isn't about her. She's pretty good with Rose when she sees her.'

He must have spoken firmly, because Louise nodded. 'And how are things between you two?' Her question was surprising.

'We're good. But we're currently in unchartered territory,' said Fay. 'We're trying out an open relationship.'

Louise's expression didn't change. 'Okay.' When she wrote down what seemed like one word, Steve wondered what the shorthand was.

'I'm not sure that's relevant, is it?' He leant forward, his whole body straining uneasily. 'It's not like we ever bring anyone home. We're still spending as much time together as a family. It happens on the outside of our' – he gestured a finger between himself and Fay – 'life together.'

'I'm not ashamed of it,' said Fay. 'We've been happily married for over twenty years. I wanted to try something new.'

*Someone new*, thought Steve with a rush of embarrassment. 'I? I?' he snapped. 'It wasn't just you who decided.'

'Yes, sorry.' Fay reached out and touched his sleeve. 'Of course.'

After a pause, Louise asked, 'Do you think this has created tensions that Rose might be picking up on?'

After Steve said yes, Fay said, 'I'm not trying to let us off the hook, but whatever was going on with Rose was already there.'

'I understand. It's complex.' Louise clicked her pen. 'But we need to look at things that might keep the problem going.'

'Lots of people don't live perfect lives,' said Fay, bristling.

'Maybe Rose isn't getting the attention she needs,' said Steve, thinking aloud. 'She might have tried to get it by bullying.'

'She gets tons of it,' said Fay. 'Too much, if anything. I feel like… like I'm always available to her. I mean, don't get me wrong, I want to be Rose's go-to person. I want to be that mum who meets her needs. But it's like whatever I give out never satiates her. She just wants more and more attention.'

'Yeah, but is it the right sort?' said Steve.

'What does that even mean?' snapped Fay. 'She's really loved.'

'I know, but our heads have been in a funny place. It might not have helped her.' Steve crossed his legs. 'I worry about that. A lot.'

Fay glanced over at him. 'You think it's my fault, don't you? Because I suggested the open relationship.'

'I never said that.'

'But you think it.'

Steve shook his head. 'No, you think it. Don't put your guilt on me.'

Fay looked at Louise. 'I'm sorry.' She gripped both chair arms. 'I didn't mean to get into that here.'

Louise put up both hands. 'It's fine. We're exploring what might trigger Rose. It's important to have these discussions.'

'We're good parents,' said Steve emphatically. 'There's a ton of love in our family, but right now we're a bit lost. We don't know why the hell things are so difficult with Rose. That's why we're here.'

Louise nodded. 'So, tell me more about her.'

/

At the front door to her cottage, Steve looks over Frankie's shoulder and what he sees shocks him. Elliot in his tux pouring champagne into a glass for Amy.

'Elliot and Amy are here?' he whispers, handing Frankie a bottle of wine that he instantly wants to take back, then turn around and leave.

'Of course.' She frowns. 'It's my birthday.'

Steve is confused. She must get something out of this, he thinks, something that he can't see. Following her into the cottage, he tells her how beautiful she looks, although she is far too done-up for his liking in a floor-length black dress and with a lacquered, immovable hairstyle. Local companies have delivered the food and hand-picked the wines, which makes him wonder if someone came to dress and style her. It wouldn't surprise him if the entire evening has been outsourced. Nothing feels real, he thinks, as she wobbles sideways on her ridiculous heels, and he leans forward to catch her elbow and steady her.

Thanking him, Frankie straightens up, then announces, 'The last guest has arrived.' When everyone looks in their direction, she introduces him to a couple standing close by who are at least twenty years older than him and way too straight-laced to appeal, but are very friendly in a jolly, parental way. Another couple shout out, 'Hello there,' and from the confident clap of their voices, he wonders if they are Elliot's sailing-club buddies. Then Elliot calls him Stephen and shakes his hand and says how good it is to see him, but the conversation between them falters after that. At least Amy is friendly and natural, the only person here that Steve can imagine encountering at a party he might go to with Fay.

'Welcome,' she says and kisses his cheek. Close up, she is fairly pretty. She has a sweet smile that distracts from eyes that are neither piercing nor large. 'Good to have you here.'

At the table, he is seated in between Frankie and an estate agent's wife who fires pointless questions at him, like where does he live and is he a Sussex 'original' and which school does his daughter go to, clearly expecting to hear him name a private one. He answers politely, but in his tight suit, at the small table, he feels squeezed and uncomfortable. The experience is headache inducing.

Elliot doesn't help. He appears desperate to control the conversation, loudly explaining what to expect as if none of them have ever been to a dinner party before. He runs through the five courses, counting off each one on his fingers – starter, amuse-bouche, main, dessert, cheese – then talks through the different pairing wines behind him. It's so utterly tedious Steve wonders if he can sustain a neutral expression. Worse still, each time Elliot has something to say, he taps his knife gently against his wine glass until everyone else falls silent.

'Stop acting like a headmaster,' says Amy after he's done that a few times.

'I'm quite softly spoken,' he says in a slightly wounded voice.

'Oh, I know, honey.' She puts her hand on his, smiling. 'Please, do not tap your glass again.'

Steve is seated diagonally opposite Amy, but she made a bit of a song and dance about moving aside the huge vase of peonies so she can see him and keep up a near constant flow of conversation. She's asked about his work and Rose and grows animated telling him about the yoga moves that will alleviate the soreness in his lower back.

As they all finish the main course – a delicious roasted shoulder of lamb which prompted an unnecessary discussion about which local farm the caterer might have bought it from – the conversation turns to holidays. Elliot says that he and Amy are thinking of visiting Cape Town in December.

'Over Christmas?' There is a morsel of lamb on the fork that Frankie puts down. She picks up her glass of Rioja. Her movements seem unhurried, her voice is calm, but Steve detects a shift.

'Yes. Maybe Boxing Day.'

'You didn't say.'

'Sorry.' Now Elliot doesn't have to tap the glass; everyone seems eager to hear this exchange. 'We only started talking about it a few days ago.'

'Hannah's coming over,' says Frankie quietly.

'Oh damn.' He slaps the edge of the table. 'I forgot.'

'Elliot!' says Amy. 'How could you forget she was visiting? Honestly. Nothing is booked, Frankie. We can easily move the dates.'

Steve waits for Elliot to reiterate this, but he only blots his mouth with a heavy white napkin. It is Amy who extends an arm across the table towards Frankie. 'We'll sort it. Don't worry.'

'I'm not.' Frankie smiles and drains her wine glass. 'Thank you, dear.'

*Dear.* Steve sits back and clenches his hands under the table. This is unbearable. He wants Fay nearby so he can catch her eye, knowing that she would feel the same. He doesn't belong here. He should be with her and Rose and Billy. It makes him emotional to think about them, Fay in particular. Christ, he hopes he's taken good enough care of her all these years.

'I must say, Frankie,' says the woman next to Steve. 'You

look wonderful. Doesn't she?' There's an echo of she does, yes, terrific.

Frankie touches her stiff fringe. 'You're embarrassing me. It's nothing,' she says, adding with a laugh, 'just a ton of make-up and effort.'

'Nonsense,' says Amy. 'You always look incredible. I would do anything to look like you when I'm sixty. You're my inspiration.'

Sixty! Steve doesn't want to feel stunned, it's a shaming reaction, but he is. Everyone around him agrees heartily, but a furtive glance at Frankie tells him she's almost gone rigid. She's mortified. When she gets up to clear the dishes, he follows her with the remains of the lamb and the gravy boat. As she piles the plates near the sink, he touches her back lightly, then watches her reach for a patisserie box and pull at the red twine tied around it.

'You aren't enjoying tonight very much, are you?' she asks.

'I am,' he says, hearing how half-hearted he sounds. 'The food is delicious.'

'So, I'm sixty,' she whispers. 'Does it matter?'

'No,' he lies. 'Not at all.'

'Go on then,' she says, still whispering. 'Tell me it's just a number.'

Steve puts his hand on her shoulder and says, 'It really is.'

Turning her head, Frankie says, 'And tomorrow when you tell me that it's over, you'll insist that it has nothing to do with my age.'

He reddens as laughter rises up at the table. 'It doesn't.' He just likes his life and his wife a whole lot more than he likes this.

'But it's over, yes?' As he nods, Frankie lifts a large Sachertorte out of the box. 'I shouldn't have asked you to come tonight. You weren't ready.'

'This isn't for me,' he admits. 'Now or in the future.' He opens the top button of his shirt, he loosens his tie.

Sliding the Sachertorte onto a plate, Frankie says, 'I agree,' then fixes her smile and walks over to the table, setting down dessert against the din of obligatory clapping.

Steve finds it much easier to be at the table now he knows he is no longer stitched into this world; he has unpicked himself, he is free. It's a remarkable feeling and tastes better than anything he's eaten here tonight. Of course, he feels bad for Frankie. Despite her smiles as they sing 'Happy Birthday' and her gracious speech about good health, family and wonderful friendships, he senses the turmoil stuck to the other side of her words.

When he calls an Uber, Amy says she'll join him – she lives a ten-minute drive from him, near the seafront, and she'll take it on. She has booked herself into an early ashtanga class and has to sleep off the booze. As they all say their goodbyes, Steve tells Frankie he will see her soon, but neither of them believes it. 'Look after yourself,' he whispers, and she says, 'You too,' and she lets him hug her and is surprisingly slow to let go.

In the Uber, they head out onto the country lanes without talking. Only after Amy has put her phone away in the pocket of her puffer jacket does she say, 'You and Frankie are a cute couple.'

'Not any more, sadly.'

'Oh. Shame.'

'It's okay.' They look sideways at each other and when she smiles, he feels so comfortable in her company that he finds himself speaking without thinking. 'The set-up.' He glances at the driver. 'Is it enough for you?'

'Enough?' she repeats politely.

Steve drops his voice to a whisper. 'Yeah. I mean, aren't you missing out on stuff? Like having your own family?'

When Amy turns to him, he regrets everything he has said. He can see immediately from the rigid line of her lips that he has misread the ease between them. 'What a presumptuous thing to say.' Her voice hots up. 'Maybe I don't want children. Maybe I don't want a full-time partner.'

'I'm so sorry.' Steve puts out his hand but instinctively realises even that is an error too, that being touched by him is probably the last thing she wants, so he draws his arm back to his side.

'I guess you want to mansplain to me about how I'm short-changing myself? How Elliot gets his cake and eats it, how he's taking advantage of me?'

'No, honestly,' says Steve. 'I don't. I was just curious.'

'Bullshit.' She says this so loudly the driver bolts up in his seat and glances in the mirror at them.

Bizarrely, since Elliot is one of those middle-aged white men that she appears to be rallying against, Amy then rushes through a monologue about the world being run by men who think they know just-about-every-goddamn-thing, but hey, guess what? Everything is about to change…

Steve stops listening as her sentences run into each other and start to make less sense. Now Amy doesn't sound as intelligent as she had over dinner. Instead, she sounds like someone who might read newspaper headlines but glosses over the articles. And yet she keeps going. Her voice is like a siren, drunken but terrifyingly loud. Steve says nothing. He's out of his depth. He wants to put his hands over his ears. He wants this all to stop.

# 17

When Fay passes Steve at the kitchen table, before she has a chance to say good morning, he says in a gloomy voice, 'We need to talk.'

It isn't necessary to ask him why, or how Frankie's dinner party had gone the night before. Fay knows he got up a couple of times in the night and went to sit in the living room, which usually means he has something on his mind. Looking at him slouched over, finger-painting the edge of his toast with marmalade, with that air of morning grubbiness about him, Fay knows he's turned. He isn't just out of the situation with Frankie; he's mentally checked out of their whole arrangement. He wants to pull over and turn off the engine, straight away.

Every time she heard him get up in the night, she was jolted into a tiny panic about what was coming, yet now, her body seems strangely unprepared. On her slow walk to the kettle, she feels almost faint.

'Fay?' Steve sounds impatient.

'I heard,' she replies.

'Don't ignore me then,' he snaps.

'Sorry.' Waiting for the kettle to boil, as she drops a teabag into a mug, she glances sideways at him in his flannel dressing gown, sitting next to Rose in her neat school dress.

*Screw you, Frankie*, she thinks. *You were on to a good thing. What in the hell were you thinking, inviting Steve to some poshed-up event with your rich mates? Didn't you get a sense of him at all?*

Steve stands up and brings his empty plate to the sink. 'So when shall we talk?' *Stop asking*, she wants to shout. Even the slop of his slippers on the lino irritates her.

'Let's just get today out of the way first, shall we?' she says curtly.

She is referring to Rose's first appointment with Louise, which has become a regular, tetchy discussion point for them. Sipping her tea, Fay examines Rose spooning in cereal and moving around a doll with her free hand. For the hundredth time, she wonders what's going on inside her and what could possibly seep out that they might not expect.

As Steve edges around behind her, she says, 'I'm just going to pop up to the office for a bit. Before I do the school run.'

'Now?' says Steve.

She glances over her shoulder. 'I need to get some work to a client today. I'm a bit behind.'

This is and isn't the truth. She is getting good at finding a small nook that she can exploit without a total erosion of conscience; after all, Emma is a client. It just happens she is the only client who Fay is having sex with and isn't paying for the website Fay has spent hours revamping and improving beyond recognition. Now she is ready to send Emma a link to the new site and get her reaction, it excites her to think how thrilled Emma will be.

'I could do the school run,' says Steve helpfully.

'No, it's fine. I have to go to the post office.' The last thing Fay needs is Michelle standing next to Steve in the playground, making digs about seeing Fay and Emma at boxing. Fay intends to do every school run until the end of term. She's worked out where to stand so Rose can spot her, but she's out of the way of Michelle and her small crew of hard-looking doppelgangers.

'Thanks though.' Fay used to believe she wouldn't be able to live with herself if she lied to Steve. *Does it make it better that I hate myself for it?* she thinks as she trudges up the stairs.

Louise greets Rose with a huge smile and serious handshake. 'Good to meet you, Rose,' adding, 'Thanks for coming to see me,' as if Rose had a choice.

Crouching down, Fay gently tugs the ends of the plaits she redid for Rose in the car. 'Tell Louise anything you want. It's just like writing in your diary. Only you have the key. I don't need to know anything unless you want to tell me. Okay?'

'That's a lovely explanation, Mum,' says Louise.

After Fay and Rose say a surprisingly moving goodbye and Fay shuts the door behind her, she feels something alive in her chest, furiously signalling that she has just handed over her child. Without Fay present, Rose has complete agency to say what she wants. What if she reveals shocking troubles that they don't know about? What if she makes them out to be monsters? And – please God, no – what if social services get involved, if they take Rose away?

At the bottom of the stairs, Fay slumps against the wall, verging on internal hysteria, and she stays that way until a courier is buzzed in. Then she forces herself to straighten up and catches the door from him as they pass each other.

In the afternoon sunlight, she is grateful to feel less jumpy. In a café over the road, she orders a latte. She briefly sits down in the only free chair, but a toddler in a pram is screaming at his absent-looking mother on the next table, so she transfers her coffee to a takeaway cup and sits in the car. Still completely preoccupied by Rose, time seems to move excruciatingly slowly. It is as if Rose is having an operation and Fay is on hold, waiting for the call to hear she has woken, she is fine.

Fay places her hands on her diaphragm, closes her eyes and focuses on her breathing. For a short time, it does the trick. She is detached from everything, filling her body with air instead of her mind with mess. When her other phone rings, she smiles, anticipating the conversation with Emma. The website is incredible, Emma will shout. You're a total legend.

'Hello, lovely,' Fay says into the receiver.

The noise at the end is stunned, hazy. At first Fay thinks there is no connection. 'Hello,' she says again, then realises Emma is crying. Such a small, tight sound, at odds with Emma's expansive personality, as if she is speaking from a confined space.

'Emma, what's happened?'

'I... I... just spoke to Richard Drake's mum.' Emma's voice is barely a rasp, dug out from beneath all her emotion. For a moment, Fay fails to understand what Emma has just said, then she connects. When Emma had written to the parents of the boy she hit with her car, she had included her mobile number and her address at the time, but when they didn't reply, she eventually accepted they didn't want to hear from her.

'Oh my God. Why now?'

'Richard's dad died recently. His mum found my letter in his personal papers. He'd never told her that I'd written.'

'Well, how was she? What did she say?'

'She wasn't very nice.' The controlled weeping starts up again. 'She said she didn't wish me any harm, but that I'd taken her son away. She told me to never get in touch again.'

Fay is aghast on Emma's behalf. 'She telephoned you to say that?'

'That's what I asked. She said she wanted to know what I sounded like. Then we both started crying. I said I was sorry for her loss. I meant her husband, but she shouted, "Which one?" It was horrific, Fay. She hates me.'

'It was an accident. A terrible accident. You must never forget that.' Fay glances at the clock on the dashboard. She has less than ten minutes before she must collect Rose, and Emma has unravelled too far to be put back together in that time.

'She said that every day she thinks about the man Richard would have grown into,' weeps Emma. 'He walked in front of *my* car, Fay. I wasn't driving recklessly. I wasn't. It was an accident, it was...'

Fay can't interrupt, she can't say she must go and be fresh and focused for her own troubled child. Instead, she lets Emma talk while she quietly gathers her belongings and gets out of the car.

'I've told work I've got a stomach bug and can't do my shift tonight. Can you come over?' Emma's voice shivers from all the tears. Fay locks the car and walks to the building door and buzzes Louise's office. 'Of course. I can pop over later.'

'Not now? I really need you.' Hearing Emma cry again, accompanied by a rare display of neediness, Fay's heart loosens. She quickly works out her timings. 'I can be there in an about an hour or so.' Louise's voice sounds through the intercom. 'Hi, it's Fay,' she replies, and then returns to her conversation with Emma. 'Sorry, I'm picking up Rose from an appointment. I need to take her home, feed her. I'll be there as soon as I can.'

'Okay.' Emma blows her nose. 'Do you mind bringing some booze?'

Fay can't drink, not tonight. Steve wants The Big Chat. She can't even stay long, or he'll go nuts. But Emma is crying again and saying, 'I never meant to hurt anyone. I'm a terrible person, aren't I?' and Fay charges up the steps saying, 'You're wonderful. Hang in there, darling, I'll be there in a bit.'


When Fay was pregnant with Rose, in spite of her incredible joy, she sometimes felt strangely claustrophobic, as if invisible walls were closing around her. This wasn't even late in the pregnancy, when her arms and legs swelled, and it felt like Rose was sucking up her entire body. From early on, she often had to stick her head through an open window to feel like she was properly filling her lungs.

This is how she feels when she and Rose are in the car. She is chasing her breath. She is also desperate to beat the traffic, darting down a myriad of side streets instead of the main roads, hoping this will buy her time.

'Would you like to tell me how you got on, sweetheart?'

'It was fine.'

'Just fine?' Fay smiles sideways. When Rose doesn't say anything else – she doesn't even move – Fay persists. 'Just fine?'

Rose shrugs. 'Do you have a snack?'

'I don't.' Fay takes a corner, fast. 'Did you like Louise?'

Rose nods and scrunches the hem of her dress between her hands. 'She's nice.'

'Good. Did you talk about what's been happening at school?'

'You said I didn't have to tell you what we talked about.'

'That's true. You don't have to tell me a thing.' It isn't smart to push; Rose needs time to process. Selfishly though, Fay wants to shake information out of her quickly, so she feels better about going to see Emma. 'But remember that I'm here to listen if you need it.'

Fay's phone – her other phone, which Rose thinks is strictly for work, recently replaced by a guilty Steve – beeps and keeps beeping. Message after message from Emma arrives. Fay doesn't touch it, still hoping Rose will share something from the session, but instead she is now sucking her thumb and looking out of the window. As they slow for traffic lights, Fay resigns herself to Rose's silence and picks up the phone, quickly scrolling through the snippets of message from Emma on the screen. Her random thoughts about the mum and Richard. How she can't live like this, it's too hard. How Richard's mum said Richard would have been a wonderful adult. If Fay can bring Chardonnay not Sauvignon Blanc—

'I told Louise you were always on your phone,' says Rose.

'Uh-huh.' Quietly, Fay slips the pinging phone into her side-door compartment. Rose has only spoken the truth. For obvious reasons, Fay is attached to her phone. She leans over and touches Rose's cheek. 'I am. I'm sorry.'

When Rose jerks away from Fay's fingers, Fay swallows

hard and clutches the steering wheel with both hands. It's not Rose's fault. It's not her job to assuage Fay's immense guilt. No, Fay must keep smiling and remain an open, neutral vessel for Rose to pour in any amount of scorn or hatred necessary to get herself back on track.

As the traffic lights turn green, Fay has to catch her breath again.

/

Steve calls out 'Hi there,' and Fay attempts to genuinely smile at him as if everything in her world is settled and normal.

'She's in the bath,' Fay whispers before he can anxiously ask for an update. 'She hasn't said much. I don't think we should press her. She should come to us.'

He nods and kicks off his trainers. 'Yeah. Agreed.'

'She's had fish fingers and beans.' Now Fay avoids his eyes as she adds casually, 'See you about nine.'

'What? Where are you off to?'

'Yoga.' She gestures towards her yoga bag and mat by the door. 'I told you.'

'No, you didn't. Don't you think Rose needs us tonight?'

'Steve, I've been tied to her side since we got home. We've watched cartoons, we've sung along to her favourite Little Mix songs. We've had lots of cuddles. I'm done in. I've already said goodnight to her. She'll be in bed in half an hour.'

'What about our talk? I texted you today about it, but you didn't reply.'

'Sorry.' She smiles. 'Busy day. Anyway, I won't be late,' says Fay in a sing-song voice.

He pauses. 'Okay, see you in a bit.' He's obviously decided it's better for Fay to be relaxed before he sets about reining them in again. 'We'll talk then.'

'Sure thing.' Fay thinks he says something else, but his voice is trapped in the slam of the door and by the time he opens it and is standing on the doorstep, she is in her car, waving at him, as if she isn't ignoring him, as if she is not heading towards the place where she is leaving more and more of herself these days.

On the way, Fay parks on a double line outside an off-licence and runs inside. In the queue, she cradles two bottles of Chardonnay in the crook of her arm like a newborn baby, while she taps out texts to Emma with her free hand.

**Fay**

On my way. Hang in there lovely.

**Fay**

In a long queue. Getting wine.

**Fay**

OMG. Woman in front can't decide what red wine to get. It's just red wine, lady!!

Back in the car and on the way, Fay keeps messaging.

**Fay**

Road works and temp traffic lights. Total drag!

**Fay**

Change green already!

Fay is sure Emma will be amused by her stream of messages; she loves a bit of silliness from Fay, and she doesn't get to see it that often. Not that Emma has replied to any of them. Fay figures she's taking a nap – it's the cocktail waitress in her, grabbing sleep when she can – or having a bath. Emma likes a long, candlelit soak.

**Fay**

Here! Just parking

By the time Fay gets out of the car, she still hasn't heard from Emma, but Steve has texted her several times.

**Steve**

You left your yoga stuff by the door.

**Steve**

Yoga, my ass.

**Steve**

You're a shit, Fay. This isn't on.

Fay stands in the street, panting slightly. Stress scrapes at every bit of her. She can't reply. It will only be another lie. Putting her phone away, she waits outside Emma's building until she is buzzed in, then she heads up the stairs, trying to push Steve out of her mind with every step. She needs to restore some balance.

When Emma opens the door to her flat, Lewis shoots out. 'Hey,' he says to Fay, barely moving his mouth. He is always coming and going, keen to milk his independence.

'Call me when you get to your dad's,' says Emma.

'Yeah.' Lewis jumps the last two steps, waving a hand above his head.

Fay hugs Emma, liking how her pink silk kimono falls open to reveal a satin camisole that pours over her body like honey.

'Sorry,' says Emma. 'I just saw all your texts. I was on a long phone call.'

Fay stops herself asking, to whom? Instead, she goes ahead of Emma into the kitchen and dumps the bag of wine on the counter. 'What a day.'

'I know.' Emma holds the fraying lapels of her kimono tight to her chest. 'I feel better now though. I've cried it out.'

Nodding, Fay pushes back a curl behind Emma's ear, letting her fingertips linger on the downy edge of Emma's cheek. Without make-up, she looks so lost and bare, a little girl again. Fay kisses her, then turns and rummages through the top drawer next to the oven.

'Talking to Hamish helped,' says Emma.

'Oh yeah?' Shutting the drawer, Fay tries to reply casually. She notices Emma watching her, eyes slightly narrowed and displeased as Fay pulls open the dishwasher door. Fay stops. Her nerves are making her overly familiar – she mustn't act like she lives here. 'I'm looking for the bottle opener.'

'Behind the drying rack.'

Fay uncorks the bottle, then asks what Hamish said.

'Nothing special. But he's seen me through all this stuff. He was the first person I dated after it happened. He was there when I was a colossal shit shower.' Emma laughs and takes the glass of wine Fay offers her. 'He gets it.' She clinks Fay's glass. 'So do you. Thanks for talking me down before.'

Emma clasps Fay's hand as they kiss. 'You need to forgive yourself,' says Fay.

'I know. That's what Hamish says. Can we get into bed and snuggle?' says Emma in a small voice.

*Only for a bit*, Fay needs to say, but instead she says, 'Yes, please, I need it too,' and follows Emma into the bedroom. Apparently, Hamish insisted that Emma wipe Richard Drake's mum's number and address from her contacts, so she is never tempted to get in touch again.

'He says the same thing as you.' Emma unties her kimono and lifts the camisole over her head. 'That I have to find a way of letting go without expecting closure.'

Fay is certain she has never said anything like this but, while it's a bit self-helpy, it's not bad advice, so she stays silent. After Fay has stripped down to her underwear, Emma arranges herself so she lies with her head on Fay's bare stomach, looking up at the ceiling and talking while Fay strokes up and down her arms. She grows heightened when she mentions how upset Lewis got hearing her cry like that, which makes Fay think tenderly of Rose; in fact, she would like to mention Rose's appointment, but Emma is still talking, and it feels both unnecessary and self-indulgent to interrupt her.

They lie like this for ages until Fay's leg cramps. Then Emma goes to get the other bottle of wine, moving heavily and sadly across the room.

Fay refuses another drink. She's already had two glasses of wine and has been there almost an hour and a half. This is her limit in both respects. Actually, she's starting to get angsty, knowing she really must leave, but she just can't bring herself to do it. *Five minutes*, she keeps thinking, but then another thirty minutes pass.

After Emma has uncorked the bottle and poured herself another glass, she suddenly says, 'The website!' She sits up. 'I totally forgot. I looked at it just before the call came. It's incredible.' She leans forward and, in between passionate kisses, whispers, 'You're so great.'

'It's nothing,' says Fay exactly as she had planned. 'I'm pleased you like it.'

'I love it.' Emma gazes directly at Fay, and in Fay's head, those words morph into *I love you*. She can even feel the pull to say those words back when Emma turns her head. Reaching for her phone off the bedside table, she says, 'I need to look at it properly.' Scrolling as she drinks, she points out bits of the website she particularly likes, eventually saying, 'I can see why you're paid big bucks.'

'Hardly.'

'Talented and hot.' Emma puts down her phone and swivels around to face her. The sex is not expected and yet inevitable. It is also different than before. More tender, less energetic.

Afterwards, Fay sits up and pulls on her clothes as Emma's hand traces her spine. Making an appreciative noise, Fay curls into her fingers, startled when the intercom buzzer goes. She turns to Emma, who is frowning, her eyes still closed.

'Shall I get it?' asks Fay when it goes again twice, short and fast.

Emma yawns. 'No, I'll go.' She reaches for her kimono and puts her arms through the flapping sleeves. 'It's probably for Carlos upstairs. His friends are such spliff heads,' she says on her way out of the room. 'They always get the wrong bell and just laugh at the other end. It's so annoying.'

Fay can hear Emma talk and giggle into the intercom, her voice dropping in and out. When she pads back in, Fay is fastening her bra. 'Was it Carlos's friends?'

Emma shakes her head. 'It was Fred.' She gulps water from the pint glass on her bedside table.

'Who's Fred?' asks Fay.

Emma wipes a drop of water off her chin with a fingertip. 'A guy.' Her smile is shy, mildly apologetic. 'Someone I've been seeing.'

Fay feels like she could topple forward onto the bed. 'Oh... sure,' she says in a voice that even sounds remote to her, as if she is trapped underwater. She pulls on her T-shirt, her jeans. She thinks she is smiling – she hopes she is smiling.

'It's nothing.' She hears Emma say this twice.

*Well*, Fay wants to say, *it's not quite nothing*. Fred exists. Fred is someone.

Attempting to maintain an air of composure, Fay doesn't ask Emma anything about him. She's not even sure she's allowed. Emma never asks after Steve, after all. The difference is that Emma knows about him. Fay is amazed at her own naivety. You stupid woman. Of course Emma will want to see others. What does Fay have to give, properly give?

'He's gone,' says Emma. 'You don't need to rush.'

'No, I need to get back.'

'Fay, are you okay?' asks Emma, adding quietly, as if she is reading Fay's thoughts, 'You are married.'

'Absolutely,' says Fay to both questions or neither; she

doesn't know. She feels so weakened, as though she might dissolve if she hangs around any longer. 'Get some rest,' she says at the door. 'You've had an emotional day.'

'I will. Thanks for coming over.' Emma plants light kisses on Fay's lips. 'And for the booze and the website. I'm really grateful.'

The words are heartfelt, the arms around Fay are tight, but everything Emma is giving her feels like a consolation prize. The crappy gift in a Christmas cracker.

On the street, Fay rushes to her car. She gets in but immediately gets out to pace up and down a bit, desperate to expend this terrible mounting energy. Then she has no choice but to drive home. Steve is telephoning and texting her furious messages and he meant it literally when he said he was waiting for her. He opens the front door before she's closed the gate behind her.

'Nice to see you.'

'Sorry,' she says.

'Are you? I mean, really?'

Walking past him into the kitchen, Fay drops her keys onto the counter. He follows behind her and, as he stands in her eyeline, she can see he has shaved his head and groomed his stubble. A good professional job. Strong, sharp lines. The sort of cut she loves. He must have gone to the Turkish barber near his work. It shocks her that she hadn't noticed on her way out.

At the sink, she drinks cold water straight from the tap, letting it flow into her mouth and down the sides until big wet patches appear on her T-shirt. Straightening up, she rubs her face with a tea towel. Only then does she see the stems from a bouquet of flowers sticking out of the bin. Steve follows her eyes.

'That was a waste of forty quid, wasn't it?'

'No. They're beautiful.' She squats down to lift the flowers out of the bin and remove the two white roses that are bent and broken. What if Fred returned to the flat after she left? She stands up, tears stinging her eyes.

'Fay—' says Steve without anger.

But before he can say anything else, she cuts in. 'I can't stop seeing her. Not yet.' And then she sits down at the kitchen table, holding the flowers close to her chest, waiting for whatever comes next.

# 18

'Did I wake you?'

Steve lifts his head off the pillow and squints sideways at the alarm clock. Three seventeen. 'Of course you woke me. What is it?'

Since her announcement a few nights ago that she could not let Emma go, Fay has been sleeping in Billy's old room. Steve didn't ask her to; he wasn't able to string any words together clearly at the time. Instead, he had left her at the kitchen table clutching the flowers and gone upstairs. As he lay on their bed, filled with a terrible sense of dread, he heard Billy's door open and shut and her decision felt appropriate. Let her sleep on Billy's old futon. Steve was the good guy here and the good guy got the new, firm mattress and the expansive front bedroom. And frankly, as childish as it was, having the upper hand over sleeping arrangements was something. He was losing at everything else.

'Can I get in?' she asks.

'It's your bed too.' Moving his legs over, Steve wonders which version of Fay he will encounter. These past few days she has morphed from the most consistent person he knows into someone whose emotional dial seems broken. He's seen her go from morose and teary to brittle and angry in minutes. Unusually, he's caught her sitting down in the daytime with her eyes closed although she isn't asleep, but at other times her focus is either intensely on Rose or her phone. He swings between feeling rejected and angry to genuine concern about her state of mind.

But feeling her body next to him for a few empty, pure seconds, it is as if the cracks between them are imagined. They are just ordinary Fay and Steve again.

'Steve, are you alright?' Her question explodes his little fantasy. The quiet, sealed-up anger that he has worked hard to keep down is pushing up again. She has already asked this a couple of times this week – it's a favourite check-in. Of course, they both know what she really means is, are you alright with me wanting someone else?

'Tired,' he says, knowing this is not the answer she hopes for. Fay craves the intimacy of confession. She always has.

'Me too.' Has she been awake in Billy's room all this time? He's stopped asking her anything, probably because the only question that really matters to him, the only one he dreams about asking is, do you love Emma? It's taken every bit of self-control to keep that one to himself.

Now lying there together feels as awkward as it might on a first date – although not their first date. They'd had sex within hours of leaving the pub, fitting together so magically they had high-fived afterwards, then repeated it twice again before dawn.

'I shouldn't have woken you,' says Fay.

He turns his head. 'Are you crying?'

She nods. 'I'm so, so sorry, Steve.'

'What about exactly?' His breath whistles tight through his words. Perhaps there has been a development, one that merits this unexpected middle-of-the-night visit.

'All of this,' she says vaguely.

She edges her legs apart, so her feet touch his, as if her body is starting a conversation with his. He doesn't stop her.

'Can we talk?' she asks.

'Now?' He pauses. 'No.'

'Soon?'

He wants to say, *yeah, when you tell me you've given up*

*your girlfriend. When you've decided that I'm enough for you.* But that's not something he's ready to announce because he won't be able to come back from it. He'll be one of those weak people who don't deliver on their threats.

'Maybe,' he says and turns over on his side. 'Night.'

When he gets up around his usual time, Fay is still curled tight into herself. He leaves her asleep and goes down to the kitchen, where he becomes disproportionately upset to find that Rose is already up and fully dressed. Is he becoming surplus to requirements? A terrible longing to be needed assails him until he notices her dress is inside out. 'Come here, poppet,' he says gently, acutely grateful for the chance to help her lift it over her head. 'Mummy's still asleep,' he says. 'Let's give her a lie-in, shall we?'

It's conspiratorial and fun to creep around and talk in exaggerated whispers. After he has brushed her hair and teeth, he is in the hallway putting a banana in the side pocket of her backpack when Fay appears on the upstairs landing in her sweatpants and a T-shirt, clutching her hair, a little wild-eyed.

'Morning,' he says. He maintains a cordial outward appearance for Rose, but he doesn't meet Fay's eyes.

'You should have woken me.' She rushes down a few stairs, then back up again. 'Hi, darling,' she calls out to Rose. 'I'll be five minutes.'

'I'm doing the school run.' Steve slots Rose's arms through the backpack loops, then pats her shoulder. 'We forgot your water bottle, sweetie. Can you go and get it? It's by the sink.'

As Rose makes her way into the kitchen, Fay says, 'No, really. Let me.' She runs her hand through her hair, pushing it up, away. 'You go to work.'

'I'm doing it.' Steve's voice resumes its defiant hardness now Rose is out of earshot. 'Stop trying to control everything.'

Fay clings to the banister, nodding, then drops onto a step, hugging her arms around her knees as he opens the door and walks out behind Rose.

'Steve,' shouts Fay.

He looks over his shoulder. 'What?'

'Nothing.' Even her voice has collapsed. 'I'll see you tonight.'

When they get to school, Rose runs off straight away. Steve almost can't believe what he's seeing, but it appears that Rose is playing with another girl. He feels an unexpected surge of happiness, like he does when he notices a lone bright flower push through the cracks in the pavement. It's not a perfect set-up; as they jump on and off the low bench under the classroom window, the girl is calling all the shots. Telling Rose how and when to jump and what mistakes she's making. This would usually concern him, but he doesn't care this morning. Rose has someone to play with and Steve feels more hopeful than he has in days.

But then, as the blonde mum in the pink velour tracksuit and her mini-me daughter weave their way through the class crowd, it is as if the flower he has admired is being trodden on. From what he can see and overhear, the pair of them are shoving party invites into the hands of excited kids. Yet they walk past Rose and her playmate as if they don't exist.

When a couple of kids grab each other and shout about a bouncy castle, Rose and the other girl stop jumping. Their feather-light playfulness has gone. Instead, they stand together silently, as if they have rocks in their pockets. Hold on, Steve wants to say. Let's not leap to hasty conclusions. But when the last invite is delivered, he knows his instinct is correct and an insurmountable fury carries him along as he turns around and approaches the gathering of mums.

*We are good people*, he thinks. *We deserve better*.

'Morning.' Steve doesn't recognise any of them except Olivia's mum, Michelle. She's always been pretty friendly, even giving him and Fay her number on the first day of term in case they needed anything.

There is a collective reluctant murmur. 'Morning.' 'Hi.' 'Hello.'

'So, someone's birthday?' he asks.

'Yes, my daughter. Rebecca,' says the blonde.

'A class party, I guess? Judging by all the invites you've handed out.' Steve smiles. 'I wondered if you had Rose's invite? And the girl she's playing with?'

'It's not quite a class party.' The blonde's flush is almost cartoonish, two round scarlet patches on her cheeks.

'Oh, really?' Steve glances around with fake enquiry. 'It looks like everyone else is going.'

'That really isn't your business.'

Steve knows he needs to walk away. No good will come of this. They will be the family that is ostracised, unwelcome at every school. The *Daily Mail* will find them and write a scathing article and yet, he can't stop. All he wants is for him and Rose to be treated fairly and decently. Is that too much to ask?

'You've only left a couple out, haven't you?' he carries on. 'Shame on you. They're just kids.'

'I do not appreciate this attack,' says the blonde. 'This is very uncool.'

'I don't care if it's cool. My... my... kid has feelings.' Steve almost hiccups out his words. He stops and starts. Later, when these mums dissect this incident, he imagines they'll imitate his pathetic voice.

'After everything the girls have gone through, Rebecca doesn't want her there,' the blonde says, her tongue flicking nervously to the corners of her mouth.

'Rebecca is six,' he snaps. 'You're her parent. Why aren't you modelling good behaviour? Teach her about forgiveness.'

Michelle takes a step forward. 'It's a bit rich, you talking to us about right and wrong.'

'Michelle, don't,' says the blonde.

'Rose knows what she did was wrong. We know she was wrong,' says Steve calmly. 'It will never happen again. Can't we just move on?'

Michelle acts like he hasn't spoken. 'Model good behaviour? Don't make me laugh. Like your wife knows anything about that.'

'What does that mean?' asks Steve.

'Michelle, enough. It's not our business,' says the blonde. 'I don't want to be part of this.'

Michelle swishes her ponytail back over her shoulder. 'I'm just saying what we're all thinking.'

At that moment Miss Floss opens the classroom door and, as the kids charge towards her, the mums disperse. Steve goes over to Rose. Holding her hands, he tells her that only some of the kids have been invited. When she stares at him disbelievingly, it takes all of his strength not to scoop her up and carry her away.

Rattled by the encounter, Steve cycles back to the house to tell Fay instead of heading off to work. He is unclipping his helmet when she comes out of the kitchen.

'Why are you back?' Now she has showered and changed, she looks far more prepared for life than when he left.

'I had a horrible run-in with one of the mums,' he says.

'I knew it.' With her hands on her hips, Fay shakes her head. 'She's such a cow.'

'Who is?' he says.

Fay blinks a couple of times. 'Michelle. Olivia's mum.'

'I wasn't talking about her.'

Fay swallows. 'Oh, okay.'

'What happened with Michelle?'

'Nothing. I just don't like her.'

'No, come on.' Steve walks behind her into the living room. 'Tell me.'

Fay is already on her knees, tidying up Rose's toys, dropping them in the colourful boxes that fit neatly under their mid-century sideboard.

'Well?' He stands in front of her. Holding a Lego piece in her hand, she says something he can't understand. 'What?' he asks in a less pleasant voice. When she sits back and stares up at him, her anguished expression tells him that he's about to be in for a whole load of new pain. He almost wants to tell her no, forget it, I don't want to know.

'Michelle saw me and Emma together a couple of weeks ago. In the changing room after a boxing class.'

'So? Emma could have been a friend.'

Fay shakes her head as she sits on her hands and rocks back and forth, chewing on the inside of her cheek.

'What were you both doing?' A throbbing starts up in his head. He almost moves his hand towards his crown, trying to swat it away. 'Were you messing around in the changing room with her? Like a pair of teenagers? Jesus Christ, Fay. Can't you control yourself?' Jealousy rips through him. He imagines them parading around naked, touching each other whilst Michelle looks on. 'And you didn't think to tell me? You know, give me a heads-up?'

Standing up, Fay can hardly meet his eyes. 'I was too scared. I'm sorry.'

'No wonder you haven't wanted me to do the school run.'

'I know.' She is shaking her head. 'It's not good, it's not. I know it.'

'That's the understatement of the year.' He runs a hand over his mouth and tries to breathe as he walks around in a small, pointless circle. 'I've gone and preached to those women about modelling good behaviour. We're going to be pariahs.'

'I'm not ashamed of what we're doing, Steve. There's nothing wrong with having an alternative relationship.'

'That's a joke, surely?' He stands still, momentarily speechless. Either he is losing his mind or Fay has lost hers. 'Who the hell are you?' he shouts. 'Don't you have any self-respect? Is holding on to this woman all that matters? Whatever the cost?'

'Of course not—'

'Bullshit. It's just become a whole lot of words with you. That's it.' He cuts the air with a hand. 'You don't get to decide when we stop. I've had enough. This experiment is done. Finito. It hasn't worked for us. Now it's over.'

Fay shakes her head as she says, 'No, no,' over and over. 'No?' he shouts.

'I can't yet,' she whispers. 'I don't know why. I just can't.'

He looks to the window, then back at Fay, severely bewildered. 'I used to feel smug about our marriage. I thought we were so lucky.' He jabs his finger at his chest. 'What an idiot I was.'

'Not everything is black and white.' She raises her voice to match his. 'Not all the time. Not day in, day out for twenty-two years.'

'Forgive me, I didn't know it was a prison sentence!'

'Of course it's not! You know I don't think that.'

Neither of them seems to know what to say next. Fay speaks first. 'Steve, we can get through this. Hear me out. You want to stop, I don't. There might be a way.' She edges towards him tentatively and he knows she's about to offer him a solution that will hold everything together for her.

'SHUT THE FUCK UP.' He is overcome with rage for the second time that morning. 'I don't want another plan.' And before he can stop himself, he reaches out and grabs Fay's wrist, pulling her close to him and rubbing her hand over his cock. 'This not good enough for you any more? Well, keep your girlfriend. I'm done.'

And then he releases her hand and sees her crumple into herself as he leaves the room.

/

Steve stays in the locked bathroom for twenty minutes. He is lying in the dry bath in his clothes, finding some comfort in the hard narrow walls holding him in. When he goes out to the garden, Fay is at the table, smoking a cigarette. It must be from the pack she stashes away for when Katie comes over and they shut themselves in the kitchen with expensive wine and cheap snacks. He doesn't say anything when he sits down opposite her. He stares at her, not really knowing what to think. He feels painful tremors between them, the aftershock, and he's utterly weakened. But he's here, keeping his head above water: the worst has happened.

Fay crushes the cigarette end in the ashtray. 'I wish I understood what I'm doing.' Her voice is a whisper. 'I'm so confused.'

'You need to move out.' As he stands up and presses a hand flat onto the table, she watches him, frightened.

'I really don't want to.' She also stands up and rushes at him, but he pushes her away with his elbow. 'Please, Steve. Let's talk this through.'

'No, I've had my fill of you. I want some space. I can't think straight.'

Fay steps back. Her face is rice-white. 'Okay… That's fair. Completely fair. I've had my fill of me too,' she says, trying not to cry again.

'Right, let's make this about you again, shall we?' he snaps, then walks back inside.

While he is at work, they trade perfunctory texts about practical details. Katie leaves for Leicester in the morning because her mum has just gone into a hospice, and the kids are staying with Matt, so Fay can move into Katie's spare room. Steve has sorted this – he controls the agenda now. He tells Fay that they'll inform Rose that Fay's dad has broken his big toe and can't easily walk around, so she has moved in to help him. Steve insists they need to make it sound like a silly injury, rather than anything serious so Rose doesn't add it to her worries, to which Fay replies 💯. Fay will still do school drop-offs and pickups and be at the house as often as possible to keep things normal for Rose. She agrees to everything. Eventually, he puts his phone on mute.

When he gets home, Rose greets him at the door. 'I'm going to the party,' she says excitedly and shows him the invite Rebecca's mum gave her and her new friend Courtney after school. At least one good thing has come out of today. He hugs her against him, reluctant to let go.

While she and Fay have lasagne, he has a bath. When it's time for Rose to go to bed, he goes into her bedroom and play-wrestles with her for a bit before kissing her goodnight. Fay watches them from the doorway. It's the first time they've been in the same room since he got home. He leaves her to put Rose to bed, sitting in the living room until the front door closes and he knows she's gone. Then he heads into the kitchen and puts on the radio to clear the silence. He opens and closes the fridge. He hasn't eaten all day, but he still hasn't got much of an appetite. When his phone rings, he is eating gherkins straight from the jar.

'Billy! What's for supper, big fella?' It's a running joke how Billy is always cooking whenever they speak, regardless of the time.

'Hey, Dad, I'm on my way home. Train gets in about nine.'

'Why?' Steve puts down the jar. 'What's wrong?'

'Nothing. Thought I'd pay you guys a visit.'

'Billy, tell me what's up.'

After a pause, Billy says, 'Caroline and I split up.'

'Oh, son. I'm sorry.' Steve will miss Caroline. He's only met her a couple of times, but he liked her. She might have a timid persona, but she's potty-mouthed and says hilarious, awful things about her family while insisting that she really does love them.

'I can't pick you up,' he says. 'Mum's out and Rose is asleep.'

'It's fine. I've got my bike.'

An hour later they are hugging on the doorstep. Billy looks well but different. He has a scrappy beard, more piercings and a finger tattoo that Fay won't approve of. Then again, maybe she won't care now she's got so much of her own mess going on.

Steve decides not to tell Billy straight away that she has temporarily moved out. He can't easily find the words and it seems a rough thing to put on him, minutes after he gets home.

Over a beer and sausages, which Billy brought with him, Billy offers scant details about the break-up. They were together six and a half months, and it was his first proper relationship, but Steve thinks he seems alright. Perhaps a bit pensive, reluctant to show how bothered he is; Steve can't really tell. Fay is better at getting that sort of emotional truth out of him – out of everyone, in fact. Billy says he might stay with Otis, one of his best friends, who is in telesales and lives in a flatshare in the centre of town. From the smell of him, Steve suspects it's because Billy likes smoking weed with Otis more than home comforts.

'How's Rose doing? Mum told me about the therapist.'

Steve drains his drink. He recalls Rose pushing her fingers into his cheeks as she happily told him about the party invite. Then he thinks of how he pushed Fay's fingers into his cock, and he is disgusted with himself again, and exhausted from the voices in his head swinging him from light to shade.

'Dad, you're crying.'

'Shit.' Steve swipes tears away with the side of his fist. 'Sorry.'

'What's happened to Rose?'

'Nothing. Honestly, she's doing better. She got invited to a birthday party today. She's over the moon.' He clears his throat and shakes himself upright.

'Dad, you're freaking me out. Is it Mum? Is something wrong?' Billy scrapes his chair around the table to be closer to Steve. He asks again as he puts his hand on Steve's back and, for a moment, Steve thinks he would like to hold Billy tight, but in fact this isn't the case. He would do anything to be held.

# 19

Fay sits on the stool in the corner of Emma's bedroom, draining a glass of water. Her head throbs, she is completely dehydrated, but she has no one else to blame but herself. It was a stupid act of self-sabotage to do coke, falling for its charms again when she knows how grim she can feel only hours after the fake happiness.

There is also the paranoia – anxious thoughts about the first bit of the evening have been consuming her since she woke. She doesn't think either of them offended her client, but she honestly can't say for sure. It wasn't the smartest move to invite Emma along to the Pets Matter Awards ceremony, but she had acted in a panic. Emma had just told her she was seeing Fred, and Fay worried that he would have the freedom to pursue Emma in bigger, bolder ways. It felt stupidly like a competition.

Fay shakily puts the empty glass on the dressing table. She needs to get going; it is almost ten o'clock. Standing up, she makes the mistake of glancing through a crack in the curtain. When the morning light slaps her face, she winces and steps away. That was rough.

It's too much effort to find her tights, so she just puts on her black dress and heels, then locates her handbag. Everything takes ages as if she is moving in slow motion. Dealing with such a terrible hangover on a midweek morning makes her feel like a student, especially since Steve will have already taken Rose to school and will be at his desk. It seems bizarre that he doesn't know that she stayed up all night nor does he have to find out – even if, out of habit, the urge to text and tell him keeps surfacing.

She doesn't bother creeping around since it's almost impossible to wake Emma, who is a ridiculously heavy sleeper. She is lying on her back, with a red silk eye mask on, snoring while Fay zips up her dress, then checks her handbag for keys to Katie's house. Katie was the first person she called after Steve insisted that she leave. Although Katie had an idea that something had happened from a text exchange with Steve, and despite her misgivings about Emma, she still sounded so shocked and upset, confirming that the situation was ridiculously serious, almost impossible to conceive. 'I thought you'd get bored with an open relationship. I never thought you'd end up here. You guys are the most solid couple I know,' Katie had said in such a grave voice that Fay had to hang up because she couldn't speak for tears.

In the living room, as Fay retrieves her scrunched-up jacket from the sofa, she sees a message flash up on Emma's phone lying on a cushion nearby.

### Hamish

Lewis told me he got highest grade in the year for art. Go boy! Takes after his talented mum. X

*That's sweet*, thinks Fay as she pulls on her jacket and leaves.

/

As soon as Fay met Emma outside the hotel on the seafront which was hosting the awards ceremony, she understood that she had set Emma's expectations too high. Emma was wearing shiny red flared dungarees over a sheer black shirt and chunky platform heels. Her fingers were jammed with vintage rings. It was a devastatingly good look, but more suited for an interesting club night.

'I've got coke for afterwards,' Emma had announced immediately. 'My treat,' she added as she finished her cigarette before they went inside. 'To thank you for all your brilliant work on the website.'

'Not necessary, really. It was my pleasure.' Fay felt uneasy as she shook her head. She did not want to do drugs. She felt hollow enough as it was, and she had been ethically opposed to cocaine for years. But Emma was smiling at her so expectantly, waiting for some gratitude. 'Well, at least let me pay half.'

Emma didn't seem that surprised by Fay's offer. 'Thank you. That's very generous.' She crushed her cigarette underfoot and looped arms with Fay. 'Let's go have a laugh.'

'Apologies if I'm not the best company,' Fay said. 'I've had a crap couple of days with Steve.'

Straight away, she wanted to take her words back. She deliberately never referenced Steve because it didn't feel right. And Emma was never curious. She seemed to blithely accept Fay's other life.

'Oh, darling,' said Emma. 'Sorry to hear that.'

Fay gestured with her hand. 'It's nothing. Now, this is a work situation,' she warned as they headed into the foyer. 'They don't know about us. You're a good friend, that's all.'

'Don't worry, hun. I'm the soul of discretion. Oh my God, look at this place,' said Emma as they approached the ballroom. 'And free fizz!' Watching her rush towards the bartenders carrying trays of champagne, Fay found it impossible to match her excitement. Access to these events over the years meant that now all she saw was an adequately decorated room, but one which lacked any real flair, like a big wedding done on the cheap.

Within minutes of introducing Emma to her client, a veterinary franchise across the south-east, Emma held all of them in her thrall. She was indifferent to everyone's hierarchical positions in the company and had no regard for formality, which they seemed to admire.

'Icebreaker!' she shouted as soon as they were all seated. 'Let's all go around and say one thing about ourselves that no one else would know.'

Fay had automatically cringed at the theatrics, but the others loved the idea. Within minutes Emma knew more about Fay's clients than she had in five years of working alongside them. Then Emma picked up the bottles of red and white wine that were placed centrally on the table and walked around topping up everyone's glass.

'Once a bartender, always a bartender,' she called out. They were the noisiest, most vivacious group in the room and others glanced over enviously. Fay even started to relax. In fact, it was a relief to be carried by someone else. It meant that others might be less likely to notice that her own energy was fading and unpredictable.

But Emma was drinking a lot, quickly. She squeezed Fay's arm and hand twice. When she leant in too close and grazed Fay's cheek to whisper something disparaging about the mushroom hors d'oeuvre, Fay grew nervy. This was a good client. A constant, reliable stream of work. She could not afford to lose them.

By the main course, Emma's interest had clearly dwindled. Now Fay was worried that Emma would start to see the evening through a muted prism and realise this was simply a hotchpotch of ordinary people at a dullish work do.

By the time coffee was served, all of the awards had been called – Fay's client did not win, but they were gracious in defeat – and Emma's attention had almost completely collapsed.

'Do you have any rituals when you're doing your art? I have a friend who can only write if she's drinking coffee from a particular mug.' The company accountant on the other side of Emma attempted to draw more glittering conversation out of her.

'No, not really.' Emma's voice was vague, half-hearted. She had stopped listening. She did not ask questions or want to play any more games. She had taken her phone out and was scrolling and tapping. When she spoke, even to Fay, it was as if she was thinking about something entirely different and separate. It made Fay realise what she must have been like recently with Steve, intermittent and remote.

When Emma stifled two yawns in a row, Fay's anxiety grew. Feeling Emma pull away from her was unbearable, so she leant in to her and whispered, 'Fancy doing a line?'

'Do I!' Emma whispered back excitedly, and her demeanour changed once again. It was as if she had been plugged into an electricity meter. She even curtsied playfully to the rest of the table after making a too-loud announcement that they were heading off for a wee and a sneaky smoke.

Fay insisted they had to use the separate toilet for disabled people on the first floor, rather than the busy loos near the function room. Watching Emma cut up the coke on the toilet cistern, it felt like Fay's moral integrity had almost completely dissolved. There seemed no point having principles when they crumbled so easily. But after she had snorted one of the two narrow lines, she forgot about this – she forgot about everything that had been dragging down her thoughts. She straightened up and smiled. The zing of the coke was like a flash of tiny, unexpected lights up and down her body. Her stomach immediately cramped. Did she need the toilet? No, she was fine. Thank God, her body was going to behave.

'Good, isn't it?' said Emma. 'Zak's the best.'

After Emma had inhaled her line and rubbed some residue powder on her and Fay's gums, she started saying something, but now Fay was leaning against the wall not really listening. She felt so alert, a controlled kind of euphoria. Why hadn't she done more coke these past few years? When Emma started singing along to the Beyoncé track coming up from the room below, Fay moved away from the wall and joined her, grateful for this woman who made these moments happen.

'Let's make our excuses and go,' she said.

Since half the table were off dancing, Fay told one of the marketing guys that she had babysitter issues and had to leave. She was sure not to stand around for too long, or engage in lengthy conversation, even though the second, fatter line of coke they had before leaving the toilet was pulsing false confidence through her.

On the street, she closed her eyes, loving the smell of the sea. Its freshness was so liberating. She insisted they cross the road and head onto the beach.

'You're a lunatic,' Emma shouted as Fay ran barefoot and screaming to the sea edge. Her toes soon felt the cold and her nose was wet. But she couldn't stop moving about. At first Emma was laughing. She loved the wildness in Fay, but Fay must have been yelling too loudly, because when three teenagers passing by stopped to stare and laugh, Emma called out, 'Hey, Fay, calm it.'

Fay stopped and picked up her heels and tights. 'That felt so good.'

Emma smiled. 'I could tell. Come on, let's go back to mine. We've still got a load of gear to get through.'

Once home, Emma set the atmosphere. She manipulated the lights to perfection, dragged out the floor cushions and turned the music up loud. When she sat down with the wrap of coke, she was eager to take control of carving up, keen that Fay didn't get more than her. With every line, Fay could feel the drugs spiralling inside her. Her voice was like a race car taking the corners fast, a little jerk here and there, unsure of whether it could keep going at this speed. At one point Emma received a text from a customer at the bar confirming he wanted to commission a large collage from her, and this prompted ideas for a solo art show, possibly even taking it to London or abroad. She had such huge, lofty plans after just one commission. And yet, right then, it seemed entirely possible to both of them.

After a while, Fay's head began to reel, and she had to

rush to the toilet to throw up; it had been years since she felt this wired. She squeezed out the last of the toothpaste, rubbed it over her teeth. Then she automatically unclogged Emma's hair from the plughole and dropped it in the bin, before clutching the sides of the sink and smiling dreamily at herself for ages in the mirror, taken with how large and shiny her eyes looked. She actually looked quite pretty and young.

'Fay!' Emma's shout was animated and urgent. 'Come on. What are you doing in there?'

By the time they finished the coke, Fay was feeling so out of it that all she wanted to do was dance. In her desperation to get inside the music, she stripped down to her bra and knickers and made Emma dance with her.

But when they both quickly got caught up in their own separate worlds, Fay decided she needed to connect them again. She clutched Emma by the back of her head and kissed her with such passion that she felt as if she might explode.

'Christ, you're so sexy like this,' Emma said, and they fitted together on the sofa in the living room with the blinds not yet pulled down. Someone was awake in the flat over the road; they could see his shadow move across the window.

'Let's give them a show.' Fay dragged Emma to her feet and started dancing and gyrating close to her while they laughed their heads off before eventually slumping back on the sofa.

'You're so much fun,' said Emma. 'Way more than Fred. I told him it was over, by the way. I'm not seeing him any more.'

Fay sat up, feeling an incredible surge of superiority. 'Fuck Fred,' she shouted. 'Fred's dead.'

Emma laughed. 'Fred is dead. All he did was talk about his visits to the gym.' She also sat up and flexed her upper arms. As she kissed each bicep in turn, she said, 'I love you. And I love you,' and they both laughed hysterically again.

'I really needed tonight,' said Fay a little while later.

'I should say so. You're on fire.' Emma reached over and looked at her phone. 'My God. It's ten past five. How did that happen?' She walked to the windows and released each blind in a clatter. The room darkened. 'Won't Steve mind that you're out this late?'

Fay was surprised at the mention of his name. She reached for the roll-up that Emma had left in the ashtray ready to smoke. 'No.' She lit it and took a long drag. 'We had a huge row.' She stopped short of announcing that she had been kicked out.

'Oh no, that's not good.' Emma didn't ask Fay to elaborate. She walked into the kitchen, came back with two large glasses of water, then reached over and took the roll-up off Fay. 'You'll sort it out,' she said, exhaling. 'Lord knows I've had my share of rows and dramas.'

Nodding, Fay tried not to feel hurt by Emma's glib response; she wouldn't have minded a flicker of jealousy. 'Maybe. It's never happened before. Not like this.' Fay stopped. If she said anything else, Emma might realise how central she was to their argument. 'Sorry, I don't mean to be heavy.'

'It's fine,' said Emma. 'Don't worry about it, babe.' Then she abruptly announced that she needed to go to bed and beckoned for Fay to follow her.

Once they were under the duvet, she shut her eyes whilst Fay lay on her side on an elbow, looking down at her. 'Are you tired?' Fay asked in surprise.

'Yeah, I'm one of those freaks whose sleep isn't affected by coke.'

Fay touched the four studs in Emma's ear. She traced her jaw, her chin, her clavicle. Fay had never had this quiet, unfettered time to examine and touch Emma before and she didn't want it to stop. Even after hours in her company, Fay never felt like she got enough of her. She always had a craving for more, to keep hold of the carefree energy that Emma infused her with.

'Emma,' she said, and it was almost as if Emma could feel the heaviness of Fay's thoughts because she didn't open her eyes.

'No, love, I'm done in. Come on. Lie down.'

As Fay reluctantly lay down, Emma said in a lilting voice, 'Lovely Fay. Lovely, lovely Fay,' which immediately flooded Fay with anxiety. There was something so gentle and wistful about the way Emma had said her name. Something that made Fay think of endings. She held Emma's hand to her mouth and kissed her knuckles and she thought, *no. Not yet, please.*

/

After Fay leaves Emma's flat, she walks back to Katie's. She showers and changes quickly, then heads down to the café two streets away. She isn't late, but Billy is already sitting at a window table with his headphones on. They have seen each other most nights since he got back a few days ago, but always in the company of Rose and Steve. Immediately, the sight of him lifts her spirits. Noticing her make her way across to him, he stands up and lowers his headphones to rest around his neck. Fay hugs him too hard. She can feel his resistance. When he pushes back, she releases him, and they both sit down.

'I could have made you some lunch at Katie's.' Fay hangs her bag over the back of the chair.

'I don't want to see you living anywhere else,' says Billy. 'That would do my head in.'

'I get that. It's strange for me too.' She glances at the menu as a waitress approaches, then says 'Same, please' after Billy orders a vegetarian fry-up.

'You look awful,' he remarks.

Fay nods. 'I had a terrible night's sleep,' she says truthfully. 'And I've got a massive headache.'

Billy looks like he doesn't care too much. He pushes his beanie off his face. 'Dad's in bits, you know. He might not show it, but he is.' Clearly, Billy has come prepared with this criticism.

Nodding, she leans over and sweeps her hand down his

face. 'This must be so hard for you.' She has to stop herself crying. 'I'm really sorry, Billy. I hate seeing you upset.'

Billy flicks her hand away. 'What about seeing Dad upset?'

'It's complicated,' she says gently.

'He's done everything for you.'

'I've been good to him too, you know.' Fay tries to keep the tartness from her voice, but she feels defensive. She has loved Billy fully with everything she has. In fact, secretly, she has always thought he was her child, that he belonged mostly to her. Why is he taking Steve's side?

'Yeah,' says Billy. 'But we all have to bow down to you. It's always about you.'

Fay stares at him, so hurt by his comment. 'Is it?' she says, almost in a whisper.

'Yeah, we can all see how much Dad loves you. Whatever is going on is something that you're doing.'

'You don't know anything about it, thank you.' Fay tries to keep her voice gentle, but her heart is pounding, reminding her of when she heard Billy's heartbeat for the first time during her pregnancy and it was so strong and intense, like a wild horse galloping along. *All bow down to me?*

'I didn't mean that,' says Billy. 'It came out wrong.'

'Is that what you think?' asks Fay. 'Is that what I'm like?

'No, you're not. That wasn't right. I'm sorry. You're just…'

'What? Bossier than Dad? More controlling?'

When Billy nods, Fay has to collect herself before speaking. 'Sorry. That's a crap trait for a mum, isn't it?'

Billy squirms in his seat at her sudden collapse in defensiveness.

'I'm not easy like your dad. I push harder. I know that. And I'm sorry.' She reaches for his hand and squeezes it. 'I think it was the only way I knew to keep the plates spinning. There are lots of plates, Billy.' She releases his hand and sits back, thinking of Rose and their businesses and their parents and

Billy living away. It feels overwhelming. And that's without figuring in her needs.

'And guess what? I still managed to drop most of them,' she adds emotionally. 'But you know, if I hadn't hassled, would you have found your way to the great job you've got? It's all coming from a good place, Billy.'

'Yeah, I know,' he says, nodding. 'But everything's messed up.'

'Right now, it is. Nothing stays the same,' she says, trying to be reassuring.

'Are you going to come home?'

'I don't know.' Fay leans back as her filter coffee and glass of water are placed in front of her, then she rummages around her bag for her Nurofen. Her head is still thumping. Billy slouches against the window, and then, both lost in their own thoughts, they sit and silently watch all the people passing by.

# 20

Steve has only just got home from work. He still has his cycle helmet on as he bends over, watching Fay's clothes slosh around in the washing machine. 'You can be so selfish,' he snaps at her, straightening up. 'I had a load of Rose's school clothes ready to go in.'

'I'm sorry,' says Fay. 'Katie's machine is playing up. I needed some clean stuff.'

'Rose needs clean stuff too. Or doesn't that matter any more?'

'Don't be stupid, Steve. I just didn't know.'

'No, because I'm running the show now.'

He can tell Fay is fighting with herself to challenge that comment – she has been at the house so often it's like she hasn't left, which in itself is an issue for him, but one he can hardly do anything about, or else Rose's happiness will be jettisoned. Fay sighs. 'Sorry. I was thoughtless. Again. *Rose*,' she calls on her way over to the door that opens on to the living room, 'come and lay the table.'

She has to ask twice before he sees Rose reluctantly drag herself into the room. 'I don't want to lay the table.'

'You have to,' says Fay in an upbeat voice. 'Come on now. Everyone has jobs.'

'I don't want a job. I'm a child.'

'Just lay the table, Rose.' The shift in Fay's voice shrivels Rose into moving towards the cutlery drawer without re-airing her feeling of injustice. Once Rose has haphazardly laid the table and returns to the television, Steve checks on the cottage pie that he took out of the freezer for Fay to put in the oven.

'So I'm away cycling in the Peak District for a few days end of July,' he says, closing the oven door. 'And don't forget I'm taking Rose surfing third week in August. It's all on the calendar.'

Fay nods and rubs her face. 'Yes,' she says, 'of course.' He's sure that his talk of plans makes her anxious, as if she never expected him to take charge of the future without her. But if she thinks he's going to retreat and wait in the wings, she underestimated him.

'I miss Billy,' she says. 'It was so good having him back.'

Steve doesn't really acknowledge her, he doesn't want regular chit-chat, but he also misses Billy like mad. He kept trying to push Billy out, on to Otis and his other friends, but Billy insisted he couldn't be bothered. Every night he cooked for the family and, after Fay left, he drank beer with Steve, and they played *FIFA* or watched episodes of *Seinfeld*. This touched Steve deeply. It made him feel good about himself to have a kid who looked out for him.

One morning Steve watched Billy jump around on the trampoline with Rose like a big kid. Rose was hysterical with laughter. The fun they were having made him smile, but it also made him furious with Fay all over again, so he took a photo and texted it to her. She took hours to reply with just one word, *Lovely*. He didn't know whether she'd been busy or wouldn't let herself be manipulated. She probably knew it was his way of trying to hurt her, by showing her what she was missing. But he doesn't feel bad. He's got a lot of hurt to share out and it's her fault.

Since Steve won't engage in conversation, Fay sits at the table with her open laptop. 'The Wi-Fi is slower at Katie's. I couldn't send this big file before,' she says apologetically. She is tapping away when Rose shouts for her. Fay ignores her. Eventually Rose comes in and drapes herself over Fay, with her hands clasped around Fay's neck. 'Watch this episode of *SpongeBob* with me. It's so funny.'

Rose drags on Fay's T-shirt until Fay says, 'Careful, sweetie, you'll stretch it.' She gets up, leaving her laptop open. 'Come on then, missie, let's see what's so funny.'

When Fay is no longer at the table, Steve goes around rearranging Rose's attempt at cutlery-laying. The laptop is open, the screen still active. Yes, he looks. And yes, he sees that one of the emails near the top of her inbox is from Emma French and is a response with the subject header, *Re: website gone live, woo hoo!* Steve feels sick even seeing her name. He shuts down the laptop and puts it to one side.

As soon as Fay puts Rose to bed, Rose gets out. Standing at the top of the stairs, plucking at the waistband of her pyjama bottoms, she looks down at Fay and says, 'When is Grandad's toe going to be better?' Steve hovers in the doorway to the living room, listening.

'Soon. Go to bed, sweetheart,' says Fay. 'I'll see you at breakfast. Love you to the moon and back.'

In the living room, Steve sits down. He opens his book and pretends to read as Fay shuts the door. 'How do you think Rose is?' she asks as he looks vaguely at the page at the same time as pulling the ring on a can of beer.

He takes a sip, glances up. 'Oh, we're probably damaging the hell out of her,' he says in a neutral voice.

'Please don't say that.' Fay looks pained.

'Well, let's see what the psychologist tells us tomorrow.'

'Are we going to tell Louise we're living apart at the moment?' asks Fay.

'No, let's tell her we've never been happier, shall we?' he snaps. 'I'm surprised you don't have to carry a notebook around with you, so you can keep track of your lies.'

'Thanks for that,' says Fay.

'Well, there you go. I feel mean. Goodnight.' He takes

another sip of beer and turns a page of the book. *Please leave*, he thinks. *Just go*.

Instead, Fay sits on the edge of the chair opposite and says sadly, 'I've lost control of everything, Steve.'

Although this admission startles him, he keeps his eyes fixed on the page. 'And?'

'And nothing.' She shrugs. 'I just wanted to tell you.'

'Well, great. Thanks for sharing.'

'Can you please keep your voice down?' she says. 'Rose will hear.'

'What do you expect?' Keeping his book open, he puts it down next to him and looks at her. '*I've lost control*. That's just bullshit. I don't buy it. You're always in control, Fay. You made all this happen. And you've kept it going.'

She nods. 'I know. I've acted appallingly.'

She says it with such meaning he can tell that she really does think that about herself and that finally she has stopped with the mental gymnastics that have taken her away from the truth.

'And that's it? Not going to do anything about it?' he snaps. 'What good is that to me?' He bats the air dismissively as she attempts to say something else. 'What I want to know is…' He stops and swallows hard. 'Is it more than sex?'

She sits back. She bends her legs to her chest and holds them there, looking at him before letting her legs go. 'Yes,' she says and covers her mouth.

'Finally, a truth.' He nods numbly. 'Do you love her… love Emma?' He presses on the sides of the beer can. He hates the sound of her name. He hates making her real, but she is and neither of them can deny it.

Fay shakes her head. 'No, I really don't think I do,' she says slowly. 'But she's got inside me.'

Steve's heart feels pummelled. He crunches the can so hard that beer squirts out the top. 'And what about me?' he asks. 'Do you still love me? Or are you not sure about that either?'

'You know I do.'

Steve feels a rush of gratitude that her voice is so distinct and immediate. 'But it's not enough, is it?' he says.

Fay presses her fingers to her temples and looks down. 'I don't know. I've got no idea what I feel at the moment. My head is all over the place.'

Swearing under his breath, he leans forward and stares at the fireplace ahead of him. 'That's good to know,' he manages to say.

'Steve. I didn't know this would happen. I thought I just wanted to have sex with someone else. Have an adventure. That's all. I really didn't think it was about anything more.' She shakes her head. 'I never expected to end up here.'

He rotates his head to look at her hugging her knees again, rocking gently. In that moment, he feels as if he is completely disconnected from the situation, as if he is playing himself in the film of his life, but a revised, scripted, make-believe version. Because this should not be happening to his actual life, not to someone like him.

'I can't believe I agreed to this fucking experiment,' he shouts. 'I didn't even want to do it.'

Fay stops rocking. 'Here we go.' She sits up and plants her feet on the floor. 'You can't put it all on me. I won't have that. No one held a gun to your head.'

'You wanted it,' he shouted.

She stands up. 'You could have said no. I was very clear that you had to want it too. Own it, Steve.'

He sits back, weakened. 'You're right. I should have followed my instinct and refused.' He drinks from the can, then swipes his lips with the back of his hand. 'But it's not down to me that you've acted like a complete bitch.'

Fay looks as though he's slapped her. 'No, I did that all on my own.'

Watching her pick up her bag and leave, he is shaking with emotion. The conversation is still alive in him, breaking him apart. He knows he should sit for a while and calm down, but hearing the door shut, he goes to his backpack and takes out his laptop. Without Billy around to distract him, Steve only has himself to rely on and it's not enough. He needs to see the new website Fay and Emma were emailing over. He knows what he's doing is ruinous, that letting in new thoughts is like exposing himself to a virus that will be hard to get rid of, but he needs to see the woman who has brought his marriage to its knees.

He has googled Emma French so many times the past few weeks her full name appears in the search bar after the first three letters. Fay had mentioned her name months ago when Emma was nothing to them both and she was telling him how Emma had been a mild celebrity at college for all the wrong reasons. For killing someone accidentally, which is a terrible, terrible thing to live with and he wouldn't wish on anyone, not even someone who is having sex with his wife.

The same several Emma Frenchs always appear first. One who died in a yachting accident the year before. One who lives in Newcastle and advertises accountancy services. Another who beams out from small-town America. He reads down, moving through to the next page and the next until he sees a website: Emma French Art. This wasn't here the last time he searched for her.

Hearing himself inhale sharply, he clicks on it. There is an uploaded video on the home page and the image that beams out is presumably Emma French, who is sitting in front of two cheese plants with several arty collages behind her. She is dirty blonde, attractive yet not really pretty. He doesn't recognise her. He definitely hasn't seen her before.

He presses the Play button and in a smooth, charismatic voice, the woman says, 'Hi, I'm Emma French, mother, artist, cocktail waitress.' As she talks on, Steve thinks about her speaking to Fay as they have sex, and a ringing starts up in his ears. He presses stop, then he just moves around the site, lingering a while on the mediocre art in the gallery.

Excruciatingly, he knows her website has Fay's style imprinted all over it. He can hear Fay's voice in the copy, he can see her creative hand on the layout. She probably arranged that curl hanging down from Emma's loosely tied knot. She might have bent forward and kissed Emma before Emma applied her ruby-red lipstick.

For a moment, Steve wants to smash the laptop like he did with Fay's phone. This woman has infiltrated every part of his home and his life. And yet, he still can't stop himself looking. He reads through the bio where Emma says she works in a bar which makes the best old fashioned in town, he opens another tab and searches locally for the best old fashioned. In about two seconds, The Nine Bar pops up. This is, of course, a shortcut to self-destruction. He's far better off not knowing any of this, because now he is compelled to do something with that information.

He takes a mental note of the address, shuts down the laptop and calls Kyla. He apologies for the late notice and asks her if she can come over for a couple of hours.

'I'm sort of busy, Mr A.' Her laughter sounds muffled. He imagines her pushing her boyfriend's hand away.

'I'll pay you double. And for an Uber over here. Bring your boyfriend. Fay's out and it's a bit of an emergency.'

Now she's taking him seriously. He can see her sit up, touch the piercing in her eyebrow like she often does when thinking. He hopes that after all these years, she'll say, *sure, Mr A, I want to help. I hope it's nothing serious*. Instead, she says, 'Did you say an Uber home too?'

As soon as she arrives, Steve gets into his car and drives fast across town. He goes through two amber-about-to-change-to-red lights, hearing someone beep at him. But tonight, he has a lack of respect for the systems that supposedly exist to maintain some order. He's always done everything he should. Where did it get him? He parks outside the bar, half on a double yellow, half over a loading bay – screw you, council – and looks at the dark closed-up-looking bar painted entirely black with a discreet name sign hanging under one small light.

At the door, a man with a grey bun in a black suit greets him. 'Hello, how are you this evening?'

'Good, thanks.' Steve likes the calm atmosphere, the way crowds of people are almost hidden in tall booths shaped like clamshells.

'Are you meeting someone?' If he's fazed by Steve shaking his head, he doesn't show it. 'Let me take you over to the bar. Mario will take care of you.'

Steve is passed over to the bartender who also has a bun and an expression of misplaced self-importance. Mario barely looks at him, Mario is doing his thing. Squeezing a lime. Pouring a silver teaspoon of a brown liquor into a shaker, then a measure of gin. Occasionally, he glances up to see if he's garnered an audience. Eventually, sick of being overlooked, Steve says, 'Hey, how about I get served?'

Mario looks over, clearly surprised that the old guy at the bar hasn't just wanted to sit and watch him. 'Certainly. Sorry, sir.'

Steve drums his fingers on the bar. *Yeah*, his curt nod signifies. *Cut the apologies and get me a drink.* He tells Mario he'd like an old fashioned and, minutes later, Mario delivers it to him and watches, wiping his hands on a tea towel as if he expects something from Steve. Steve pays with his card, then takes a sip. It's delicious. Still, he gives Mario nothing but a nod, a muted thanks.

When he sees Emma for the first time, she is moving fast alongside the bar as the door blows shut behind her. His heart starts thumping and he automatically rounds over his drink, wanting to hide but not hide, but then he straightens up. He has nothing to feel ashamed about.

'Did you go to Seville for those?' says Mario as she hands him a net of oranges.

'I bumped into that guy, Luke, in the Co-op. You know, that loony antiques dealer who used to come in and drink neat bourbon. Now, he's got some stories.' Laughing, Emma launches into an anecdote, and while Mario listens and slices into an orange, his body language changes. He looks engaged and relaxed. He throws his head back and laughs with her. Watching them, Steve swallows; Emma is like a neon sign in this dark bar.

Then she disappears. She passes back and forth a couple of times, carrying a tray of empty glasses or tapping orders on a small pocket tablet. Steve keeps staring at her, almost willing her to turn her smile on him, the one she turns on everyone in this bar. The one she used to get and keep Fay's attention. But she doesn't seem to even notice him.

Twice she leans into booths and says something. She waves at a woman about to leave and calls out 'Hello, darling' to a man joining a group of people. Steve can hear her laugh bounce all over the place. She appears to belong to everyone. He wonders if this causes Fay pain or whether it makes her want her even more. Fay begrudges anyone stealing too much of her space, but she can be possessive of people around her.

When Emma appears again, Steve prepares to stand up. He's ready. This time he won't let her waft by, but he'll grab her, he'll tell her who he is. Instead, she approaches him. He isn't even off his stool when she glides in between him and the couple who have just sat down at the bar and are intimately leaning into each other.

'Don't I know you?' As Emma scratches the side of her nose, he sees the red varnish on her thumbnail is badly chipped. He's surprised the management allow it. She doesn't wait for an answer. 'Yes, I do.' Her voice is frosty. 'You're Steve. Fay's husband.' She seems unhappy about it.

Steve is stunned. 'How do you know that?'

'I've seen photos of you,' she says. 'When I came to your house that time.'

Steve stares at her. 'You came to my house?'

She nods uncertainly. 'Yes. Sorry, I know I shouldn't have. Fay told me off. I never did it again.'

'Uh-huh.' His voice sounds hoarse. This woman must have picked up photos of him and put them down. She's had these past couple of months to know who he is, to decide that he is or isn't a threat. 'What the hell were you doing in my house?'

Emma looks sheepish. 'I had some puppets I thought Rose... your daughter... might like.'

Steve knows the puppets she means. Rose has made him play with them a few times. He shakes his head gently. He could ask this woman anything. She doesn't seem to have the ability to lie.

'I see... well, anyway, this was a good old fashioned.' He drains his drink. 'Not the best but good.' She looks puzzled. 'You said on your website that you worked in a place that served the best old fashioned in town? Website looks great, by the way. Fay did a fantastic job, as usual.'

Emma sighs and crosses her arms over her chest. 'She did.'

'Yep, it looked really flash. She must have spent ages on it. Lucky you.'

'What exactly are you doing here?' Emma says crisply. When a woman calls out, 'Bye, Emma,' she swivels around and flashes her smile, then turns back to him. 'Well?'

'I wanted to see who you were.' Steve wishes he still had liquid in his glass. His mouth is dry. He hadn't expected his reasoning to sound so pathetic. 'See who my wife is involved with.'

'You guys.' Emma shakes her head. 'Fay was really unhappy when I came to your house. She gave me this whole lecture about boundaries and rules. And here you are.'

Steve meets her stare. 'True. But I had to see you in the flesh.'

'Uh-huh. Well, this is me.' She puts her hands on her hips. 'Just as well I'm used to being a curiosity. So you've seen me, now what?'

Steve doesn't have a plan beyond this moment. It dawns on him that this might be very short-sighted. In fact, he is starting to see that he might have played this very wrong. He came to examine her, to get a grasp on who she is, and for what? She owes him nothing.

'Look, truth is we're going through a terrible patch,' he blurts out. 'I just...'

'Honestly, hun…' She cuts in and presses a hand on his arm. 'I don't want to know. I've said as much to Fay.'

He is taken aback by Emma's clarity, her ability to erect a steel fence around her feelings. They could learn a thing or two from her. He leans into the bar. There is nothing else to say. He wanted somewhere to vent his anger and frustration, but now it has nowhere to go but inside him. He has achieved nothing by coming here, except he's made himself look foolish. And now he has a real imprint of Emma French on his brain. He will be able to properly picture them having sex. Christ, that's going to finish him off.

'Anyway, I have tables that won't wait on themselves.'

'Yeah. Okay.' Then, in a move that will humiliate him when he recalls it later, and for reasons he will never understand, he clicks his heels and salutes her before saying goodnight and leaving the bar.

Steve drives home slowly. He finds a parking space near the house and, once he turns the engine off, he calls his mum.

'Stephen, darling,' she says in surprise. 'We were just on our way to bed.'

'Can I talk to you about something?' He can hear the tremble in his wafer-thin voice.

'It's rather late,' she says. 'We're about to turn the lights off downstairs.'

'I just need to talk for a bit.'

'Yes, but I'm very tired. We had such a long day, didn't we, Doug?' His mum starts to talk about the boiler, about the noise it was making and the hot water splashing out from the bottom. How they've had to call a plumber and the plumber can't come until the following afternoon, and the more she talks, the more incensed Steve feels.

'Did you hear what I said?' he shouts over her. 'Do you ever listen to anything I say?'

'Stephen,' she says with a gasp. 'You're being very rude.'

'Well, how many times have I called needing to talk? Never. Not once. And you know why? Because I've always suspected that you would let me down. If I've spent too much of my marriage trying to please Fay, it's not just because I love her and want her to be happy. It's because I've always been scared she's going to leave me. And you know why that is? Because of you. Because you didn't love us enough to stay.'

Steve can hear his mum say, 'Doug, I don't understand this. I don't know what Stephen is saying,' and the phone being handled. Then Doug's placatory voice starts up. 'Steve, what's all this about? Let's calm down. Your mother's very upset...' but Steve hangs up, puts his head on the steering wheel and tries to stop shaking.

Fucking hell, he almost wants to laugh. Instead, he lifts his head and screams really loudly. He's buzzing. When was the last time he'd put himself first? Said what he felt and to hell with the consequences? He'd been a people-pleaser for too long. Always quick to smooth things over. At least now there's some rawness to his life, some real honesty for the first time in what feels like forever.

He gets out of the car and walks fast to the house, shouting out hello to Kyla as he hangs up his coat. He puts on Radio 6 Music and flits around as they wait for Kyla's Uber and, when she eventually goes, he pours himself a whiskey and takes it over to the sofa.

But as he sits there, his mood starts to sour again; his elation drains away. How did they get here? What damage have they done? And it's not just Fay's doing. He sees this now. He has been complicit. He has not been brave enough, and this sense of failing brings him close to tears.

# 21

Fay arrives after Steve. She takes a seat without greeting him and apologises to Louise. 'I thought we were meeting outside,' she explains.

'No problem,' says Louise. 'Nice to see you again.'

'I told Fay that I'd meet her up here,' Steve says to Louise.

Fay ignores him and asks Louise if she has missed anything.

'No, we haven't made a start.' Louise smiles, then jots down a note in the open pad on her lap. Fay wonders if Louise has cottoned on that she and Steve are islands and Louise is the bridge. She would be justified in writing *tensions, problem parents*.

When Louise looks up, Fay returns her half-smile and takes the opportunity to properly survey Louise's new bob, which falls to just below her ears and is dyed bright orange. It's strangely unflattering. Still smiling, Fay forces herself to look away.

As Steve gets up to retrieve a tissue from a pocket of his jacket that he has hung up on the coat stand, Fay sneaks a sideways glance. His shabby appearance is suggestive of a late-night drinking session. She knows he's been doing that frequently the past couple of weeks; she's found enough crushed cans in the recycling and his skin has those telling blotches beneath his unshaven jaw. In fact, his demeanour reminds her of how he was after his dad died, all twitches and tics and sharp edges. Fay feels a blow to her heart – if he's feeling that sort of pain, it's down to her. His undoing is entirely her fault.

Steve sits down, blows his nose, then bends one leg over the other knee and taps the sole of his trainers. Fay can see that Louise is finding it distracting. Twice she loses her thread.

'Sorry.' Steve plants his feet on the floor and knits his hands across his stomach.

'So how do you both think Rose has been?' asks Louise.

'Well, she must have told you she's made a new friend,' says Steve.

Louise's nod is accompanied by a professional smile. Fay thinks, *why are you asking when you clearly know?* It feels like a trick question, but instead she says, 'Yes, Courtney. Rose seems really happy about the friendship.'

These days, it's all about Courtney. Courtney's guinea pigs. Courtney's pink furry backpack. Courtney's special way of drawing people. Rose has even shown Fay how straight Courtney extends her arm into the air when she's vying for the teacher's attention. Fay knows, she really does know, that this is a wonderful thing, a breakthrough for Rose. She's even a little in awe of Rose's transformation – she's skipped into school a couple of times, properly skipped – but at the same time, she is also scared to trust it. That's what she hates about this. The constant questioning of Rose's innocent happiness, unable to stop thinking that it will always feel precarious.

'What do *you* think of how Rose is doing?' Fay asks Louise. She can't be bothered to skirt around. After all, they're paying Louise to tell them what she thinks. Louise must have caught the flash in her eyes, the call to action, because she straightens up and puts her pad on the table next to her.

'Rose is happier,' says Louise. 'But there are issues around self-esteem, no doubt from her experience at her old school.' Together they are looking at how to build her self-confidence and focus on how Rose might deal with her anxiety around friendships, and the difficulties with peers when they arise.

'Talk to me about her self-esteem at home,' says Louise. 'Do you find that she struggles with having confidence in herself?'

'I don't think so.' Fay attempts to trade a glance with Steve for the first time.

'Maybe we don't let her,' says Steve, still looking directly at Louise.

'What do you mean, Steve?' asks Louise.

'We're very quick to help or praise her. If something isn't going well, we're so concerned about her feeling bad that we dive in straight away.'

Louise is nodding, writing this down. Fay imagines her thinking that this is all great stuff. The honest dad reveals that the parents are fixers. That because of their own anxieties, by fixing their kid, they are in fact stunting her.

But yes, it's true, they both do this. They rush to smooth Rose out. 'I agree.' Then Fay thinks, *to hell with it, I'm just going to lay my shortcomings out there*. 'Actually, I do it far more than Steve. I find it really hard to see Rose struggling.'

As soon as Fay admits this, the waistband on her trousers seems less tight. She simply cannot keep everything in any more. Now Steve is talking about the party invite and how he handled that. 'I got it totally wrong. I should have let Rose deal with it. But it was just so cruel. I couldn't bear it.'

Louise nods. 'Well, it's completely normal for you to want to solve things for her. Especially after what she went through at her other school. It's a loving response. But it would be far more helpful to give Rose the right set of tools to deal with difficulties when they arise. And you know, sometimes children just need to realise things can be a bit rubbish.'

'Oh, I think Rose knows that by now, don't you?' says Fay.

'Of course. We know she does.' Louise crosses her legs. 'I'd like to talk about something that did come up during a session. I have Rose's permission to speak to you about it,' she says. 'We were talking about safe places. Rose has said she feels a bit anxious at home.' Louise pauses. 'She says that your voices are very different with each other. This is her way of explaining that something isn't right, like she felt at her old school.' Fay's eyes immediately sting. 'What Rose is expressing, at least in my mind, is that she feels insecure in the household at the moment.'

'Steve and I have had problems and I've moved out,' blurts out Fay. 'But Rose thinks my dad has broken his toe and I'm staying at his house to look after him.'

Louise nods sympathetically. 'I'm sorry to hear that.'

'It's me. I'm to blame,' says Fay.

'This isn't a blaming exercise, Fay,' says Louise gently.

'No, but it's my fault. Rose probably feels abandoned, doesn't she? Oh God, I'm a shit mother.'

'Can we please not make this all about you?' snaps Steve.

Fay doesn't look at either of them. She fiddles with her wedding ring, then her bracelet. She has no defence. Steve has the right to shame her. It's all true.

'But I agree, Louise,' says Steve in a calmer voice. 'Rose must feel completely unsettled by our conflict. I think we all are. She's our priority and we're getting it wrong. Thanks for sharing that with us. I'm really pleased Rose can talk to you about it.'

Louise reaches for her A4 diary off the table. She flicks through to a blank page and tears off a strip. Then she goes to the back pages, holds one finger over a name and writes something down.

'Here.' She holds the slip of paper out between them until Steve tentatively reaches forward for it. 'This is the number for Sacha Levinson, a wonderful couples' therapist. Give her a call. I feel like she could really help you both.'


Outside on the pavement, Fay says, 'That went well.' She smiles to show she's making a joke, a bleak joke. Steve zips up his cardigan over his jaw and shoves his hands in the pockets. 'I thought it was difficult but fine.'

'She gave us a couples' therapist number. She even said she knew her personally and would call to see if we could get moved up the list. That's pretty horrifying.'

'Why? She's doing her job. Trying to improve things for Rose. She can see that we're not helping.'

Fay nods. 'Yes, you're right. Look, I need to go. I've got so much to do.' She's not managing anything well and now her work is suffering. To gain sympathy and more time, she even told a client that she has a lot of personal stuff going on, which she has never done before. But he was pushing for a ridiculous timetable and in between regularly rushing home to see Rose, then trying to snatch moments with Emma and sort her head out, time is filtering away. She has never felt so overwhelmed.

'I need to tell you something.' Steve moves around nervously on the balls of his feet, as if he is shadow-boxing. He pushes his cardigan away from his mouth. 'I went to The Nine Bar and saw Emma last night after you left.'

It takes Fay a couple of seconds to compute this information. She is so shocked that she isn't sure that she has heard him correctly. That this could happen had never occurred to her.

'I didn't plan it. I was just really angry.'

They might be out on the street, but Fay feels like there is no air, none at all. This has to be the reason Emma hasn't responded to her text this morning. Until now, Fay had felt relaxed about the lack of response. She'd imagined Emma was sleeping off her night shift – she had said she might stay on for a few drinks because her favourite colleagues were working.

'What did you say to her?'

'Not much. Just that I wanted to see who she was. It was very brief.'

'How did she react?'

Steve pauses. 'She didn't seem to care that much.'

With every word, humiliation shudders through Fay; what if Steve is wrong? What if Emma went home and decided this situation is too toxic, that she's had enough of Fay?

'But in case you're interested, I didn't like hearing that she had come to the house. Jesus, Fay. How many lies are there?'

Fay doesn't want to hear it. 'I have to go.' She needs

to call Emma, apologise and put things right. As she starts to walk away, Steve reaches for her arm. 'Don't,' she says and pulls her elbow away so sharply that she almost knocks into an older woman passing by slowly, a bag of shopping in one hand.

Emma doesn't pick up her phone. Waiting for her to respond to one of Fay's three messages, Fay moves between the desk in Katie's spare room and the small garden. The house is positioned high on a hill, which affords terrific views of the city and sea, but even the calm, silvery water isn't comforting today. When she feels too unsettled to sit with the silence, she gets on her bike and heads over to Emma's flat. She buzzes and when Emma answers, she says without explanation or apology, 'It's me. I need to talk to you.'

'Hi. Sure.' This short but cool response has Fay taking the stairs two at a time. She needs to get inside and explain herself, smooth over Steve's error. But pushing on the open door to the flat, she can see they are not alone. Both Lewis and Hamish are in the living room.

'I'm sorry,' says Fay. 'I didn't realise you had company.'

Emma is in a green kimono that Fay hasn't seen before. Her hair is wet and loose. She looks different, but how? A tremor of fear runs through Fay.

'Hi, Fay, how are you?' asks Hamish.

'Fine, thanks,' she says. 'How are you both?'

Lewis ignores her. His fingers deftly play out some game on his phone. Hamish says, 'Fine, good, thanks,' then he swipes the back of Lewis's head and says, 'You're being spoken to.'

Lewis looks up briefly, mumbles, 'Yeah.'

'You won't get much out of him. Anyway, we'd better get going.'

Fay's natural instinct would be to say, no, I've interrupted you, I'll go. But she can't today. She can't apologise and leave. She needs to have this conversation with Emma. It's pressing on her insides, making her feel desperate.

'We'll catch you later.' Hamish exchanges a glance with

Emma, who says, 'Lewis, take a jacket.' Feeling stupidly excluded, Fay watches Emma and Lewis have a standard tussle about taking the jacket; Emma insists Lewis needs one, Lewis refuses, then Hamish pipes up to say, 'It's fine, Lewis knows if he's cold,' and Emma eventually says, 'Okay, okay, what do I know?'

After they leave, Fay barely waits until Emma is back in the room before she says, 'Look. Steve told me he came to the bar. I'm really sorry. It's so embarrassing.'

'Don't worry. It's fine.' Emma leans in amongst all her plants. She sets about plucking dead leaves off a fig tree and collecting them in her hands, then touching a fingertip against the soil. All the while she has her back to Fay.

'He crossed a line. It isn't fine. I promise he'll never do that again.'

'Honestly, don't stress, love,' says Emma without looking at Fay. 'It's done.'

Fay scratches at her neck, her forehead. Something isn't right. This stilted atmosphere that cramps over them isn't usual. It might not even be to do with Steve. Perhaps she missed a step and messed up somehow when they were on coke, an evening that is decidedly absent and patchy in parts.

'Emma? Are you angry with me? Please tell me the truth.'

'Of course not.' Emma turns and smiles, but it is that strange smile of hers again. Not false, but not truthful either.

'Look, I need to tell you something about Steve and me. It might explain why he came to the bar.' Fay's stomach turns over. 'We've agreed to live apart for a bit. I've moved out.'

Emma's eyes widen. 'That's big.'

'I didn't plan to tell you like this.' Fay puts her bag down on the sofa and moves even closer to Emma. When she reaches out to put her hands on Emma's shoulders, Emma steps back.

'What is it?' Fay's heart starts pounding.

'Nothing. Just got a handful of these.' Emma holds up her fistful of dead leaves, then drifts slowly into the kitchen. The back of her kimono trails after her like a wedding gown.

'Is that a new robe?' says Fay, inanely trying to plug the silence.

'It's a present from Hamish's mum. She and her sister went to Japan for a holiday.' Emma clatters the pedal of the bin, throws the dead leaves away, then touches the sleeve lovingly.

'Things don't have to change between us,' says Fay urgently. 'We can carry on as we are.'

Emma switches on the kettle. 'Fay, look…' she says calmly and, before she can say anything else, Fay cuts in desperately.

'It's been amazing, hasn't it? I mean, I know…'

'Fay.' Emma puts up a hand and says in a rush, 'Hamish and me. We're going to give it another go.'

'Hamish?' Fay's voice is scratchy and squashed. She can barely lift the weight that has just fallen onto her.

'We've been talking about it for a while. He's asked me before.' Emma shrugs. 'It feels like the right time. And he's got a new job in Manchester. A real step up.'

'No,' says Fay shaking her head. 'You can't. I won't let you.'

'Fay, sweetheart, listen to me…'

'I need to be with you,' Fay says and starts crying. 'I feel alive with you.'

'For now.' Emma comes to her and tenderly cups the side of her face. 'But it won't last. You know that. Especially without Steve.'

'That's not true. What we have is special.'

'I'm a hot mess, Fay.' Emma puts her arms around Fay and speaks so close to her face Fay smells bitter coffee on her breath. 'I told you that from the start. And I'm always going to be a mess.'

'I don't care.'

'Not now, maybe.' Emma's voice is small but clear. 'But you will.'

'No, I won't,' says Fay fiercely.

'You *will*.' Drawing back, Emma stares into Fay's face. 'You've got a good life.'

Fay reaches for Emma's hands and squeezes them. 'But I can help you with yours.'

Emma shakes her head. 'I'm not someone people stay with. I'm not.'

'So how can you be with Hamish?'

'Because he gets my mess.'

Fay shouts. 'I get your mess. You said so.'

'It's different. Hamish and I had Lewis together. I'm more honest with Hamish than anyone else because I have to be.'

'You can be that way with me.'

'Listen to me, Fay. You're an amazing, incredible woman. You don't want me. I'd ruin you.'

'No,' says Fay. She takes Emma's hands and turns them over in hers and kisses each palm over and over.

'I ruin everyone,' says Emma. 'You'd leave me. You think you won't, but you will. Everyone does.'

Fay leans forward and kisses Emma on the lips with an urgency that overwhelms her. She puts her hands inside Emma's kimono, she feels her smooth, cool skin, and then she drops her head on Emma's shoulder and she weeps. She has never felt so unmoored, so out of control. She kisses Emma's throat and chest whilst tears lash down her face.

'I'm already ruined,' she says, holding Emma tighter than she has ever done before. 'I am.'

# 22

'Daddy!' Rose's voice is distant enough for Steve to ignore it. He's still half asleep, lying there dozing, thinking about nothing much, but he likes it there. He doesn't want to leave. *I'm so tired*, he thinks as Rose pulls on his arm. When the pull turns into a hard pinch, he sits up, squinting.

'Ow.' He rubs his forearm. 'What y'doing, Rose? Cut that out.'

Now he's more awake, waves of pain pound against his forehead and the events of the past few days catch up with him – no wonder he could justify getting through so much beer last night. Drinking gives him a lack of clarity about himself. When he's sober, he doesn't feel strong enough for all the hurt in his life.

'Daddy, I can taste lipstick,' says Rose. 'It's making me feel sick. And you've got it all over your chin.'

After Steve rubs his eyes open and focuses, he can see her uneven eyeshadow, sticky black lashes and red stained lips. Oh God, he had agreed to let Rose put make-up on them both to lift her spirits after Fay texted to say she wasn't well enough to pick up Rose from school. Had he said they needed to wash it off? Probably not. Why would he have cared? What's a spot of make-up on the pillow when your wife's lover lights up every room she walks into?

Steve reaches for Rose's soft, smooth hand. 'Let's go and clean ourselves up, sweetheart.'

'What were you doing?' Rose is looking down. 'What's this?'

'Huh?' Swinging his legs over the side of the bed, Steve stares bewildered at the sea of clothes on the floorboards. And then it comes to him: drunk and furious, yet impotent as ever in knowing how to be constructive with his rage, he came upstairs with a black bin bag and attempted to fill it with all the clothing he'd ever worn to please his mum.

'What did you do, Daddy?' says Rose.

Steve looks at her anxious face and attempts a big, silly smile. 'Honestly? I was getting rid of shit that I won't need again.'

Rose covers her mouth, but her eyes tell him she's smiling. 'You swore.'

'I did.' Suddenly his head really hurts every time he moves, as if a door is opening and slamming. When he slumps down on the edge of the bed, Rose sidles up next to him.

'Can I swear too?' she asks. When he nods, she says, 'Shit.' At first her voice is hesitant, almost a whisper, but she quickly gets into the swing of it. 'Shit shit shitty shit shitty…'

'Okay. Great job,' he says.

Rose stops. 'Mummy won't like me swearing,' she says in a mildly delighted voice.

'Mummy's not here,' says Steve roughly, but she should be. Fay has always been the one to see Steve, properly see him. She would have tossed bits of clothing into the air and made Rose laugh, her way of covertly offering Steve praise for long-overdue action. But Fay isn't here, and he hates and misses her at the same time.

In the bathroom he finds a half-used bottle of face cleanser and cotton pads. With Rose lying under the duvet, he sits on the edge of the bed and wipes the make-up off both their faces.

'I know it's a school day,' she says after he has kissed her fresh cheeks and held her soft body to his. 'But can I have pancakes?'

'Yeah, why not?' It seems such a small ask. 'With Nutella, I presume?' he adds, and Rose claps her hands excitedly. 'So, you have to go and get dressed for school really quickly, then come and fill the bin bag for me. Deal?'

As Rose scrambles out of the bed, Steve pulls back the curtains and opens a window to release the stench of his beery sleep. Then he notices the blue-and-white-striped formal shirt strewn by the chair. His mum had made Doug give it to him last Christmas, but Doug had quietly passed him the receipt afterwards and said, 'Change it by all means. I'm not sure it's your style.' Doug, now he's a good man. Steve wells up. Years ago, out of the blue, his mum had asked Steve to start calling Doug dad, even though his own dad was still alive, and she had sent Steve to Coventry for his refusal. How long hadn't she spoken to him for? Was it two or three weeks? He can't remember.

Steve kicks at the clothes. She had it coming. That isn't a nice thought, but it's a fair one. But for now, he's got other, more pressing problems and maybe they're all linked, maybe they're not, but they're the ones he has to focus on.

/

Ten minutes before Fay is due to arrive and walk Rose to school, Steve receives a text.

## Fay
Sorry I can't come bad tummy

This is the second text like this. More than her flakiness, Steve hates that she hasn't even mentioned Rose or sent her love. Doesn't she realise how reliant Rose is on their fake attempt at normality? She needs the stability. Furiously, he starts to draft a mean text, then erases it. It would be too painful to find out if she was, in fact, feeling fine and just too happy spooning Emma in a warm bed. He doesn't need to know if she's giving up on them and giving in fully to her desires. He'll find out soon enough.

Once he tells Rose he's taking her to school, she lights up

with questions. Well, a million variations of the same question, not far from the one he has. 'What's wrong with Mummy's tummy? Why can't she come this morning? Why didn't she come yesterday?' Fudging every answer, Steve plays the big, fun, reliable daddy and gets Rose out of the door, then heads to work. After lunch, feeling a nervousness rise in him, he goes for a run on the beach. He thinks about everything, but mostly he thinks of Emma's hand on his arm, saying, 'Honestly, hun, I don't want to know,' and it infuriates him that her dismissal of him is the line that is on repeat in his head.

He is back at his desk working when his phone rings. He recognises the number, and he instinctively stands up to take the call from the school. 'Rose is fine,' says Miss Floss immediately. 'I'm with her in the school office. Unfortunately, Mrs Ariti hasn't come to pick her up.'

'I'm so sorry. I don't know what's happened. I'm on my way.' Steve cycles fast and recklessly to the school. His initial anger has turned to fear. He rushes into reception without even bothering to lock up his bike and after over-apologising to one of the admin staff, he takes Rose's hand and leads her outside. 'Doesn't Mummy want to see me any more?' she asks as they walk alongside his bike, and her voice is so shrunken Steve can hardly talk at first.

'Course she does, darling.' He bends down and hugs her. 'She sent me a text saying tell Rose I love her so much. She's still looking after Grandad, but now she's poorly. Really bad tummy. She forgot to tell the school. Anyway, I'm going to go and see her. Take her some medicine.'

At home, Steve calls Kyla. She's in town on her way to Urban Outfitters, but she can help if it's an emergency, which they both now recognise is code for double money. Her friend drives her over and when she arrives Rose stares at both of them and starts sucking her thumb, then she starts crying and says, 'Don't go, Daddy. Please. I'll be good.' And Steve's heart, which is already stamped on, bent up, takes yet another knock – any more and he'll be bleeding out on the floor, needing surgery. 'You are not just good, Rose. You're brilliant. You're the best. This is about Mummy not feeling well. Not you. Yeah? Give me a high five… and a low five… and a behind-the-back five… that's my girl!'

For the second time that day, Steve cycles in a panic. At Katie's house, he rings the bell and simultaneously knocks hard on the door with the side of his fist. Fay doesn't answer, but his instinct tells him she's inside, so he jumps over the separating wall and knocks on the neighbour's door. When the old man eventually puts the door on the latch and looks out, he recognises Steve from all the times they used to come over before Matt and Katie split and he gives him a spare key.

Steve lets himself in. 'Fay,' he shouts as he runs from room to room. He opens every door, even the one to the airing cupboard. Then he takes the stairs to the attic room where someone, something, is huddled under a sheet on the double bed beneath the huge roof window. The room is so hot he gasps. Hearing a faint noise, he pulls back the sheet and finds Fay lying on her side with a radio on low next to her head.

'Oh, thank God, Fay. Thank God.' Steve sits on the edge of the bed and almost starts crying. His back is prickly with sweat. His breath is slowly catching up with him. He stares at her, hating her for scaring him on top of everything else. And yet, he loves her, his whole body pulls towards her with love.

'What happened?' he says. When she doesn't answer, she doesn't even move, he says, 'Tell me. I deserve that much.'

When she says something that he doesn't understand, he has to ask her to repeat it. 'It's over with her,' she says eventually in a clearer voice.

'Why?' he says, taking strands of sweaty hair out of her mouth.

'I don't know,' Fay whispers and pulls her legs even tighter into herself.

When she doesn't say another word, he realises trying to extract conversation from her is pointless. He needs to take charge. 'Come on. Time to get up.'

'Leave me,' she says. 'I want to be left.'

'I can't do that.' He gently tugs on her arms until she is swivelled towards him, slumped over. Then he grips her under the arms and pulls her to standing. 'Think about the kids. We owe them.' She doesn't respond. It is like holding up jelly, another Fay he has never seen before, every safety pin that has held her in place, gone. 'Let's get you freshened up. And I'll make you something to eat.'

When she is sitting in the bath, he sprays warm water over her. As he soaps her back and underarms, something he has never done for her, the thought that she is hurting over the loss of another is like a slither of glass stabbing at him.

After he lifts her out and towels her dry, he rummages through her suitcase and finds clean trousers and a shirt. Then he dresses her, makes her scrambled eggs and watches her while she gently, wordlessly, spoons it in. Halfway through, she looks up at him and starts to sob.

He doesn't know what is running through her mind, but he doesn't ask. He just says what he realises she needs to hear. 'Fay, you'll be alright. You'll get through this. You will.'

# 23

## Four and a half months later

Around this time every Tuesday, Fay eats her lunch on one of the sea-facing benches near the old pier. Today she lifts a cheddar cheese and marmite sandwich out of its Tupperware, takes a bite, then uses her iPhone to photograph it. She had promised Rose she would message evidence that she has tried this ridiculous food combination.

## Fay

Check it out! And it's pretty yummy! See you in a bit. Love you. xx

As Fay eats, she stares out to sea. It's not a warm day, but the clouds drift against a flimsy blue backdrop, the water glistens. *Breathtaking*, she thinks. Even more so given that a few months ago, she could have sat for hours and not noticed a damn thing because her mind was still eating itself, bingeing only on bad thoughts. Today though, she even notices seaweed trailing between the few swimmers who bob about by the pier. She cranes forward. Who's in the water today? She's bound to know some of them. She's been a regular in the sea since the summer, often several times a week, first wading in her bikini and then her gloves, woolly hat and sea socks when the cold began to bite.

Her phone pings. Of course, Rose has already replied with a GIF. Her iPad is always in near reach. Is that a dancing dog or a bear shaking a pair of maracas? Fay really can't tell. Rose seems to have access to an inexhaustible number of odd, animated characters, a regrettable outcome of her having her own iPad.

Fay would be the first to admit that she bought the iPad out of guilt because, for a few weeks, she could not mother Rose at all. She could hardly look after herself, let alone know what homework Rose had to submit or what trip she needed a packed lunch for or how things were with Courtney. So, if a scratched second-hand iPad has in any way helped, if it means Rose can contact Fay whenever she is scared or happy, distract her and give her an edge over some of the girls, then great. So be it. There are worse things; yes, Fay *knows* there are far worse things.

After checking the time, she flaps out crumbs from the front of her sweatshirt. She still has five minutes and Rhona's flat is barely a two-minute walk. Fay is slightly dreading today; she doesn't want to be early. She keeps looking at the time on her phone, then reluctantly gets to her feet and makes her way to a block of flats overlooking the seafront. She presses the buzzer, waits for the main door to click open and takes the lift to the fourth floor.

Is she ready? Possibly. Possibly not.

/

'Hello there,' says Rhona. 'Come in.'

Fay follows Rhona inside and down the hallway. As always, every door in the flat is shut, except that to Rhona's counselling room, concealing Rhona's life from the scrutiny of her clients. A few times Fay has heard a man's voice and today she walks through the faint smell of fried bacon.

Steve had found Rhona. A week after Fay had told him that she and Emma were over, he announced very matter-of-factly that she needed a therapist. 'I can't help you and you really need help.'

It was true; the way Fay was behaving could not go on. It was not right to yearn for sleep the moment she woke, because she could not bear her dark, circular thoughts, nor could she keep calling Steve in the early hours to apologise and ramble and cry. Because what it came down to was this: if the experience with Emma had given Fay so much life, it felt as if her absence had taken it away.

'What a beautiful day,' says Rhona as she sits down in the chair opposite Fay and rearranges her neck scarf.

'Gorgeous,' says Fay, although hardly any sky filters through the narrow window into this shady room. The first therapist Steve found her had a far nicer room than this, large and soaked in morning sunshine. But the therapist sat impassively and silently in the corner, waiting for Fay to do the talking. Which, frankly, was near impossible at the time, when all Fay could do was drop into a chair like a stone and cry. So, Steve asked around again, and it was Katie who told him Rhona came highly recommended, with the caveat that she was not a conventional therapist.

Rhona lacks all the traditional qualifications that the old Fay would have insisted on before handing over her emotional life. She is cavalier about taking bits from many therapeutic approaches to suit the client, and her one diploma is not even framed in glass, but clipped between wooden hangers, next to the poster listing this year's sea tides and full moons. But the first time Fay sat down, Rhona reached into a chest for a heavy yellow blanket and said in a compassionate voice, 'Why don't you wrap that around you? It might stop you shivering,' and Fay knew she had come to the right person.

Rhona leans forward, hands resting on her knees, and smiles at Fay. 'How are you?'

'Okay. I've had a pretty good week.'

Rhona gestures with a hand for Fay to continue.

'Well, I guess it's really about this one thing that happened. I was in the farmers' market in the square with

Rose. I had just bought these beautiful roses and some coffee beans. Rose wanted churros, so we sat down at a table next to the cart while she ate them. I was sitting there, stroking her hair, looking at everyone milling around, and I suddenly felt so light. Honestly. Carefree.' She pauses. 'Like Emma made me feel.'

Rhona smiles. 'So, it was inside you all along,' she says in her throaty voice. 'She didn't take that energy with her. You can see that now?'

'I think so,' says Fay.

'It's powerful, isn't it? Understanding you can give yourself what you need.'

Fay nods. 'And then the next day, I don't know if it's related… but I barely thought about Emma at all. I mean, I was shocked to realise it was late afternoon before she came into my mind.'

Rhona smiles and leans back in her chair. 'What a long way you've come since our first time in this room.'

Fay nods. In that session, Rhona had asked lots of questions, and then five minutes from the end, she had moved her hand over her heavy wooden necklace and said, 'Emma woke you from your slumber. I suspect… and, of course, we shall find out in our time together… that this was at the root of it.' And Fay had looked through the window that gave a view on to nothing much and cried without touching her face. Maybe this was right. Fay had no idea. Nothing about her life made sense in that moment. All she knew then was that she had a terrible longing for Emma.

'But even after all this time,' says Fay, spreading her hands, 'I still don't know how it happened. How I,' she aggressively points at her own chest, 'let it happen. I hurt Steve so much.'

'Well, sometimes it is okay not to know,' says Rhona.

'Steve said something interesting last week. He said he thought we'd been focusing on the wrong things. How did he put it…' Fay frowns. 'Like we were so busy trying to move forward all the time we forgot about moving down, going deeper.'

Rhona presses her hands together and says, 'Absolutely. So, how are things between you?'

'Okay, getting better every day,' says Fay. 'We've decided to start couples' therapy. A therapist who has been recommended has space for us. Although we'll keep living apart for the time being. That hasn't changed.'

'I think that's an excellent idea,' says Rhona. 'Now we're finishing up here, it's a perfect time for the two of you to do some work together.'

Fay can feel that the painful memories are starting to slowly exist outside of her and Steve, like a trailer attached at their back. It's there, they pull it with them, but sometimes they can look ahead and forget about its presence. On his birthday last week, she stayed over at the house instead of returning to the studio flat she had been renting the past few months. It was late after they had all watched a couple of Disney films and played board games and eaten too much pizza and Fay's one-room place could feel so lonely at the end of a good day at the house. After Rose had gone to bed, she had given Steve a card. Inside, she had written, *Thank you for everything you did for me. I will never forget your help when I deserved it least. You are the best human being I know.* And Steve had welled up a little and said, 'Yeah, thanks, now where's my present?' and they had toasted him with a glass of champagne, then Steve suggested he make up Billy's bed for her.

And while saying goodnight on the landing, they had come together and briefly kissed. She hadn't known they would, but she had touched his stubble and he felt good and real and there was a shift in her; she wanted him. She did. But she wasn't ready and nor was he. He might not feel as angry as he had, but she knew, because he had told her, that the hurt was a long way off from leaving him.

In the darkened hallway, as she passed him to go into Billy's room, she said, 'I love you so much, Steve,' and she understood why he said thanks and goodnight but did not say it back. Would he ever again? Would they be able to start over, mesh together the old and new versions of themselves? Who knows? Not her, not yet.

'So, we've been working towards today for some weeks now,' says Rhona. 'It's our last session. How do you feel about ending?'

'Pretty scared,' admits Fay. 'Sometimes I feel ready, but then I freak out. What if I forget how to be truthful with myself? With Steve?'

'I believe you'll know,' says Rhona. 'I do.'

'Thank you for everything. You've helped me so much. I couldn't have got through the past few months without you. I mean it.' Fay tries not to cry.

'Thank you, Fay. And you know…' says Rhona quietly, 'it's never really over. The dialogue between us lives on forever inside you.'

Fay nods. 'Can I hug you?' she asks. 'Is that allowed?'

/

A few weeks later, Fay stops by Sainsbury's on her way to the house. She is in the canned-vegetable aisle, bent over, trying to remember the brand of chopped tomatoes they prefer, when her phone vibrates in her coat pocket. With a can in one hand, her reading glasses slipping down her nose, she gasps.

## Emma

Hey honey, was just thinking about you. Tried the other phone but it's dead.
How's tricks? Things didn't work out with Hamish but I like Manchester.
Except the bloody rain! Here it comes again. Cue Eurythmics 😩😁 xxx

Fay leans into the shelves as if she has been punched in the stomach. She reads it and rereads it, searching for a secret message, a code, until she realises there isn't one. Emma is probably lying around, bored. Fay pulls her trolley into her to let others pass by. Then, when she feels she can move, she abandons it in the aisle and shakily walks out of the store into the car park. In the car, she stares at the message. She knows she cannot reply. It must never start up again; her life, her sanity is at stake. But as she deletes Emma's text and telephone number, then blocks her, Fay realises that in fact she has no desire to message back or hear from Emma. And as she closes her eyes with her phone still in her hand, she feels herself breathe more easily, knowing that the end has finally come.

Arriving at the house twenty minutes later, she calls out hello and lets herself in. Noticing the Hoover and bucket of cleaning products in the hallway, she remembers that Patricia and Doug are coming for lunch tomorrow, their second visit here in the past two months, which has made Steve happy. Fay hadn't a clue that he had blown up at his mum until he told her on their first walk alone on the South Downs, a month or so ago.

'Only took me nearly thirty years,' he had said and laughed, but Fay said, 'Don't do that. I'm proud of you. It was a hard thing to face.' And they had sat for a while at the top of a hill, agreeing that there were lots of things that were hard to face.

Fay wanders through as if she still lives here. Which she does in so many ways. Sometimes she will visit several times a day. All her post and deliveries come to the house. She does the school runs, she often makes breakfast and dinner, she loads and unloads the dishwasher and cleans the toilets. Sometimes it feels like she only showers and changes in her studio flat, other times it's where she feels she needs to be. But her soul is still here, that's for sure.

In the cold kitchen, as the din of a saw strikes up, Fay realises why the doors are slightly open and no one is inside.

The arborist is here. She buttons up her coat and wanders out, calling hello, and Steve turns and smiles. Rose is on the trampoline with Courtney. 'Mum's here,' she shrieks and unzips the surround to crawl out while Courtney waves and carries on jumping and singing to herself.

Rose runs to Fay and says, 'I did two forward flips,' adding in a whisper, 'Courtney still can't do them.'

'Well, are you helping her?' says Fay.

'Yes,' Rose says. 'I'm showing her what I do. And she's trying her best.'

'You are such a kind girl.' Smiling down at her, Fay tucks Rose's curls behind her small ears. Thank God for Louise, who saw Rose weekly for nearly three months. Sometimes it hurts Fay that they have needed someone else to help shape their daughter, but Steve thinks the opposite. 'We're getting the whole house therapied up,' he likes to joke, but he also points out that now Rose goes into school happy. Her mood is better. And she has a friend, a good friend, in Courtney. Fay agrees. Courtney can be as frowny and bossy as she likes; Fay always welcomes her with open arms. She has taken Rose away from a troubled time.

As Rose walks back to the trampoline, Fay moves closer to the smoke tree to stand next to Steve. She thinks about Emma's message. She will tell Steve about it later, the moment they are properly alone. They have promised each other honesty, even when it's painful to hear.

'It's sad,' she says, watching the guy harnessed to the tree, cutting away. Already the branches are falling noisily.

Steve nods. 'It really is.' They watch together, which takes a while. The tree had grown so big and protective.

After the arborist has gone, Rose sits on the small blonde stump and Fay holds her cup of tea and experiences the tree's absence. It is odd. With every leafy branch gone, she can see straight over the fence into the garden next door and the sky feels so expansive, glaring down at them. But she doesn't feel the need to move. She can cope with the exposure today.

'What are we going to put in its place?' says Steve.

Rose shouts, 'Another big tree!'

'Or maybe something completely different?' Steve surveys the long flower bed. 'Get rid of those bushes. Create a vegetable patch.'

'A vegetable patch!' Rose jumps up and down, holding on to Courtney's hands as they both chant, 'Veggie patch, veggie patch.'

Steve looks at Fay. 'What do you think?'

Fay doesn't know the first thing about growing vegetables. 'Why not?' she says. They can learn.

## THE END

# Acknowledgements

Thank you.

To my fabulous, wise agent Rowan Lawton at The Soho Agency for your unwavering commitment and the phrase 'don't go global', which has become a firm favourite. Thanks also to Eleanor Lawlor for back-up and Helen Mumby for your help with the book to screen journey.

To Cari Rosen, my editor, for your loveliness and collaborative spirit. Thank you for caring so much about *Permission*. To the rest of the team at Legend for everything that publishing my book involves, in particular Olivia Le Maistre for working tirelessly to get it into people's hands.

To fellow writers and friends Rebecca Whitney, Beth Miller and Alex Hourston for your great support and a mutual love of good food and cocktails – special thanks to Alex for also being a terrific champion, sounding board and critic from the get-go.

To Emily Gajewski for reading chapters so eagerly and to Sarah Marx for answering all things therapy.

Thanks to my parents, sisters, and friends for always believing in me.

But most of all, to Jonny and Samuel for the love and the laughs. You're the best! Thank you, always.

Follow Legend Press on Twitter
@legend_times_

Follow Legend Press on Instagram
@legend_times

'Prescient, completely believable and slightly terrifying. *Permission* looks at the age-old dilemma of whether monogamy can ever be enough. I was drawn to Fay and her need to define herself outside the confines of family life, while every other character navigates their own, sometimes rocky, often exciting, path through non-monogamy. Brilliantly drawn, I loved it.'

Rebecca Whitney, author of *The Liar's Chair*

'A total binge-read. Characters you can fully invest in, stunning dialogue and a satisfyingly unpredictable story – one of my favourite reads of the year so far.'

Fiona Mitchell, author of *The Swap* and *The Maid's Room*

'Bravo to Jo Bloom for writing the novel all married people, especially women, want to read. *Permission* is an honest, thoughtful, entertaining and intricately-crafted novel about the realities of marriage in middle age. The alternating points of view work especially well and both the husband and wife, Steve and Fay, feel totally familiar and real but also fresh and nuanced enough that it's impossible to stop turning the pages.'

Elyssa Friedland, author of *The Intermission*

'A very sensitive and thoughtful approach to a complex and emotive issue... the characters really came to life on the page and have stayed with me.'

Laura Barnett, bestselling author of *The Versions of Us* and *Greatest Hits*

# Praise for
# Permission

'I was completely absorbed by this fascinating contemporary story about love and marriage. It lays bare some of our most cherished beliefs about romantic relationships, then delicately tears them apart. Beautifully written and subtly observed, it's full of believable characters whose every feeling and behaviour makes perfect sense. It's written with such emotional intelligence but it's also a pacy page-turner; I sped through it and now need to read it again more slowly to savour it properly. Highly recommended.'

Beth Miller, author of *The Missing Letters of Mrs Bright*

'Intelligent, finely written, morally complex. Perfect for book clubs seeking their next 'what would you do' read.'

Tammy Cohen, author of *Stop at Nothing*

'I loved *Permission*. A deep-dive into a contemporary marriage, it asks a deceptively simple question – what happens if we want more? – and answers with a story that is utterly compelling; full of surprises, yet always real. A novel of our moment. I couldn't put it down.'

*y House*